Midway through the Sunday sermon, Lindy wished she could put her head down to rest. It was throbbing. She was glad that the young people's choir didn't have to sing today, and she could sit in the audience. She avoided her grandfather's eyes as he steered clear of hers. She noticed, however, that today he looked exceptionally tired. Was it because he was up half the night waiting for her? Lindy felt bad about what had happened, and she wanted to ask her grandfather to forgive her. Her grandfather was right. The devil was always tempting Christians to stray from the path. She realized that she could not give Nick up, but she could give up the other things. If Nick really loved her, he would have to do right by her.

*To Crystal
Many thanks,
J. Michael*

LIFE IS NEVER AS
IT SEEMS

J.J. MICHAEL

Genesis Press Inc.

Obsidian

An imprint of Genesis Press Inc.
Publishing Company

Genesis Press, Inc.
P.O. Box 101
Columbus, MS 39703

ISBN: 1-58571-153-5
Manufactured in the United States of America

First Edition

Visit us at www.genesis-press.com
or call at 1-888-Indigo-1

DEDICATION

For my daughter
Michelle
and
Granddaughters
SeDona and Siyah
Dreams do come true.

ACKNOWLEDGMENTS

I give thanks to the Creator and all the Celestial Beings that have guided me through this life time. And thanks to my family and friends for their continuous support of my writings. Special gratitude to Leticia People, a pioneer publisher in black literature, for her guidance, support and belief in my talent. I must thank Pastor Sidney Foster, Jr. for encouraging me not to give up on any of my dreams. I am grateful for the guidance of my editor, Angelique Justin of Genesis Press and for the knowledge and skills of Deatri King Bey in editing this work.

CHAPTER ONE

Spring of 1967

Reverend Perlie Johnson of Mount Olive Baptist Church eased his aching body onto the purple seat cushion of the old African wooden chair. He breathed a sigh of relief that at last he could sit down. The chair, with its detailed Egyptian carvings on the back, wasn't the type of chair you would ordinarily find at a church pulpit. It stood out and was a bit much for most traditional Baptist churches. However, it supported Reverend Johnson's heavy frame and aching back. At sixty-seven, Rev, as he was called by his congregation, didn't care what others thought of him.

He was drained of energy, for the Holy Spirit had descended on him. It wasn't the first time this had happened in his forty years of preaching. This Sunday morning he felt tired and old. Maybe, he thought, it was time to retire from the only thing that he loved and knew how to do—preach. The problem was who would take his place? God had not granted him the gift of a son, and he was not about to turn his church over to any of the up and coming young ministers who thought they knew everything. No, somehow he had to find the way to go on until God was ready for him to stop.

He had been wrestling all week with how to get a message across to his congregation. It all started with a conversation he had had earlier in the week with his right-hand man, Deacon Willie Coleman.

"Rev, you heard about all that mess going on at Howard U?" Deacon Coleman asked.

"You mean those militants or Black Panthers, whatever they call themselves, stirring up the young people on the campuses across the country?" Rev replied.

"Yeah, they're the ones," Coleman confirmed.

"They're at Howard, uh."

"Yeah, they're the ones that closed down the administration building."

"What's wrong with the president and deans over there, letting those rabble-rousers on the campus? They're a bad influence on the young people, teaching bigotry, hate and separatism. We got to do something."

"I don't know how much you can do, or anyone else for that matter," the deacon replied. "This movement is strong. It could turn out to be a pretty nasty fight. Do you want the church to be involved in that type of battle? You never know what side people will take."

"You got a point there, Coleman. The least I can do is start right here with our church family. We have to make sure our members, and especially the young people, are not involved in any of these goings-on. If they are, I want them to get out!" Reverend raised his voice. "The only cause they need to serve is the Lord's! That damn war in Vietnam isn't helping this country any. Our young boys are being sent over to some foreign country to be killed, maimed and hooked on drugs. What's this country coming to?"

"I don't know, Rev. Things haven't been right since Kennedy was assassinated."

"I tell you it's nothing but the devil taking over the minds of our young folks. Look at how they're dressing. Any young woman with any respect for herself would not go prancing around in those skirts that stop at least ten inches above the knee. If she bends over, you would see what God gave her. They better not try and wear any of that mess around here. Thank God my granddaughter Lindy is not involved or influenced by any of that mess."

Deacon Coleman could see how riled up his minister was. "Now, Rev, the movement has some good points. It is giving our kids a sense of their roots, self-esteem, and taking pride in how they look," the deacon said, readying himself for a challenge as he looked the Reverend dead in the eye.

"I don't mind them taking pride in themselves, but they cross the line when they foster violence, anti-white messages, and disrespect what we worked for all these years. That's all I am saying. These Black Power people are wearing those loud-colored African dashiki shirts, and if that isn't bad enough, look how they are wearing their hair. It is a disgrace to the Negro race."

"We are not called Negroes anymore, Rev. We are black folks," Deacon Coleman pointed out. "Don't you listen to the Godfather of Soul, James Brown? 'Say it loud, we're black and we're proud!'" He laughed. He liked to taunt his old friend.

"Black? Man, there is not a black spot on me, or you for that matter. We are colored folks, Negroes, and don't you forget that," Reverend Johnson chided him.

After that conversation, Rev went into prayer and asked God to show him or tell him what to do. During the week, he worked on changing his sermon, but the words he wanted wouldn't come. On Sunday morning, he proceeded with his original sermon, "Getting Your House in Order," when midway through the message, he felt the Holy Spirit rise up in him. He always knew when it happened. He would get hot, hotter than normal. Even his voice changed. Then the words would just pour out of him. Rev came from behind the pulpit and stared out at the congregation. They knew the Spirit was upon him. They had witnessed this many times.

"We got to get order in our houses," he began. "God's house is in order. God didn't put us in a disorderly world. We create our own disorder. I think there is a lesson here for us to learn. When we have children, we have to have our houses in order. Why are we letting our daughters, our women, flaunt themselves in an ungodly manner? They're not living a Christian life."

Several people hollered, "Amen, Rev. Come on, preach the word!"

"Our women have been dressing like harlots, wearing dresses and skirts that only have a yard of material. And pants that don't cover the area that don't need to be seen! What do they call them? Yeah, *hot pants*!" Rev's voice screeched as he said the last two words.

"They cover their faces with cakes of makeup that make them look like Jezebels…"

The congregation was silent.

"You know that they are up to no good when they put on their Jezebel costume. Because that it exactly what it is, a costume. They're doing the devil's work, enticing the men to fall and sin. All that makeup, that nakedness, and that big hair is the work of Satan. We can't let Satan into this house. No, sir. We have to keep order in this house. Satan is trying to confuse us by making women think they should wear the pants. Next thing you know, the men will be wearing dresses."

He paused, and the congregation laughed. Rev knew humor would lighten the mood.

"Satan is at work here," he went on. "Strike him down, Father. Send him back where he belongs—to Hell."

"Amen!" screamed the congregation in unison, as if someone had held up a cue card.

"Don't come into this Lord's house dressed like harlots. Get right with God." Rev held the Bible up at the congregation. "Put on some decent clothes to worship in the House of the Lord, and going to school and work. Jesus ran those money-baggers out of the church. He'll run you out, too."

Some of the sisters of the church stood waving their hands in agreement with the minister.

"We're not going to sit by and do nothing and let this church, city and country go to Hell. I am here to tell old Satan: Get back. We are Christians, and we are going to fight you, Satan. We are not giving up on our Christian sisters and brothers without a battle. So get back, devil."

Rev stopped for a moment as if he were listening to someone speaking to him. By now the church members were on their feet urging the minister on. Finally Rev Johnson turned and strutted back and forth across the dais. He was speaking so fast the congregation could hardly understand what he was saying.

"The Holy Spirit is telling me this morning that you young people need to show some respect and appreciation for your elders instead of giving them backlash. Your parents work hard for you every day so that you can go to school and college to help raise up our Negro race. And what do you do? Drop out of school, and get involved with drugs and the wrong crowd. Talking about 'they're my friends.' Friends? Let me tell you who they really are—demons! You called them friends. Child, they want your soul. They frequent those places you hang out at—you know what I'm talking about—wearing disguises, the big hair, short dresses and dashikis. What do they do? They give you cigarettes, sex, marijuana, and alcohol, promising you a good time. What do you give them? Your soul. That's right, your soul.

"You think you know everything. We old folks, as you call us, don't know anything. You know it all. You think we weren't young once. The devil, he's just laughing, as he sets that trap for you. Then when you are down, whom do you blame? You point the finger at your parents, the government and the church. Don't fall into that trap. Save yourselves. Get right with God. Obey your mother and father. Honor your mother and father. It's called God Power."

Rev stopped and wiped his forehead then leaned on the podium for support. "I'm tired, children. I'm tired now. You know what you need to do to get right with God. God doesn't like his children not obeying. He will punish you. It all starts in the home and church. We old folks have to see that there is togetherness and order in the home. Obedience starts in the home and church. When order is seen in the home, it will reflect itself in the community. Don't let these fast-talking, slick devil workers pull the wool over your eyes. Walk with the Holy Spirit. Talk with the Holy Spirit, and see with the Holy Spirit. Won't you join the church today? Let the Holy Spirit move you today. Remember, say it loud: God Power!"

"God Power!" shouted the congregation. They clapped their hands, held them up to receive the Holy Spirit and shouted as the Spirit took over. The organist struck the keys to "We are Soldiers in the Army, We Got to Fight," and the gospel and young people's choir began to sing.

Several visitors came forward and joined the church. Reverend Johnson smiled to himself as he thought of how he could still arouse the Holy Spirit in himself and others. At least 700 or more people, from what he could tell, were packed into the church; even the balcony was full. He silently thanked the Holy Spirit. If someone didn't like his sermon or wanted to complain, he would tell them to complain to the Holy Spirit, for it wasn't his words that Sunday morning, but the words of God.

Silently, he thanked his grandfather and father. Both had been southern Baptist preachers from Virginia. He had been ordained into the ministry by both of them. The difference between him and them was that he went on to divinity school. Rev soon found out that he learned more from watching his father and grandfather than from the school.

He could hear his father saying, "Boy, you got to make them shout, cry, and call on the Lord. Fall down on one knee and look up to the heavens, and pray as if the devil was after you," Papa John would chuckle.

Rev recalled watching his father strut back and forth across the pulpit, mesmerizing the worshippers with his heartbreaking stories. Then he would call on Jesus Christ and the Holy Spirit. "Get control of them early and always keep them in the palm of your hand," Papa had told him. "Moreover, whatever you do, invoke the power of the Holy Spirit." It always worked.

As he made his way to his chair, Rev took the white linen handkerchief from the pocket of his robe and wiped away the beads of sweat that had formed on his brow and nose. His grayish white hair was almost plastered to his skull. He wore his hair long to cover the thinning around the top of his skull. He ran his hands through his hair to make sure every strand was in place.

Rev shifted his weight on the chair to lean on his side, to get a better view of the Sunday school children as they marched down the center aisle of the church, until they all stood in front of the dais. The podium blocked part of his view of the congregation, which he thought was good. He didn't have to stare into their faces after he gave the word. Sometimes the extremely severe message was targeted at a particular member or members. Rev could then retreat and study their reaction by sneaking a look around the podium.

He barely heard the young people reciting their poems. His mind kept drifting in and out. He wiped the sweat from his brow again and reached for a glass of water. He was exhausted from preaching for over an hour, and the weather was unbearable. One would think that it was already August in DC. It was near 90 degrees, and it was only May. The sweat kept pouring down the Rev's face. Another hot Sunday like today and he was not going to make it. He made a mental note to tell his daughter Margaret to set the air conditioning at a lower temperature next Sunday if it was still hot. One could never tell about the weather in DC. It was as fickle as their football team, the Redskins.

Rev remembered when the church didn't have air-conditioning, and they had to suffer through those long hot days. He wasn't going to do that anymore. Through the years they had raised funds and reno-vated the church, bought the property next to the church, and built a parsonage, all thanks to the efforts of Margaret. She chaired the com-mittee that was responsible for the renovation and restoration of the church. It took several years to complete the project. Many board members opposed the restoration of the church that included the building of the parsonage, saying it cost too much. Margaret fought them tooth and nail until she got every penny she needed to do the job.

Coming up 16th Street going north toward Silver Spring, one couldn't help but notice the large gray brick structure with the well-kept lawn and the large sign that read: The House of the Lord, Mt. Olive Baptist Church, Pastor Perlie Johnson. The interior décor was just as beautiful as the exterior. Rev's dream had come true.

It seemed like only yesterday that he was a young man attending Howard University Divinity School. He had left southern Virginia after that awful thing had happened with his beloved Amanda, and his father had passed. Rev felt a slight pain in his chest. After all these years, he still felt something whenever he thought about those years.

He tried to forget that time in his life. He had told the founding members of the church that he was reborn the day he left out of Virginia. He brought his mother and baby daughter with him. It was rumored that his wife had run off with another man—a white man. But he never talked about his past, and they never asked.

He worked nights at the main post office sorting mail. It was a good job for a Negro man. During the day he attended school. Rev dreamed about having a big church on 16th Street, the Gold Coast and spiritual corridor of Washington, DC. He knew that previously closed doors of Washington society would open to him. He found people in DC to be very cliquish. Nevertheless, he knew that money, time, and having the right skin color would win out.

Rev figured he had a lot to be grateful for. The church was getting ready to celebrate its fortieth anniversary. It was thriving, and more and more people were joining every week. Margaret's health was better; the spells had subsided. Rev prayed everyday that God would relieve her of her misery, or at least let him get some rest from it. His only granddaughter had just graduated from Howard and was getting ready to go to medical school in the fall. *Yea, God is good,* he thought.

Reverend Johnson looked to his right at the young people's choir. He could not see the face of his granddaughter, but her brownish blond hair could not be missed. Rev closed his eyes and remembered the first day he had looked at her in the hospital crib.

She had startled him when she opened her eyes. The violet blue eyes of his wife Amanda stared back at him. As the years passed, Lindy grew to look more and more like her grandmother. What worried Rev was that she also acted a lot like her grandmother, and this was not good.

Rev's watery eyes caught those of Deaconess Walker. He quickly looked away, as he didn't want to lock eyes with that woman. She had become a pain in his side. They used to have fun together until she got too serious, and he had to drop her. She was talking about leaving her husband, his good friend Deacon Walker, so that they could be together.

Rev knew that he couldn't afford a scandal like that. The church folks of Mount Olive Baptist Church would run him out of there, even if he had founded the church. Rev could see the headlines in the *Washington Post* talking about the senior pastor of Mt. Olive Baptist Church expelled from the church for adultery. No way was he going to let that happen to him. Besides, he had had to let her go anyway. Lately, it had been difficult getting the old boy to perform. After all, he was in his late sixties.

He caught a glimpse of Miriam Williams; she had recently joined the church, a widow from North Carolina. She was soft-spoken, not a bad looking woman. Her striking feature was her body. She was hippy with big legs, something he'd always found attractive in a woman. Maybe it wasn't too late for him to settle down.

He had almost remarried years ago, soon after he had moved to Washington. Julia Palmer was her name. He thought about how she kept pressing him to get married. Julia was a good woman and would have been a good mother for Margaret, though he doubted whether Margaret thought so.

But Julia had given him an ultimatum to marry her or she would leave. Just when he had almost given in, he'd had that damn dream again. It had started soon after he left Virginia.

He would wake up in a sweat, with tears running down his face. At first, he couldn't remember the details, just a sketchy outline of the events. Eventually, he began to remember bits and pieces of the dream.

He would barely lay his head on the pillow before he would hear this buzzing sound, and bells. After many years, Rev realized that the sounds were bells—faintly, but nevertheless bells. As the buzzing sound got louder and the bells dimmer, he felt as though he was being sucked out of his body. He was in complete darkness. Fear gripped him, and then these horrible, grotesque faces appeared in front of him. Rev could not see their bodies, but he sensed that they were trying to pull him down. Just when he thought they were going to engulf him, Rev felt another presence, a light, in the distance.

Instantaneously, he started moving toward the light. He could still feel the power of the others trying to get him. Whenever the fear gripped him,

Rev moved back toward them. The bells got loud again, and he felt this feeling of love, and he tried again to move toward the presence. The presence was Amanda. Her arms were stretched out reaching out for him. She was standing at the gateway to a city called Shamballa. Rev tried calling to her, but no words came out of his mouth. He woke up frightened out of his wits...

He had the dream one night that he and Julia spent together. He felt her shaking him.

"Perlie, Perlie wake up, you're dreaming."

He'd opened his eyes and stared at her. She had a troubled look on her face. He felt tears running down his face. His chest was heaving. After a few seconds, he was able to speak.

"I was dreaming. It's OK; I'm all right, go back to sleep. I had better leave now before it gets light. I don't want Margaret looking for me."

Although he had the dream quite frequently, he and Julia never talked about it again. She knew it was the same dream, because he always tossed around in the bed and screamed out the name Amanda.

Julia suspected that something terrible had happened to him or his wife before he came to Washington. She tried to get him to talk about it, but Perlie would give her a cold stare. She felt him drifting away from her. Was it the dream coming between them, or was he still in love with his wife? Julia begged him to go get help, but he was too proud to see a psychiatrist.

"What would my congregation and my daughter think about me seeing a shrink? No," he would tell her. "It was just a dream."

After the dream, he would be withdrawn for days. Julia couldn't get him to go anywhere. He would stay cooped up in his office or the church. He didn't have time for her. Julia decided to give him an ultimatum. Get help so they could move on, hopefully to get married, or she was leaving. She never heard from him again. Julia decided the best thing to do was to move back to Florida to care for her aging parents. Many years later, Rev heard that she had married her high school sweetheart.

All he had left of Amanda was that dream, until the suitcase came. It came with a letter informing him she had died of malaria in Africa. Her body, as she wished, was buried there. All her belongings were in that one battered suitcase.

He took the old suitcase and put it up in the attic. It was months before he opened it. When he lifted up the lid of the suitcase, he could smell her. His eyes watered and his heart ached. Rev quickly looked through the things. He pulled out a Bible that was marked with writing all through it. Amanda had neatly filled in the family genealogy, hers and his. His remorse turned to anger; he tore the pages out, and then felt badly that he had desecrated the Bible.

He moaned as he read the title of the second book, *The Book of Life*, by Two Adepts. Two adepts of the devil, he thought. The book brought back old hurtful memories to him. Amanda had changed after she had started reading it and going to those meetings with the white folks. They'd acted as if Amanda was one of them. When he'd asked her about them, she would clam up.

Papa John told me that I had to put my foot down, Rev thought ruefully. He had raised me to be a man and not to be led around by the apron strings of a pretty woman. Those white folks were putting ideas in her head, making her think that she was better than the rest of us because she looked like them.

Rev had found two pieces of her jewelry: the ring he had given her on the day they got married, and the gold heart-shaped pendant he'd given her when Margaret was born. He put the jewelry in his pocket and tossed the books back into the suitcase. Rev squeezed the suitcase under some other junk in the attic. He vowed to throw it away one day, but for right now he decided it was best left alone.

When Margaret turned sixteen, he gave her Amanda's ring. She never wore it. On Lindy's sixteenth birthday, he gave her the gold pendant. She never took it off. It was like having Amanda back, and that was what worried him. The though of her and all those old memories made Rev want to scream. *Why, Amanda, why did you do it?* It was over. Let it die.

LIFE IS NEVER AS IT SEEMS

The Sunday school children finished their program, to the joy of all. Rev wiped away the sweat now mixed with tears.

CHAPTER TWO

Margaret Johnson Lee watched her father from the back of the church as he delivered his sermon. She had to admit that, at his age, he was still very good. The congregation was holding on to his every word. They loved him. Nevertheless, she admitted to herself he was showing signs of aging. He kept forgetting things, and was not moving as fast as he used to.

God, she thought, if I had only been born a boy, there would not be a problem with my taking over! All her life, Margaret had wanted to be a minister.

When she was in her early teens, her father would let her read his sermon. On most Saturday afternoons when other young people were out having a good time, she would be listening to her father practice his sermon for the Sunday service.

By the time she was a young adult, Margaret knew the King James Version of the Bible forward and backward. She could recite chapters and verses as well as her father. She taught Sunday school and was her father's unofficial manager of the church. Margaret had her hand in every group or committee of the church, from the senior and junior choirs, to the usher board, to the missionaries, to the deacon and deaconess boards.

The members feared Margaret as much as they feared her father and God. She was the power behind the power. Margaret had the ability to get things done. When she finished Dunbar High School, Margaret wanted only one thing—to be a minister in her father's church and someday take over when her father retired. Years ago, she had approached her father with the possibility of his ordaining her. She never forgot the discussion between them.

"Papa, this is a wonderful sermon you are going to give tomorrow," she had said, handing the pages back to her father. "Remember that time you let me give a testimony?"

"Yes, Margaret," Rev responded as he put his glasses on to make a few corrections on the message he planned to deliver the next day.

He was proud of his daughter. She was a big help to him in running the church. In Bible Study, she demonstrated her abilities to interpret the scripture. Margaret was natural like her mother, but in a different way. Margaret didn't mix the Bible with all that rubbish or mystery teachings that her mother Amanda had tried to get him to include in his sermons whenever his Papa John let him preach in the old days.

Rev looked at his daughter as if he was seeing her for the first time. She took after his side of the family in appearance, the same olive skin, brown eyes and dark brown hair. She was even physically built like the Johnson's, tall and broad.

"Papa, I want to be a minister. I don't want to go to college to be a teacher. I am happy doing what I do now, running—I mean, helping you to run the church. Will you ordain me?" Margaret asked her father as she looked into his deep brown eyes.

To her he was one of the most handsome men in the church. He had a little gray hair at the temples, which made him look so distinguished. The sisters in the church were always after him. He seemed to ignore them. He was happy with just the two of them, and so was she.

"Margaret, you know that there are no women Baptist ministers. I would probably be expelled from the Baptist Association. Besides, this is not for you. You are going to make a great teacher. Think of how many young people you will be able to save by helping to educate them. No, I want you to go to Howard or D. C. Teacher's College and get an education."

"But, Papa, isn't this our church? You started this church. It was your dream, and now it is my dream. I want to be a minister!" Margaret cried as she gripped her father's arm.

"Girl, get a hold of yourself. You know as well as I do that we have a Board of Trustees that makes decisions regarding the affairs of this church. Now stop this nonsense; I don't want to hear any more about this." He patted her head and turned back to his sermon.

Margaret left his study with tears streaming down her face. "Somehow, someday, this church will be mine, all mine!" she said to herself as she stormed toward her room.

Margaret now watched as the second offering was being taken. The ushers would bring the plates to her after the collection. Deacon Coleman or one of the assigned deacons would accompany her to the church office, where they would count the money. Margaret didn't trust anyone. It was just too easy for someone to take a few dollars from the plates and envelopes. Every Monday morning she banked it. It had always been like that.

When she was younger and Papa had just started the church, times were not as prosperous as they were now. Some weeks they would not be able to meet all of the church obligations, and other weeks they hardly had enough to give Papa a salary. At one time, Papa had refused to take a salary, and they lived off a special collection taken for the pastor each Sunday. They never had to worry about food, because the good sisters of the church provided dinner for them every night. Those had been lean times in every other respect.

Margaret remembered Sister Julia, whom she thought Papa really liked. Then all of a sudden, Sister Julia had just stopped coming to the church. Margaret was glad she was gone because she took up too much of Papa's time anyway. Nevertheless, she wondered what happened to her, and to other women that Papa would take an interest in. After awhile, Margaret recognized that her father had discreet affairs that never amounted to anything. Therefore she could stop worrying about sharing him with someone else. When she was around fifteen years old, she overheard her grandmother and father talking about her mother.

"A suitcase came today with her things and a letter. Did you see it?" Rev asked his mother.

"No, I don't want to have anything to do with that woman. Some things need to stay buried."

"She's dead," Rev went on. "Died in Africa of malaria."

"Good!" his mother said sharply. "It's best for everyone, especially

Margaret. We didn't want her being exposed to those people, anyway. Just as Papa John said, 'the devil got her soul.'"

This time Papa didn't say anything.

"How did they know where to find you?" his mother asked.

"That's just it; I don't know."

"Well, don't worry about it. They're not going to bother us now. They got what they wanted. We can now lay this to rest."

Margaret never forgot that conversation. Years later she found the suitcase in the attic. It contained a letter, her mother's clothes, and some old books. As she read the letter, for a second she felt something. She asked herself, was it sadness or anger? She decided that she really didn't have any feelings for her mother. She didn't even know what her mother looked liked. Her mother had left her when she was only a few weeks old. She didn't love her. What mother would go off and leave her newborn baby? Margaret was essentially motherless.

No one talked about her mother. It was as if she didn't exist. Margaret knew nothing about her mother's people. She'd been raised by her paternal grandmother and her father. Her grandmother died when Margaret was in high school. Her father had left his job as a postal clerk to become a full-time minister, and Margaret assumed her rightful role as first lady of Mt. Olive Baptist Church.

Margaret attended DC Teacher's College. In her senior year, she met Benjamin Lee, a young doctor just starting his residency at Freedmen's hospital. He was a few years older than she was, but it was the kind of match that her father expected of her. Benjamin was a devout Christian, and at one time had thought about going to theological school.

They married soon after she finished college, and she was pregnant before they were married a year. Her husband never got a chance to see or hold his baby daughter. In one of the worst snowstorms of the century, Benjamin Lee returning home from the hospital was involved in a four-car collision. He died instantly. The baby was born two months after the fatal accident.

The voices in Margaret's head started the day her father brought her and the baby home from the hospital. Margaret was in her room when she heard someone say, "He loves that baby more than you."

"No!" she'd cried out. "That's not true."

"He calls her his little angel."

"Papa loves me. Go away."

No matter how hard she tried, she could not get the voice to go away. One time the voice told her to get rid of the baby; then Papa and she could be happy again. She fought it. The voice called her names: whore, bitch, stupid.

"No!" she would scream, and began to break up anything she could get her hands on. Margaret screamed to drown out the voices, but they would not stop. She slept, and spent most of her time in her room. She wouldn't even go to church on Sunday. Margaret stayed away from the baby. She could hear her crying at night. Papa would beg her to take care of the baby, but she was scared that she would hurt her. She couldn't tell him that. What would he do with her?

It was the worst period of Reverend Johnson's life since he had left Virginia. His daughter acted as if the devil possessed her, and he had a baby granddaughter who looked exactly like the woman he had been trying to get away from in his mind.

Rev got Deacon Coleman's wife to help him take care of the baby. He knew he could trust her and Deacon to keep quiet about Margaret's behavior. The tongues started to wag anyway, after Margaret refused to come to church or take on any of her old duties. The members of the church blamed her condition on the loss of her husband. Rev never told them anything different, because he really didn't know what was wrong with his daughter.

After a night of a crying baby and screaming mother, Rev couldn't take it anymore. The restless nights were taking an effect on him. He finally put his foot down and made Margaret go to the doctor. The doctor told them that she suffered from postpartum depression. Margaret was sent home with a bottle of tranquilizers that kept her doped up most of the time. The medicine quieted her down.

The same way she went into the darkness, she came out of it, so

Rev thought. He returned home one afternoon from visiting the sick and shut-ins when Deaconess Coleman practically dragged him into the baby's room. Margaret was sitting in his mother's rocking chair holding her baby daughter. She just looked up at her father and said, "She is so beautiful, with those violet blue eyes. I am going to call her Linda Johnson Lee."

Margaret resumed her old position of running the house and church. The first thing she did was to send Deaconess Coleman packing. She was getting too close to her father and church affairs. This was Margaret's legacy, and she planned to keep it that way.

As the ushers made their way down the center aisle with the collection plates, Margaret looked at her daughter singing with the young people's choir. Margaret knew that her daughter was different. Lindy's violet blue eyes and blondish brown hair made her stand out among the others. She not only looked different, she acted differently.

As a young child, Lindy preferred books to dolls and preferred to be alone except when she was with her grandfather. What unsettled Margaret was the way Lindy stared at her, and she often spoke about things that Margaret didn't understand.

"Mommy, I see eye colors around you."

"Stop it, Lindy. There's no such things as eye colors, or whatever you called them."

"Mommy, there's black around here." She pointed to Margaret's head. "Does it hurt, Mommy?"

"I told you stop it, Lindy!"

"But I see them, Mommy!" the little girl protested. "Different colors, not just on you, but on everyone. You always have the black one."

"I am losing my patience with you," Margaret said sternly. "I am not going to tell you this again. There are no such things as eye colors. I don't want you to ever talk about this again, or I will have to take you to the doctors. Do you know what doctors do with little girls who talk nonsense?"

"No, Mommy," a frightened Lindy answered.

"They take them away from their families and put them away with other crazy people."

Margaret knew she was frightening Lindy, but the child was too powerful. The voice told her so. Lindy never mentioned the eye colors to her mother again.

Twenty years later, Margaret admitted to herself that she was still baffled as to how Lindy knew about the pain she felt in her head. The voice told her to be careful, or someday her own daughter would take away from her what she loved the most, her father and the church.

Margaret stole another glance at Lindy. She had managed through the years to keep her daughter and her father apart, although lately Lindy had been gaining ground with Papa. And that was not good!

CHAPTER THREE

Lindy pulled down the trap door to the attic. The stepladder came forward without any effort. Her mother had had the steps installed to make it easier for them to have access to the attic. Lindy gracefully ascended the steps and looked hopelessly at the several boxes facing her. She had put this job off long enough. She had promised her mother she would at least start to go through the boxes of clothes, books and toys to decide what she wanted to keep and what to give to charities. She had to finish before she left for medical school in August.

Lindy took a deep sigh as she moved one of the boxes to make room to sit down. She pulled several stuffed animals out of one of the boxes. These were her favorites, and she hated to give them up. She put the animals back into the box and marked it "Charity." In a couple of months, she would be leaving home for the first time. It was time to put childhood things behind her.

Lindy figured that the year she spent on the campus of Howard University didn't count, because she'd spent most of her awake time, if not in class, at Founder's Library or at home. Dorm life was not for her. Her first year living in the dormitory had been a nightmare. She was put in a large room with three other girls. One roommate spent most of her time in the student canteen playing bid whist, one cried for home constantly, and the third one talked about her boyfriend from sun-up to sundown. Lindy was what they called a bookworm. She had nothing in common with these girls.

She was a loner. It had always been that way. Her mother kept telling her that the other girls were jealous of her because of the way she looked. Lindy thought it was more because she was not like them. She didn't want to chase after boys. She'd rather read, study, and watch the stars.

Before sealing the box, Lindy pulled out a little stuffed collie dog. It was her favorite. She hugged it to her, and the day that she got it flowed backed through her memory. Her grandfather had given it to her as a peace offering if she promised not to do those bad things anymore.

Her eyes became cloudy as she remembered how that day in Sunday school she had picked up the coat of one of her Sunday school classmates. She began to rub the fur collar as if it was one of her stuffed animals. Bright pictures flashed before her eyes. She could see little Johnny Robinson lying on a table. There were bright lights all around him, and people dressed in white were standing over him. When little John's mother took the coat from Lindy, the only words that came out of her mouth were "His stomach is going to burst."

A couple of days later, her grandfather called her into his study and told her never to do that again. At first, Lindy didn't know what he was talking about. Nevertheless, he looked into her eyes and held her shoulders, shouting at her, "Don't ever tell anyone again about what's going to happen to them, or what has happened to them. I don't want them to think that the devil got you, too."

She stared at her grandfather as he kneeled at his chair and began to pray. As she left his study, she could hear him saying, "Please, God, don't let it happen again. I am your faithful servant. I have not broken my vows to serve only you. Spare this one."

That evening, her grandfather came to her room and said, "Remember your promise, Lindy." When she came home from school the next day, the collie dog was sitting on her bed.

Years later, Lindy learned that little Johnny had emergency surgery for appendicitis the same day she told his mother that his stomach was going to burst. The Robinson family never returned to the church.

Lindy put the collie back into the box. *It's time to let go of the old and move on with life, she thought.* However, in her heart she knew that part of the old would always be with her.

Lindy crawled over to a corner of the attic. She moved one of the bricks from the wall, reached in, and pulled out a small book. It was her diary. She had to hide it because her mother often searched her room. She could never figure out what her mother was looking for. Lindy took the key off the chain she wore around her neck with the pendant her grandfather had given her. She turned the lock that recorded her life's secrets. She had no one to talk to about the strange occurrences, so she kept a diary recording whatever she saw, heard, felt and sensed that was beyond normal comprehension.

Lindy flipped through the pages of the diary until she came to the list.

By the time she was in her mid teens, she had devised a list of the many shades of colors she saw around people. She called them her rainbow eye colors. Beside each color she listed a series of words that corresponded to the color. If someone was "red," for instance, she discovered that it might mean that they were angry, energized, impulsive or sexual. People with blue around them like her grandfather like to talk a lot. What disturbed her was the black color around her mother's head and heart.

Lindy also recorded any unusual incident involving the eye colors that pertained to a person's health. She surmised that dark, murky colors indicated someone was ill or would eventually get a disease. Sometimes she could actually see the diseased organs inside the body. So many times she wanted to tell the person or even try to help them, but Lindy remembered her promise to her grandfather. For this reason, she had decided to become a doctor.

She turned to the page in the diary dated March 10, 1963, and began to read the words that she had written four years before:

One of the girls in the dorm had a Ouija board. I didn't want to play. I had a bad feeling about the board. The other girls insisted and kept after me until I gave in. I sat in front of the Ouija board, and before I could put my hands on the indicator, it started moving. It spelled out the words "wake up." I screamed, not because the indicator was moving on its own, but because of those two words. The girls were all screaming and moving back from the table. The indicator began to move again. One of the girls grabbed the board and threw it in the trash. I looked at her in total bewilderment.

"What did you do that for?" I asked.

"Did you see what it was doing?" the young girl with a deep southern accent screamed at me. She was shaking, she was so scared.

"Did you make that happen?" another one asked me.

"Of course not! I don't know what happened. I only wanted to see if it would continue to do it. Forget it. It's no big thing." I could hardly get the words out.

My voice quivered and I felt my jaws tighten up. I tried closing my mouth and it wouldn't. I just stood there with my mouth wide open and saliva running down the side of it. I couldn't talk. I pointed to my jaw. They looked at me as if I was a freak. The one with the deep Southern voice ran out of the room. She came back with the floor mentor who took me to Freedmen's Hospital.

Lindy stopped reading for a second and ran her hands along her jawbone. The doctors told her grandfather and mother that they could not find any physical condition. They believed the problem was psychosomatic, and that Lindy needed to see a psychiatrist. Grandfather didn't want her to see one. He said that it would always be on her records. Lindy didn't know what records he was talking about. It happened again and again, until finally he relented.

She went to see Dr. Stanley Higgs, a prominent Negro psychiatrist, several times. She never told him about the eye colors or reading minds because of her promise to her mother and grandfather. She feared being committed to an institution for insane people. Dr. Higgs asked many questions about her home life. She told him only the good things. After a few hypnotic sessions, the problem with her jaw went away. Dr. Higgs told her mother that she needed to socialize more with people her own age. The following September, she entered her sophomore year at Howard. Her mother bought her a car, a Volkswagen Beetle, and she commuted to Howard.

Was there some connection between the Ouija board, the illness and the dream? she wondered. The Ouija board spelled out the same words that were part of a dream that kept recurring since she was a child. Lindy turned to the page where she had recorded the dream:

I was alone in an area that reminded me of a desert. The sand was white and hot. The sun overhead was brilliant. I tried to shield my eyes with my hand as I looked up at the sun. I could see sunrays circling the sun. Something or someone compelled me to look straight head. In the distance I saw a figure. I didn't know if it was a man or woman. The person was walking straight toward me. As it got closer, I felt this overwhelming feeling of love. My heart started to beat faster. I faintly heard bells. It sounded like it was saying, "Wake up, wake up, it's time." And I would do just that, wake up. It didn't make any sense to me, but the warm feeling of love would stay with me for days.

Lindy closed the diary and put it back into its safe haven away from her mother's prying eyes. She turned her mind back to the task at hand. She had only gone through two boxes. She quickly started to go through box after box, being careful not to get caught up in reminiscing about each item. A cramp in her right leg made her stand up and take a stretch. She stood on her toes, threw her head back and reached for the ceiling of the attic. The ceiling wasn't that high. Then she bent over from the waist to touch her toes. Coming up from the position, her eyes caught a glimpse of a brown object buried under piles of boxes and furniture. Lindy couldn't remember ever seeing it before. She began to lift the furniture and move the boxes to get to the object.

It turned out to be just an old, beat-up suitcase that probably belonged to her grandfather. As Lindy lifted it to put it back where she found it, the contents fell out, a few dresses and some books.

A noise at the bottom of the steps shocked Lindy into action. She quickly shoved the contents back inside the suitcase as she saw the top of her mother's head appearing at the opening of the attic.

"Lindy, you have been up here for a couple of hours now; have you made any progress?" Margaret Johnson Lee asked.

Lindy looked at her mother and responded, "It's slow, but I am making progress."

"You look so flush, your cheeks are pink. What's going on?" Margaret had a skeptical look on her face as she began to inspect what Lindy had done.

"Oh, nothing, Momma; I'm just a little tired from moving furniture and boxes," Lindy replied as she lifted a box in front of the suitcase to make sure that her mother didn't see it.

"You really haven't done much. I don't see how you ever made it through Howard. You're so slow." Her mother's remarks stung, but Lindy knew she was looking to start something, and that it was best not to respond to her.

"Meanwhile, your grandfather thinks he can run around the country participating in marches and sit-ins as if he is your age. He is just too old for this type of carrying on. He needs to stay put and leave that kind of thing to the younger men in the church," Margaret said as she daintily smoothed back her hair as if a strand was out of place.

"Papa is taking on too much," she went on. "I worry about his heart. In fact, I am going to schedule a medical appointment for him. Have you noticed that he has been out of breath lately, Lindy?"

"Yes, Momma, I did," responded Lindy. "He does look a little tired." She wanted to tell her mother that her grandfather was more than tired. A dark murky green color had formed around his heart. Through the years, Lindy had watched it grow from just a small speck of green to the size of a quarter. Her grandfather was in pain. She wanted to touch him to make it go away, but touch of any kind was not a part of the Johnson-Lee household. When she reached the age of three, her grandfather, the only adult in her life who had shown her any physical affection, had stopped hugging her.

"I want these boxes finished," her mother bossed her. "So take your head out of the clouds and do what you have to do."

Lindy watched as her mother maneuvered the attic ladder. At fifty-five, Margaret was still very agile and, Lindy thought, physically beautiful, but she had a heart made of steel and ice in her veins. She was at least 5'6" tall, with a slim but broad frame. Her hair when untied from the knot that she wore pulled back on her neck was long and wavy, with a streak of gray going down the center, which only made her more striking. Margaret dressed impeccably, wearing only the best clothes from Garfinkel's, Lord & Taylor, and Cissy's, the boosters' personal store.

Lindy wished that she could have known her father or at least his family. All she had of him were photos and the occasional story her mother would tell her about him. When she pressed her mother for more information, Margaret would say, "Let the past stay where is belongs, dead."

Lindy pulled the ladder up so her mother could not intrude on her again without warning. She lifted the suitcase out of its hiding place and opened it. Her small thin hands pulled out a letter that informed her grandfather about the death of her grandmother Amanda.

"Africa?" Lindy said aloud, her eyes open with amazement. Her grandmother had gone to Africa. *What did she do in Africa?* "Malaria?"

No one had ever told her of these things. She knew she looked like her grandmother, but that was all she knew. Maybe the books had more information. The large Bible was old and worn. The pages had turned yellow and some in the front were missing. Words were scrawled along the side of the chapters and verses. As she tried to make out the wording, Lindy got the impression of a young woman sitting with a group of other women reading the Bible. She could not see the woman's face, but around her neck was the same locket that now hung around Lindy's long slender neck. The woman, Grandma Amanda, Lindy assumed, was focused on a particular verse in the Bible. The names Mary and Jesus floated through Lindy's head. She tried to see what book in the Bible the women were reading, but the vision disappeared as quickly as it had materialized.

Lindy sat on the attic floor holding her grandmother's Bible to her chest, wishing she could share the image with her grandfather and mother. She quickly dismissed the idea out of her head. She read the title of the second book aloud, *The Book of Life* by Two Adepts. Lindy opened it to the front page and read the inside inscription: *The world is not as you imagine it to be. If you are reading these words, your soul is awakening from maya. The mysteries will be revealed to you.* **Wake UP.**

CHAPTER FOUR

Summer of 1967

Lindy slipped on a plain dark blue wraparound skirt and white sleeveless blouse. The flat, dark blue sandals matched the skirt perfectly, thanks to her mother. The clothes were expensive and conservative. Lindy looked into the mirror. The image that stared back at her was one of a good Christian girl.

A couple of months ago, her grandfather had given a sermon on the proper dress attire for Christian women. He didn't allow his sheep, as he called his congregation, to stray too far from the Christian principles. Women were admonished if they wore too much makeup or flashy jewelry. It was against God's will, he told everyone. God forbid if they wore slacks or a pantsuit to church. Lindy laughed to herself as she imagined Rev and the deacons chasing any woman who would dare to wear slacks out of the church. *It would be a sight for sore eyes,* she thought.

Looking in the mirror that hung on the back of her bedroom door, Lindy saw a tall, lanky girl with small breasts and hardly any butt. She wished that she were more developed. Her long straight hair just hung down her back like strings. If only she could get it to curl up. The bush was in. Everyone was shouting, "Black is beautiful!" Regardless of what her grandfather said, straight hair was out. Where did that leave her? They wouldn't let her cut it. What were her grandfather's favorite words?

"Women are made to have a head full of hair. My mother had hair down to her waist. It's your crowning glory," he would preach at her.

"You don't know how blessed you are. Come here," her mother would grab her by the arm and parade her over to the mirror that hung over the mahogany server in the dining room.

"Forget this nonsense about cutting your hair. Other women would die to have hair like yours. It's thick, and straight as any white person's hair. I wish mine was straighter. If anything, I wish I could get rid of this." She would touch her strands of gray hair.

Pulling her hair into a ponytail, Lindy let the image fade from her consciousness. She glanced at her watch and realized that she had to hurry. She pulled the drawer out of the nightstand and reached behind the drawer for the taped object. She had to be careful.

Now to get out of the house without too much questioning. At twenty-two, they still treated her as if she was twelve. Earlier Lindy had told her mother about her plans for the evening.

"Tonight I am meeting some of the students I tutored to celebrate our graduation," she'd casually mentioned.

"Graduation has been over for weeks. Kind of late for celebrating, isn't it?" Margaret responded.

"Graduation parties can go on for weeks. I won't be out too late."

"Make sure you aren't. Tomorrow is Sunday and you have an early rising."

One Saturday while driving through Rock Creek Park, Lindy had accidentally found the perfect spot for what she needed to do. It was a picnic area, full of people having fun until dusk. Lindy called it her special place as she eased the Beetle into one of the parking spaces.

She emptied the contents of the bag on the seat next to her. She had done this many times recently, until it had become a routine. She adjusted the front rearview mirror where she could look directly into it.

The young girl picked out the black eyebrow pencil and began to outline her upper and low eyelids. A trace of blue over the black outliner accentuated her violet blue eyes. She added black mascara to make her eyelashes longer and darker. Lindy pinched her cheeks until they turned red, giving her the effect that she wanted. She rummaged through the several items on the front seat until she found the hot red lipstick to match her cheeks. She reached under the driver's seat and pulled out another bag. This one contained her prize possession.

Twisting her hair into a bun, she easily slipped the large black Afro wig into place and snapped on the dangling silver hoop earrings.

She stole another glance at herself in the mirror. The girl who stared back at her was not the one she'd looked at earlier. "Not bad," she said, "for a girl who usually looks like a plain Jane."

"One last thing to do, then I will be ready," Lindy mumbled to herself.

She untied the wraparound skirt and lifted up her hips to pull it from under her. Black hot pants now covered her hips and less of her butt. Lindy folded the skirt neatly and put it on the back seat of the car. Next off came the white blouse to reveal a red halter-top. She stepped out of the car to get the platform shoes that were hidden underneath the spare tire. Lindy quickly put them on. They added two inches to her already tall frame. Before she could get back into the car, she had attracted the attention of a group of guys playing soccer. The catcalls confirmed what she already knew in her heart. "I'm black and I'm beautiful."

Lindy arrived at the Kenyon Grill, the local hangout for the Howard and DC crowd, a little after 7 o'clock. The place was packed with the usual Saturday night crowd. She spotted Nick at the far end of the bar with a drink in one hand and the other hand moving as if he was painting on a canvas. Nick was an artist. Knowing him, he was probably trying to get his point across by painting a picture in the air.

The bar was smoky and dark, even thought it was still light outside, as Lindy made her way through the crowd. *God, he looks good*, she thought, her eyes on Nick. His smooth dark brown skin looked good against the white shirt. He had a sports jacket on with dressy black slacks. Was this her Nick? Lindy was used to seeing him in jeans, a sweatshirt and a fatigue jacket.

She walked over to him, and he put his arm around her waist and kissed her on the lips. Lindy acknowledged his friends and then looked at him. He had a red circle of light around his head. Something had happened to put him in this mood.

" Hi," she said. "You look so different, I almost didn't recognize you. What's up?"

"Baby, baby, talking about me, look at Ms. Lindy." Flashing big white teeth, Nick let out a low whistle of approval. "You look sexy as hell in that outfit."

Her eyes lit up when he mentioned how great she looked. He had given her the money and helped her pick out the wig.

"We're going to a party in Georgetown," Nick announced. "My professor, the one from Israel, is having a party. We are going to mix with the enemy." He always referred to whites as the enemy.

"Nick, I wish you would stop calling them the enemy."

"Oh yeah, I forgot about that side of you," Nick kidded. "How long do we have before you turn into Cinderella?"

"Don't worry about it. Let's go," Lindy replied, a little irritated that he was treating her as if she was a child.

Nick got behind the wheel of Lindy's little black Beetle and headed for Rock Creek Park. Traffic was heavy as they made their way through the twists, turns and curves of the park. They were quiet on the way to Georgetown. Each lost in his or her own thoughts.

Her life had changed when she met Nick in her senior year. He was everything she wasn't. He was a free spirit and popular on campus, even though he was not a Greek. He didn't believe in the fraternal brotherhood. He attended Howard on a full academic scholarship. When things got tough, he worked for the government's Work-Study Program. For years the football and basketball coaches tried to get him to play ball. Nick refused, and kept his head in books and painting. Sports were not for him. He was an artist and he knew it.

During the first half of his senior year, he ran into some problems in his math class. He had put off taking the class as long as possible. He knew that math was not one of his strong subjects. His scholarship was in jeopardy for the rest of the year because he was failing the class. Lindy was recommended to him by his math teacher to tutor him. At first she refused him, but he persisted. She would find him waiting for her outside of Douglas Hall after her English literature class. He begged her until she agreed to tutor him twice a week for a month. They agreed to meet at Founder's Library every Tuesday and Thursday.

Lindy found Nick easy to talk to. He shared his artwork with her and talked a lot about black art and black history, about Africa, and about his dream to go to Paris to study art. She confided little things to him about school and wanting to go to medical school. He gradually broke down all her barriers against him.

One Thursday afternoon, he refused to go into the Library to study. He pulled her along as he began to walk toward Fourth Street.

"Today is too pretty to be cooped up in the library. We are going to the Howard Theater." Nick looked at Lindy.

Before she could respond, he added, "If you could see the look on your face. It's OK. I got tickets to see the one and only Marvin Gaye, a black boy right from DC." He started dancing in front of her.

"What about your lesson? We just can't abandon studying." She laughed at him as he did the Hitch Hike, imitating Marvin Gaye.

"Oh yes, we can. That's the problem with you. You need to have some fun."

"My mother thinks that I'm in the library."

"Girl, you are going on twenty-two years old. Get a grip. You are legal. Besides, I thought all the women loved the Stubborn Kind of Fellow."

"I'll go, but I am going to quiz you as we walk, and I have to be back for my afternoon classes."

They stayed for two shows. Lindy missed her afternoon classes; it was the first time she had ever cut classes. She felt a little guilty, but being with Nick made her forget about the guilt and what her mother would say. Lindy never forgot that day. She fell in love not only with Marvin Gaye but also with Nicholas Lewis.

Nick intrigued her with his way of thinking. He wanted to save the world, he would tell her, and especially his people. Lindy would correct him and say, "Our people." Then he would go into his Southern dialect and make fun of her.

"Why Ms. Lindy, what in the world do you mean 'our people?' Honey, you are sure enough white. The Master has been fooling around with your mama. You're a house nigger. This little field nigger is going to save you. Ms. Lindy, I'm going to teach you how to be black and proud."

She read about Marcus Garvey, Paul Lawrence Dunbar, Nat Turner, Harriet Tubman, Phyllis Wheatley, W.E.B. DuBois, Ida B. Wells, and Mary Church Terrell. She watched as the Black Power movement took place on Howard's campus. The Greeks were no longer in power on campus, as evidenced by the loss of the coveted home-coming queen election to a candidate sponsored by the movement. As much as she wanted to participate in the movement, Lindy feared the wrath of her grandfather and mother more. She knew that they were against the movement. Nick was an avid supporter of the movement. It was through him that she touched the part of her heritage that had been denied her for most of her life. She was beginning to find out who she was.

Nick knew her darkest secret, her ability to know things about peo-ple. He had taken her to the public library to find information about the eye colors. There wasn't anything. Lindy was happy because Nick didn't think she was crazy, nor was he scared of her abilities. Lindy told him about how she knew what ailed people. She didn't understand how it worked, but she could look at someone and information about that person or that person's health would come to her. At last she had some-one to talk to.

Now, as the drove to the party, Lindy felt Nick's big warm hand cover hers. She smiled at him, and his heart missed a beat. She was so beautiful, he thought. Who would have ever thought that he would wind up with this half-white woman/child? Although he knew she was quite strong-willed, she always looked so helpless. He took a quick glance at Lindy and realized that the helplessness that she exuded was more of a child-like innocence. She really didn't know who she was. He figured that her mother, the great Margaret Johnson Lee, and her renowned grandfather, Reverend Perlie Johnson of Mt. Olive Baptist Church, had brainwashed her, or tried to anyway, into thinking she was better than others because of her damn near white skin. Nick figured that their brainwashing didn't work, because she was with him.

He was the son of a poor Alabama sharecropper with a whole bunch of sisters and brothers. He didn't have a pair of new shoes until he was a teenager. At the age of thirteen he was 6' 2" tall and wore a size thirteen shoe. His father and brothers were all around 6' and had to look up to him. He was the baby boy and his mother's favorite.

Nick's brown, near-black skin tone and six inches of nappy black hair definitely would not fit into Lindy's family's plans. He knew that they couldn't take a chance on Lindy having a brown kinky-head child like him. They planned for Lindy to marry a doctor, lawyer or Indian chief. He had to be high yellow, with plenty of money and the right social status. Nick was from the wrong side of the tracks. He knew this was the reason Lindy had never invited him home with her.

Everything had been going according to schedule until he met Lindy. It was not in his plans to get emotionally involved with anyone right now. In his pocket was a letter from the University of Paris informing him that he had gotten a one-year fellowship. Nick thought about how he had waited all his life for this piece of paper. The professor had given him an outstanding recommendation, and he had managed with the help of Lindy to pull his math grade up to a C. Why wasn't he elated? He asked himself. He glanced over at Lindy and realized that he didn't want to be apart from her for a year. He couldn't believe that he was actually falling for her, not now. It really didn't matter, he told himself. They were going to be separated anyway. She was going away to medical school in the fall.

Nick hated to come to Georgetown because of the parking. He had to drive around the area until he found a parking space that was usually two or three blocks from the professor's house. He figured the slaves who lived in this area years ago probably never thought there would be a problem with parking when they built their homes. Nick chuckled to himself. Here he was, a son of a sharecropper, being invited to the home of one of his rich white professors. Life was good.

CHAPTER FIVE

Harvey Goldstein taught political science at Howard University; and his wife, a black civil rights attorney, participated in the sit-ins and marched with Dr. King. They had lived a number of years in Israel and traveled extensively in Europe and Africa. Professor Goldstein had taken a special interest in Nick's artwork and his life. Nick had taken his class as an elective. The professor liked the young man's spirit. He was always questioning him and not taking anything the professor said as gospel truth. Professor Goldstein saw something in Nick that the others didn't see, the desire and power to get ahead against all odds. Nick reminded Goldstein of himself when he was younger. They had struck up a friendship and had a small business arrangement on the side.

The party was crowded when Nick and Lindy got there. Most of the people that the professor introduced them to were diplomats, politicians, and lawyers. Nick and Lindy were the only students. The other guests questioned Lindy and Nick about the Black Power Movement on campus. They wanted to know about the movement from the viewpoint of a black American and a white American student. Lindy and Nick looked at each other and laughed. They realized that the guests thought Lindy was white, even with the wig on.

Nick had gotten used to the confusion over her identity, and even though Lindy was making light of the mistake, he knew that it really bothered her. She was tired of being left out. Nick encouraged her to find out about her ancestry. Where did her people come from? What did they do? Who were they? When she approached her mother and grandfather, she got basic answers. They were from a small family in southern Virginia. Her grandfather was from a family of preachers. She was told that there was no one left in Virginia, except for some distant cousins.

She later found out, quite accidentally from a conversation she had with her grandfather, that her father's family had begged Margaret to let them see her when she was a baby. But, her mother had refused. Margaret didn't want anything to do with them. Rev had blamed Margaret's unwillingness on her post partum depression. Rev had told Lindy that all she needed to know was that God was first in her life and that was all that counted.

Nick was waiting for the music and dancing. Lindy explained to him that parties like these were about small talk and drinking. There would not be any dancing. As the evening wore on, Lindy proved to be right. They had circulated the room a number of times, having the same boring discussion on politics and the government. Nick glanced at his watch; he wanted to leave early so that he could spend some time alone with Lindy. However, he had some unfinished business with the professor. At that instant, Professor Goldstein appeared and grabbed Nick by the arm.

"Excuse me, young lady. Let me borrow him for one minute, I have something I need to discuss with him," Professor Goldstein said as he practically dragged Nick with him across the room through the door that led to his study.

Lindy didn't know if she should move or just stand there and pretend to be invisible, when she heard a voice behind her say, "Now, why would you want to pretend to be invisible and hide your light, child?"

Lindy turned around to face a woman dressed in a white robe. The hood of the robe covered most of her face. Lindy thought she looked rather ghostly with her head hung down. What attracted Lindy's attention was the gold belt that gathered the robe around the woman's waist. The clasp was the head of two snakes.

Lindy didn't remember seeing the woman as she and Nick circled the room a number of times. She must have just come in.

"I'm Lindy Johnson Lee," she introduced herself, still in awe of the woman's appearance. Then it dawned on Lindy. *How did she know what I was thinking? Was it a lucky guess?*

Before Lindy could ask her, the woman said, "Wake up."

"'Wake up'? Oh, my God, who are you?" Lindy asked. "What do you mean, 'wake up?'" Lindy looked into the stranger's eyes, and for a moment, she thought she knew this woman. She felt someone pulling on her right arm. She quickly turned to see Nick standing there with the biggest grin on his face

Lindy turned back to respond to the stranger, and she was gone.

"Did you see the lady I was talking to?" Lindy asked Nick.

"No. You were just standing here. How many glasses of wine did you have?" he asked her jokingly.

"Nick, you must have seen her. She was standing right here. I was talking to her." Lindy put her hands on her hips and looked at Nick with a don't-play-with-me-now expression.

"I'm serious, baby, I didn't see anyone."

Lindy took a good look at him and realized that he was stoned.

"What's the matter?" he managed to get out. After their meeting in the study, Nick had shown his acceptance letter to the professor, and they had gone out into the garden and taken a few hits off some California gold to celebrate. Lindy made Nick uptight. The gold was just what he needed to loosen up a little.

Lindy told him about her strange encounter with the woman.

"I want to talk to the professor and his wife. They probably know who she is." Lindy pulled Nick along with her as she went looking for them. They found the professor at the door saying farewell to several guests. Nick pulled him aside and explained that they needed to talk to him and his wife. Professor Goldstein invited them into the study.

The study reminded Lindy of her grandfather's at home, except for the staleness from the cigarettes and liquor that permeated the room. The large cherry-wood desk took up most of the room. The walls were lined with books, magazines and papers were everywhere.

The Goldsteins listened attentively to the beautiful Howard student telling them about a woman dressed in a white robe and a gold belt that had a clasp made like two snakes.

Ludicrous, the professor thought to himself. Nick probably gave her some hits off the California grass, and she can't handle it. *Nick doesn't need to be involved with her. He is a great artist or will be, and doesn't need this girl no matter how beautiful she is.*

The professor decided to humor her for now and get her out of his house.

"We didn't invite anyone who fits that description," he responded, peeking over his glasses. "Do you know of anyone by that description, dear?" he asked his wife.

Betty Goldstein hesitated a few seconds before answering, "No, I don't. However, let me ask some of the remaining guests if they noticed any woman wearing—what did you say?" Betty Goldstein looked directly at Lindy as she put her glass of wine on the table. "A white robe and a belt that looked like a snake."

"Yes," replied Lindy faintly.

It only took Betty Goldstein a few minutes to return to the study.

"I'm sorry, Lindy, no one saw anything."

As they left the Goldsteins', Betty reached over, kissed Lindy on the cheek, and whispered, "Call me tomorrow; Nick has my number."

Lindy tried to get out of there as fast as she could. Nick's friends probably thought she was deranged. Maybe she should see Dr. Higgs again, Lindy thought as they walked the short distance to the car. He had helped her before; although she had always thrown the Valium he gave her down the toilet.

Once they were in the car and driving to Nick's place, Lindy and Nick both started talking at once.

"I believe you, Lindy; if you saw a woman, then you saw her," Nick stated as he turned into Rock Creek Park.

"Nick, I talked to that lady."

"Betty Goldstein knows something. Did you notice how she hesitated before answering?" Nick asked her as he tried to look at both Lindy and the curves of the road. He was slowly coming down off the high. He knew what he wanted now.

He reached over and began to stroke her leg. He wished she could spend the night with him. He couldn't believe that as fine as she was she had made it all the way through Howard and was still a virgin.

Nick parked the car in front of his apartment building on Ogden Street.

"I have to come up and make a quick change," Lindy said. "Nothing else, Nick."

Nick lived on the third floor, in an efficiency apartment. After that day at the Howard Theatre, they had started having the tutoring lessons in his apartment, and that led to other things. Lindy was accustomed to the clothes, canvases, paint and books scattered around the efficiency apartment. She decided to go into the bathroom to change to deter Nick from anything else. Lindy walked through the closet to get to the bathroom. There was a rollaway bed in the closet for any of Nick's friends who got too drunk or high to go home.

"Do you have Betty Goldstein's phone number? She asked me to call her tomorrow." Lindy's voice quivered as she spoke. She was getting ready to wash the makeup off her face when she realized that Nick was standing in the doorway of the closet with a joint in his hand.

"Haven't you had enough of that?'

"You need to take a few hits to chill you out. Clear your mind, child." He smiled at her.

"Maybe you are right." Lindy didn't particularly like marijuana. She had only tried it once or twice.

Nick handed Lindy the joint as he pulled her wig off and untied her hair. It fell down her back. Nick lifted the hair, swung it over her right shoulder, and kissed the back of her neck. He unsnapped her bra, and his hands caressed her breasts. The nipples were hard and pointing up to the heavens, he would say.

"Nick, it's late" she tried to protest as he started rubbing his hand between her legs.

Lindy had taken a couple of tokes off the joint. She felt weak in the knees. She didn't know if it was from the joint or Nick's tongue darting in and out of her ear.

After a few more hits, she felt funny, like she was floating. She started dancing around the apartment in her birthday suit. Nick just stared at her. Then he pulled her over to the bed. He liked it when she got a little wild. She started ripping his clothes off as they kissed. His tongue began to caress her stomach, and she felt hot all over. He was kissing her mouth again. She lost consciousness for a brief second.

Lindy opened her eyes and Nick was gone. There was a stranger on top of her doing bad things to her.

"Get off me!" she screamed as she pushed him away. "Where's Nick?"

Befuddled, Nick lifted his large frame off her to the other side of the bed.

Lindy looked like a wild animal. He could not see her face because her hair covered it. She was waving her arms, shouting, "Call the police! Where's Nick?"

He tried to grab her, but she pushed him back and kept shouting for the police.

Nick slapped her. Lindy looked at him as if she was seeing him for the first time.

"Look at me!" He took her face in both of his hands. "It's me, Nick. You're OK."

Very softly she said, "I'm scared, Nick. Call the police."

High as he was, Nick knew that calling the police or anyone for that matter was out of the question. He still had some grass in the apartment. The meeting he had with the professor at the party was not only about his acceptance letter but to give him his share of the grass. He had promised to give it to him at the party. Nick didn't consider himself a dealer. He was the middleman. He picked up and delivered. The professor let him keep a little for himself. It was a nice arrangement. But, right now he had to get Lindy to calm down.

"Come on, Lindy, let's walk." She was crying uncontrollably now.

Nick turned on the shower and pulled her into it with him. The cold water felt good. She finally stopped crying. What was in the gold? He wondered. He remembered that someone said give a person milk to drink when he had a bad trip.

Lindy drank the milk as Nick helped her to walk around the apartment. It was one in the morning. She was in no condition to drive home. It was time for him to meet Reverend and his daughter. He wished it were under different circumstances.

Twenty minutes later, they sat in the car in front of her house.

"You don't have to go in with me. Take the car, and I can get it tomorrow."

Her head felt as if it weighed a ton. Everything looked and sounded different. Nick had dressed her, but something was wrong; she couldn't put her finger on it at that moment.

"I'm not scared of them. I just don't want you to have to face them by yourself."

"It's better if you don't come in, Nick, believe me. It will only make it worse."

Lindy looked up at the lighted house. It looked as if every light in the house was on. The clock in the Beetle said 1:50 a.m. The front door opened and Margaret just stood there.

"I'd better go before she comes down here."

Lindy took a deep breath and gathered herself together as she practically fell out of the car. Nick gunned the engine and took off down Sixteenth Street. It was early yet. He knew where he was going.

CHAPTER SIX

Lindy walked up the driveway. Her legs were wobbling and her head was pounding. She looked down at her feet and the platform shoes, shocking black hot pants and red halter-top stared back at her. *Hell*, she thought, *Nick put the same clothes back on me that I wore to meet him.*

It was too late to turn back now. As she got closer to the door and the light, Margaret let out a scream that brought Rev running from his office. He had fallen asleep in his Queen Anne chair as he often did waiting for Lindy to come home. He looked at his granddaughter with disgust and anger.

Margaret reached out and pulled Lindy into the house.

"Look at you. Oh, my God, you look like a slut," her mother screamed at her.

Lindy stood there waiting for the Lord to strike her dead, for she had surely done it this time.

Turning to his daughter, the only thing Rev said was, "Get her upstairs and out of that mess, and we will talk about this in the morning." He left the two of them standing in the vestibule.

"Who is that in your car? Where is he going with it? Where have you been?"

Margaret threw a barrage of questions at her. Lindy's head was still reeling. "Answer me, damn it! Or I will call the police and report the car stolen."

"No you're not. You're not going to do a thing," Lindy hollered at her mother, her hands on her hips.

"What do you have on your face?" Margaret grabbed Lindy's chin and pulled her close so she could get a good look at the makeup on her eyes. "Give me your purse," she demanded.

Before she could answer, Margaret snatched the purse from her, and the contents spilled out on the shining hardwood floor. The red lipstick, rouge, eyeliner and big hoop earrings all made a strange sound, or so it seemed to Lindy, as they spattered on the floor. Her mother stared at her with contempt in her eyes. Lindy's only response was to laugh. She could not contain herself as she started laughing hysterically. For the second time that night, Lindy was slapped.

The sound of a bell startled her. Lindy opened her eyes, and she was in her bed. The alarm clock had gone off. She reached over and silenced it. The draperies were drawn, but she could still see the bright sunlight filtering through the center of them. Then everything came flooding back into her head, the woman, Nick, the joint, the scene at his apartment, and the confrontation with Margaret. Lindy lay in bed for another fifteen minutes. As she tried to get up, her head was pounding. Everything still had a foggy look to it. Lindy made her way to her bathroom. She didn't want to turn on the lights. She looked into the bathroom mirror. Her eyes were puffy and red, as was her face. She looked terrible. She had an hour to get ready to teach the teen class at Sunday school.

As she moved about her room trying to get herself together for the day and to face her family, she thought about the woman in the white robe. Had she finally lost it? Lindy reached under her mattress and pulled out the book she had taken weeks ago from her grandmother's suitcase. She had brought it to her room and started to read it, but she could not focus on it. She only got as far as the third page. Her mind was on Nick most of the time. Besides, the book didn't make any sense to her. She kept turning to the inscription and read it repeatedly before turning to the next page.

The book was divided into twenty-two lessons. Each lesson was less than one or two pages in length. Lindy read the first lesson as if she was reading it for the first time. It said:

"You are a soul. The soul is neither born nor does it die.

"You are Spirit, and with each breath you take you breathe in the gift of life.

"You are made in the spiritual image of God."

Then the rest of the page was blank. Someone had written almost at the bottom of the page, "Help me, God, to know my soul's mission." Lindy recognized the same handwriting that was in the Bible.

She got out of bed, knelt down by the bedside, and recited the Lord's Prayer. "God, what is happening to me? What have I done wrong?" She prayed as she had been taught. "I'll be good. Please, I beg of you, forgive me. God, please forgive my sins. I had sex with Nick. I dressed in a way unbefitting a Christian woman and; Father, I smoked a joint. Father, I am sorry that I caused my family so much despair and pain. I ask that you forgive me, and that my family forgive me… Help me, Father. I promise never to smoke one of those things again, and to dress and act as a good Christian woman."Across the hallway, Rev was also on his knees. His hands were folded together as he silently recited the Lord's Prayer. His chest was hurting so badly, and his stomach was churning. Rev quickly finished and pulled himself up from the floor. It had to be a gas pocket in his chest. He swallowed some aspirin and Pepto-Bismol and prayed that it would at least get him through the morning service. His sermon was going to be on tithing, and he would use the Prayer of Jabaz as the Bible scripture.

Margaret had told him that the congregation needed a reminder about tithing. They were slipping, and that sort of thing you had to catch before it got out of hand. As the painkillers finally began to take effect, the Reverend could smell the aroma of the coffee, bacon, sausage, toast, greens and fried chicken cooking. He smiled to himself as he thought of the good sisters already in the kitchen preparing for today's meal.

His smile soon changed to anguish as he thought of what had happened the night before. He could not believe that his granddaughter had defied him and the Lord. He would have to do something about her. Margaret had not slept most of the night. She lay in bed thinking about Lindy and how she had managed to deceive her. Margaret realized that Lindy was more powerful than she had thought. She was glad that her father had witnessed the demonic act of her daughter with his own eyes. Lindy had to be punished. Just before dawn, Margaret realized what needed to be done. The voice had told her what to do. The first thing that she did that morning was talk to her father.

Midway through the Sunday sermon, Lindy wished she could put her head down to rest. It was throbbing. She was glad that the young people's choir didn't have to sing today, and she could sit in the audience. She avoided her grandfather's eyes as he steered clear of hers. She noticed, however, that today he looked exceptionally tired. Was it because he was up half the night waiting for her? Lindy felt bad about what had happened, and she wanted to ask her grandfather to forgive her. Her grandfather was right. The devil was always tempting Christians to stray from the path. She realized that she could not give Nick up, but she could give up the other things. If Nick really loved her, he would have to do right by her.

Lindy couldn't shake the feeling that something was terribly wrong with her grandfather. She could see dark colors around his chest. She knew if she told him this he would only get upset. He needed medical attention and soon. Maybe if she talked to her mother? But her mother was not talking to her. She was not surprised when her mother ignored her at breakfast. As a child, whenever her mother determined that Lindy was not in best behavior, her mother would stop talking to her. The silence from her mother hurt her more than the actual punishment. Sometimes Margaret would not speak to her for days.

The words "the devil has gotten in my house," shocked Lindy back to reality.

"Yes, you heard me right," the old minister said to his congregation. "If it can happen to me, God's Reminder, then it can happen to you. The devil will sneak up on you. You have to pray and praise the Lord all the time. I'm talking morning, noon and night, children. All day long if you have to get right with the Lord. You got to have everyone in your house praying with you or the devil will enter him or her when you turn your back. Do you hear me?" Rev shouted at the congregation. "If you hear me, then give me an Amen."

Everyone started hollering "Amen!"

"I'm going to ask that the deacons of this Holy Temple come forward and form a prayer circle right here in the front of the pulpit."

Deacon Coleman and the others looked at Rev in surprise. Deacon Coleman was the first to move. Rev hadn't told him or the others that he planned to have a prayer circle. The prayer circles during the sermons were different from the regular old praying in a circle. Rev had brought this with him from the country. The sinners were surrounded by the officials of the church, who prayed over them until they confessed their sins and asked for forgiveness. Rev had not done it for years. Many of the new and younger members didn't go along with such doings.

Deacon Coleman and the rest of the congregation got their second surprise of the morning when Rev said, "Now I am going to ask my granddaughter, Linda Johnson Lee, to come forward and stand in the middle of the circle."

The entire congregation turned to look at Lindy. She knew what was going through their minds. "Were her sins that bad to have Rev call a prayer circle?" The blood rushed to her faced, making her skin looked blotched. *How could he do this to me?* Lindy walked to the center of the circle. Her knees were weak and her head was still throbbing. *I deserve this*, she silently said to herself.

Rev came down from the pulpit. He began reading James 5, Verses 14-16 as the organist quietly played "Lord I Want You to Hear My Prayers."

Rev's voice sounded like Dr. King's as he read, "Is any sick among you? Let him call for the elders of the church, and let them pray over him, anointing him with oil in the name of the Lord. And the prayer of faith shall save the sick, and the Lord shall raise him up, and if he have committed sins, they shall be forgiven him. Confess your faults one to another, and pray one for another, that ye may be healed. The effectual fervent prayer of a righteous man availeth much.

"Kneel down, child," he commanded Lindy. The congregation was waiting for one thing—to hear her sins.

"First, I am going to ask each of the twelve deacons, like the twelve disciples of the Lord, to pray over you to give you a chance to think about the sins that you have committed, and how this is your hour to get right with the Lord." Rev still didn't look at her.

Deacon Coleman touched Lindy on the head as he led the group in prayer. One by one the deacons touched and prayed over her. The congregation edged them on with their "Amens" and "Praise be to the Father." Lindy felt so alone, and the pain in her head was getting worst. She closed her eyes. Her body was trembling and tears continued to stream down her face.

Margaret, standing in the back, could see how distressed her daughter looked. The voice said, "She deserves what she is getting." A smile came to her face. She quickly let it go before someone saw her. Her father didn't want to do this, but she had convinced him that it was for the best. Suppose members of the congregation saw or knew about Lindy's disobedient ways? It was best for them to acknowledge it first and do something about it.

At the end of the prayer, Rev stood over Lindy; he put one hand on her head, and just as he was about to talk, the pain hit him full force. Pain shot through his left arm. Rev clutched his chest as he fell partially on Lindy. For a moment, it seemed as if time was frozen. Deaconess Walker's scream broke the silence, and the congregation's nurse ran toward the circle.

The Rev never got out the words, "Confess your sins." The congregation was sitting on the edge of the pews anticipating her response. Instead, they watched as their beloved minister collapsed on top of his granddaughter. The congregation was on their feet trying to see what had happened to their minister.

Deacon Coleman moved Rev gently off Lindy, saying only, "Give him some air."

CHAPTER SEVEN

The aspirins that he had taken earlier that morning had probably saved his life, explained the short, curly-haired Jewish doctor. He was only a resident, but the cardiologist was on his way. The family would not be able to see Rev for a couple of hours.

The hours seemed to drag as more and more of the members of the church started coming by. Deacon Coleman set up a prayer vigil in the waiting room. They were praying every hour on the hour. The room was getting so crowded that they had to send people home and pass the word along for others not to come. This was going to be a long night. Deacon Coleman promised he would keep the congregation informed of Reverend Johnson's recovery.

It was on the six o'clock news of all the local news stations. Rev was one of the leading ministers of the District, and he sat on a number of boards. Other ministers and officials started calling in, tying up the switchboard at George Washington Hospital.

Finally, Dr. Robert Petersen, the chief cardiologist, came to talk to the family.

Dr. Petersen confirmed what the young resident doctor had explained to them earlier that day. He added that they had to do more tests, but it looked as if Rev Perlie would need open-heart surgery.

Both women broke down and cried. Deacon Coleman and the others tried to console them. They reminded them that Rev was in the hands of the Lord. He was a good man, father and Christian, and the Lord took care of his own.

Dr. Petersen led them to Rev's room. He said Margaret and Lindy could spend no more than five or ten minutes with him. Neither woman was prepared for what they saw. Both Margaret and Lindy had visited members of the church and friends in the hospital before, but this was their first experience with someone they loved. Rev was hooked up to several machines. Tubes were everywhere, in his mouth, nose, arms, and all over his chest. A nurse was checking the monitors, and told Margaret and Lindy that Rev would not wake up because of the medication and the effects of the heart attack. Every time Lindy heard that word she wanted to cry, but she fought back the tears; this was her fault.

Margaret went over to the bed and kissed her father gently on the forehead.

"Papa, can you hear me? I am here. You're going to be all right. Oh, Daddy, you can't leave me now. I need you!" she whispered in his ear as she held his hand. She looked at her daughter, convinced that she worked him into this state with the way she had been acting lately; this was her fault.

Lindy moved to the other side of the bed. She saw how her mother looked at her. It was with the same cold eyes she saw earlier in the church. She looked down at her grandfather. He seemed to have aged within hours. She couldn't believe that this was the man that just hours ago was prancing and jumping around. If only there was something she could do to help him.

Lindy kissed his hand, and started reciting the Lord's Prayer and asking God to spare her grandfather. Each woman was deep into her own thoughts when the nurse came back into the room and told Margaret that someone needed to see her immediately. Margaret had told the other members of the church to let her do all the talking to the press. She didn't want the wrong information getting out. Besides, she knew how to plug the church and give her father good press. Margaret looked over at Lindy, who was still holding her grandfather's hand and praying.

Margaret said to the nurse, "Show me where this person is," and followed the nurse out of the room.

Lindy ended the prayer with "God's will be done." Her head was still lowered when she noticed a bright light coming from the foot of the bed. Lindy turned toward the light, and the lady in the white robe was standing before her. Lindy looked into the eyes of the woman and felt the love and peace that always accompanied the dream she had. Without speaking, the women conveyed to her that they would have to hurry if she wanted to save her grandfather.

No words were exchanged between them. However, working on the commands that the woman telepathically transmitted to her, Lindy followed the instructions she heard in her mind.

Breathe deeply, Lindy, and let it out. Keep breathing and you will notice a tingling in your hands, and when your hands feel hot, place them on your grandfather's chest. Just hold them there and remember the love you have for your grandfather.

Lindy closed her eyes as she took long, deep breaths. She felt a little lightheaded, as if all the blood had rushed to her head, and then she felt a tingling sensation in her stomach, then her arms and hands. Her hands felt as if they were on fire. Lindy wanted to run and soak them in a pail of ice. Instead, she placed her hands on her grandfather's chest. She felt pain, hot piercing pain in her hands and arms, then in her chest. She cried out in pain.

"What's happening to me? My chest, God, my chest!"

Don't be afraid, Lindy. You are feeling the pain your grandfather went through. Breathe child, breathe deeply, and it will pass. Think love, Lindy, love, send him love.

The pain felt unbearable; she had a ringing in her ears, and then she heard words in a language that she didn't understand.

AUM MANI PADME HUM (always bringing me right to my heart where I dwell eternal). Repeat the words: AUM MANI PADME HUM.

Lindy began to mumble the words; they got clearer and she keep repeating them. The pain subsided, and pictures of her grandfather as a child, as a young adult, and finally of him hugging a women with violet eyes flashed before her. The pain returned, and she felt as if she was going to collapse. The words *AUM MANI PADME HUM* rang stronger in her ears. She felt cold, and suddenly saw herself as a child playing in the snow with her grandfather. The scene skipped to her grandfather teaching her to drive in the parking lot of Carter Baron Park. He was laughing as she drove the car around in circles. Lindy could feel the love he had for her. She opened her eyes, and her grandfather was looking up at her.

"It's you," he whispered, and his chest heaved as if he had an electric current run through him. His heart monitor went off and a few seconds later his nurse and Margaret rushed into the room.

"What are you doing?" the nurse screamed at Lindy. "Take your hands off his chest!"

The nurse grabbed Rev and pushed him gently back down on the bed as he tried to reach for Lindy. By then a team of nurses and doctors had come running into the room.

"Get them out of here!" Dr. Petersen ordered the two women.

Margaret and Lindy were practically pushed out of the room. By then Lindy was drained of all energy. She quietly followed her mother down the hall to the waiting room. Distraught, Margaret accosted Lindy before they entered the waiting area.

"What were you doing to Papa?"

"Nothing," Lindy lied. "He had pulled on his monitor, and I was trying to adjust it when it went off."

"You sure you weren't doing some of that devilish work?"

"I wasn't doing anything." Lindy left her mother standing in the hall, then walked into the room and sat on the brown leather couch. The few members of the church who were still there praying asked what had happened, but all Lindy could do was shake her head. She was too shaken to talk.

They waited and prayed.

Hours later, Dr. Petersen walked into the room. The six remaining church members jumped up from their seats and formed a circle around the doctor.

"Mrs. Lee, I don't know how to explain this but your father—" Before he could finish Lindy let out a gasp. "Relax, he's OK," the doctor said.

Then everyone let out a sigh of relief.

"As I was saying before, I don't know how to explain this. Your father was a very sick man when he entered the hospital this afternoon. The EKG showed that he had had a heart attack. Tomorrow we had planned to do more extensive tests to determine the extent of the damage."

Margaret interrupted him. "You keep saying 'had.'"

"That's what I am trying to say. There is no need to do any of these tests. When we rushed to his room thinking he was coding. Instead, the monitor showed that his heart was beating at a normal pace. Therefore, we decided to run some tests again; that's what took us so long to get back to you. The result showed that he never had a heart attack."

Everyone starting talking at the same time. "What do you mean?" Deacon Coleman asked.

"It's difficult to explain. We don't know. There's no evidence of damage to the heart, and he says he's feeling fine. In fact, he wants to go home. We are going to keep him overnight for further observation. We have never seen anything like this. I would like to ask the young lady who was with him in the room when he started coming to, what happened in there?"

All eyes were now looking at Lindy. She could feel tears coming to her eyes. This time they were for joy. It worked. Whatever the woman in the white robe had told her to do, it worked. "Thank you, God!" she silently said. She had not harmed her grandfather. He was going to be all right. She knew it was better to stick to the story she had told her mother.

"Nothing happened in there. He tried to dislodge his monitor and it went off."

Margaret looked at Lindy as if to say, *I know you are lying.*

During the night, Rev was in and out of sleep. It seemed as if every few minutes a nurse was poking him to take his blood pressure and temperature, or listen to his heart and lungs. He wanted to holler, "Leave me be!" He just wanted to try to recapture that moment with Amanda.

Mandy, as he often called her, had been standing next to his bed.

She looked like an angel. She was speaking in tongues. He felt her soft, small hands on his chest and this tremendous amount of love. But when he tried to sit up and talk to Mandy, the violet blue eyes of Lindy and not Mandy stared back at him. Rev knew that the devil was back again, up to his old tricks. Then he slipped into sleep again.

CHAPTER EIGHT

Lindy went right to her room when they returned from the hospital. She didn't want to tangle with Margaret any more that day. She called Nick, told him about her grandfather, and got Betty Goldstein's phone number. Lindy never talked long on the phone to Nick because she would eventually hear a click on the line. After hanging up the phone, she realized that Nick sounded distant. Was he angry with her about last night? He'd promised to meet her tomorrow.

Her call to Betty was also short. "Hello, Goldstein residence."

Lindy immediately recognized Betty Goldstein's rich voice on the other end of the phone. Her voice had a warm, smooth quality to it.

"Mrs. Goldstein, this is Lindy Lee. I met you the other night at your party."

"Oh yes, I remember you. How is your grandfather? I heard about his heart attack on the news."

"He's fine. He will be coming home tomorrow."

"That's wonderful. The media made it sound very serious."

"It was." How much could she share with her? Lindy wondered. A part of her, for some reason, wanted to tell Betty Goldstein everything. Lindy restrained herself from divulging too much too soon. *She would probably think that I am nuts*, she thought, especially after what happened at her house.

"There is something else, isn't there?" Betty questioned her. She had picked up on the stress in her voice.

"I'd rather not say."

"Lindy, can you meet me for lunch tomorrow around noon at the Florida Avenue Grill? Do you know where that is?"

"Yes, I do. I will be there."

When Margaret walked past Lindy's room, she could hear her

daughter talking on the phone. The phone must have rung while she was in the shower, she decided. She hurried to her own room and picked up the phone. She was too late. They were hanging up. But she managed to hear a female voice say something about a bar.

Margaret sat in her recliner, rocking herself back and forth. She wanted to scream. The voices, they were yelling at her. She could hear names—"yellow bitch," "slut" and "whore." She put her hands over her ears to block out the voices when she recognized the voice that was always stronger than the others.

It said, "She's winning him over. You have to stop her."

Margaret sat up straight in the chair. Her mind was racing, going over the events of the last eight hours. Something happened at the hospital when Lindy was alone with Papa, she thought. *She had a strange look on her face when the nurse and I returned to his room and the monitor was beeping. Did she heal him? She's not God. How can she do these things?*

She's just like her, Margaret thought to herself. Papa never talked about her, but she remembered hearing bits and pieces of conversations between her grandmother and her father about her mother. They said she healed people by putting her hands on them. People were scared of her, because she would sit for hours staring at the full moon, and she would wander in the woods late at night. They would see her talking to herself. They never looked her in the eye.

Margaret picked up the hand mirror off the dresser, looked at her face, and began to weep quietly.

"Why don't I have those eyes, that straight hair and that sharp nose?" she asked herself.

She pinched her nose as if to make it straighter. She had started doing that when she was a small child. She took another look at her nose, turning her head from left to right. It looked the same, big and broad on her light-skinned face. She wanted a white face and a pretty little sharp nose like Lindy's.

She had watched how Papa doted on Lindy as a baby, then as a young girl. One time she had heard him say, "Amanda, you have come back to me. God's given me a second chance. This time you'll be just fine and none of that nonsense," and he'd kissed Lindy on the forehead. He looked at her as if he worshiped her. The only time he got upset with Lindy was when she would do or say those strange things.

Ever since she was born, Margaret thought, Papa acts as if I don't exist any more!

But Saturday night, Lindy had shown her true colors. Papa saw it for himself. She was dressed like a whore and running around with strange people that we don't know, just like my mother did. Doesn't Papa know that she is going to hurt him, too?

Margaret stopped, and it finally dawned on her. Who are these people? Whoever they are, they want to destroy Papa and the church.

"I have to put a stop to this once and for all," she told herself.

Margaret rocked back and forth in the chair as the voices in her head continued to shout profanity, and her mind raced.

"How can I stop her? No…" she told herself "…how can I destroy her and anyone involved with her?"

The voice told her what to do. She randomly opened the Book and read, "Unto thee, O Lord, do I lift up my soul.

"O my God, I trust in thee. Let me not be ashamed, let not mine enemies triumph over me.

"Yea, let none that wait on thee be ashamed; let them be ashamed which transgress without cause.

"Shew me thy ways, O Lord; teach me thy paths.

"Lead me in thy truth, and teach me: for thou art the God of my salvation; on thee do I wait all the day."

Margaret closed the Book and smiled. God had spoken to her. She was special.

CHAPTER NINE

Nick had slept late on Sunday. He rolled over and looked at the clock; it was after three. He hadn't gotten in until five in the morning, and he'd been too keyed up to sleep when he did get home. Lindy had really freaked him out. He had gone to one of the after-hours clubs and partied for a while, and then over to one of his friend's pads. A couple of other guys were there playing cards and shooting the breeze about the Black Panthers and how to bring down the Establishment.

At one time, Nick had thought seriously about joining the Panthers, but he knew he didn't have what it took to be one. He was too scared. Nick knew that being a Panther meant more than putting up a good front or a lot of talk. He had to prove that he was committed to the cause, and that meant taking drastic action. Deep inside of him was still the little boy who just wanted to be a famous artist.

Nick was glad that he had returned Lindy's car. His instincts told him that those high-faluting people might sic the police on him. He had gotten one of his boys to follow him to Lindy's house so that he could drop the car off. She had called him and told him about her grandfather. He wanted to go to the hospital to be there with her, but they both knew that would be a bad move. Nick gave her Betty Goldstein's phone number when she asked, even though he was hoping that she had forgotten about that. It was one thing that he wanted her to keep under wraps. He went along with her weird stuff because it didn't interfere with anything. It was between the two of them. But last night she embarrassed him in front of the professor. What did Betty Goldstein want to talk to her about? Damn, he didn't need those two together.

As he was drifting off to sleep, the phone rang again. He let it ring a couple of times before deciding to answer; maybe it was Lindy.

"Hello?" he said in a sexy low voice.

"Hi, Nicky."

Only one person on the Howard campus called him Nicky.

"What's happening, Diana?"

"*Nada*," Diana answered. She was a Spanish major. "Can I come over?"

Nick had to think for a moment. Lindy hadn't said she was coming over. He had them trained. No woman was allowed to just pop in without calling.

"Sure, baby, come on over. I haven't gotten up yet. Why don't you join me?"

"I am on my way."

Nick decided to take a quick shower. As the water ran down his body, he thought about how good it would be to spend an afternoon with Diana. He was still horny as hell. *Women are like cars,* he thought. *Lindy is a Cadillac, and Diana is a Chevrolet. A Cadillac is something you dream about, and when you get it you know that there is nothing like it in the world. The only problem is that you have to handle it with kid gloves. You just can't be. You show off a trophy. You don't let what happened last night happen to your trophy.* Never again would he let Lindy even talk about that stuff or smoke a joint.

Diana, like the Chevrolet, is the backup. The fun car. You know that it is always going to be there no matter what you do to it. Diane was his home girl. They practically grew up together. Some folks at home said she followed him to Howard. He had been fooling around with her off and on since high school. Diana was easy to be with and lots of fun. She knew the score. He wasn't in love with her. With her, he didn't have to think or be uptight all the time. She knew about Lindy and other women he had fooled with. Diana acted as if she didn't care, as long as she got what she wanted, and he had plenty of that to go around. Lindy didn't know about Diana. And that was how he liked it.

It didn't take her long to get there. Nick opened the door and his eyes took in everything about her. She was stacked, with big breasts, a big butt and big legs. Her brown 'fro was short and neat to match her deep brown skin and eyes.

" Hi, is everything OK?" She looked at him with concern.

"Yes, come on in." He pulled her to him and, with his foot, kicked the door shut. He reached over and locked the door. Nick practically tore her clothes off and for the next hour they made love as if they had never done it before. With Diana there was no holding back.

When they were finished, Diana got up and searched her bag for a cigarette. *Nothing like a cigarette after good sex,* Nick thought. He had stopped smoking because of Lindy, but Lindy wasn't here now. Diana lay back on the bed. He took the cigarette out of her hand and took a couple of puffs.

"I thought you had stopped."

"I have, but a hit once and awhile doesn't hurt anybody."

"Nick, I need to tell you something. I am late."

"Late? What are you talking about?"

"I missed my period."

Nick had turned on his side to face her.

"I missed this month. I didn't want to say anything, because I wasn't sure what was going on. You know I am irregular, and sometimes I can go almost two months without having a period. But I'm worried." Diana's eyes were large and anxious.

Nick couldn't be hearing what he thought he was hearing. His brain was fuzzy from that grass last night. Diana was telling him she thought she might be pregnant. But he hadn't been with her for a while.

"Diana, this is the first time we have been together in weeks," Nick said to her as he put on his jeans and stood at the bottom of the bed.

"Did you hear me, Nicky? I said that I missed my period for this month. I think I'm pregnant."

"Are you sure? How do you know it isn't something else?"

"My breasts are tender and I have morning sickness. I have a doctor's appointment tomorrow, so I'll find out for sure."

"You managed to screw all right earlier."

Diana picked up a pillow and threw it at him. She gathered up her clothes and started getting dressed.

"You can think what you want. I don't fool around. This baby is yours, Mr. Nicholas Lewis." Her voice was choked and tears began to trickle down her face.

Part of Nick wanted to hold her, and the other part wanted her just to go away, like a bad dream.

Diana picked up her purse and headed for the door. Nick reached for her arm.

"Wait a moment, Diana. Let's talk about this thing." He could not get his mouth to say the word "baby."

"This 'thing' you are referring to is a baby, and there is nothing to talk about right now. You'll hear from me, Nick. I think you had better think twice about Paris. In fact, if it's a girl, I think I will name her Paris." Diana slammed the door in his face.

He started to follow her, and then he decided he needed time to think. Nick searched the apartment until he found a cigarette butt. It tasted stale and dry, but it soothed his nerves. A child meant a lifetime commitment, child support. Hell, he wasn't ready for that. He didn't even have a legit job. He had sold some of his paintings, thanks to the professor, and that was enough, if he was careful, to get through the summer. He had put all his hopes in getting the fellowship and a chance to go to Paris. Now this. He had to talk Diana into having an abortion. There was no other way.

CHAPTER TEN

On Monday morning, the house was quiet when Lindy went downstairs. Margaret's car was gone. Lindy knew that her mother had gone to the hospital to bring her grandfather home. It was just like her mother not to include her or ask for her help. This morning Lindy decided not to let that upset her; she had other things on her mind.

She wanted to see Nick and to tell him about what happened at the hospital. She also wanted to see him to make sure he was not upset with her about Saturday night. Lindy tried calling him. No answer. Was he still asleep? Nick never got up before noon. She wanted to go over there, but she never did that without calling him first. She needed to see him. Her heart won out.

Lindy quickly dressed. She didn't even take time to dry her hair. She didn't want to be there when her mother returned with her grandfather. She realized that she was not ready to face them yet.

Ogden was a quiet residential street situated between the busy thoroughfares of Sixteenth Street and Fourteenth Street. Lindy circled the narrow street until she found a parking space not too far from Nick's apartment building. She sat in the car debating whether to go into the apartment building or go find a telephone booth and try to call him again. One thing was for sure, she could not continue to sit in a car with no air conditioning. The day was hot and humid. The underarms of her blouse were already stained with perspiration. The hair that had been wet and dangling down her back when she left the house was already dry from the heat. Lindy pulled it together in a ponytail and put on her straw hat to keep from being sunburned.

She went around to the side entrance of the building. Sometimes guests or residents would leave the door propped open. She wanted to go directly to Nick's apartment, avoiding the front desk. The receptionist was a young student from Nigeria who liked to talk to her. Nick often teased her that the Nigerian had the hots for her. Lindy was in no mood today to carry on a conversation with him. She pulled on the door a few times, but it was locked. She made her way around to the front again.

The Nigerian buzzed her into the building. She had planned to ignore him and just go up to Nick's apartment, but he stopped her.

Giving her a big smile, he said, "He left twenty minutes ago. Not home."

He could see how disappointed Lindy looked. She was such a beautiful girl, he wondered why Nick fooled with those other women.

"Do you want to leave a message?"

Nick up and out so early is unlike him, thought Lindy. "No, I'll stop back later."

"You don't want to wait? I could get you something to drink," the Nigerian offered.

"Thanks, but I have to go." *You really want me to stay so that you can talk my ear off!*

Lindy sat in the car for a few seconds more, trying to decide where to go. She still had some time to kill before meeting Betty Goldstein. She definitely was not going back home, she told herself. She turned on the radio in time to hear Nighthawk, the DJ, blasting out, "Good morning, Chocolate City. Wake up! It's time to have some hot fun in the summer time. For all of you folks out there that don't have to hit the 9 to 5 this hot funky day, drop by Meridian Hill Park. It's happening there, baby. Check out the drums. Connected to your roots. Meanwhile, here's something for the rest of you poor folks slaving over a desk. Mary Terrell…"

Lindy didn't wait to hear the rest of his message. She had heard enough to know where she needed to go. As she got closer and closer to Meridian Hill Park, she felt a strange kind of excitement. She counted her blessings as someone was pulling out of a parking space. When she stepped out of the car, she could hear the drums. Forgetting about the heat, Lindy ran up the flight of stairs to the top of the park. She turned to face the east side of the park, and she began to walk toward the bench, where a lady in white sat waiting for her.

Lindy approached the bench with apprehension. Her hands were sweating, and her heart was beating fast. Although the lady had her back to her, Lindy knew who she was. She couldn't explain it, but she had felt that the words of the DJ were a message for her to tell her to come to the park. When she reached the back of the bench, the lady turned and looked at her. Their eyes locked.

Lindy moved to the front of the bench and she sat down on the edge next to the lady and said, "Who are you?"

"My name is Mary."

Lindy paused for a moment, thinking, Unbelievable. I am sitting in a park talking to the mother of Jesus. Am I crazy?

"I am not that Mary," the woman said, as if she could read her thoughts. "Because of who you are and your mission in this incarnation, your vibration is high enough to have contact with me. If you have doubt, you won't maintain it. Doubt keeps your soul closed to the teachings. Seek the truth." Before Lindy could respond, Mary disintegrated into pieces like a puzzle, and she was gone in the blink of an eye.

Lindy sat there in utter amazement, going over in her mind what had just transpired. *Seek what truth? "Incarnation," "vibration," and "teachings"* — the terms meant nothing to her. *What did she mean by "who you are" and "your mission?"*

The heat was unbearable, but Lindy could not bring herself to move, when she felt a hand on her shoulder. Lindy quickly turned, hoping that Mary had returned. Instead, she found herself looking into the familiar face of Cissy the booster.

Besides attending Mt. Olive Baptist Church, Cissy sold expensive clothing to many members of the church and other prominent people in the City. Margaret was one of her best customers. It was rumored that Cissy shoplifted to get the clothes. Others said she got them from her New York connection. Lindy knew that her mother didn't care. Cissy would stop by their house two or three times a month. She often could hear Cissy and her mother either haggling over the price or gossiping about others. Lindy went out of her way to avoid Cissy. Cissy had dark colors around her. Lindy didn't know exactly what that meant, but her instinct, coupled with the dark colors, told her that she didn't want to tangle with Cissy.

"That's a pretty white lily. Where did you get it?" Cissy asked in her nicest voice. Cissy had tried to be nice to this one, but this one turned her nose up at her. Whenever she came to the house, this one acted as though she didn't exist. *What is she doing in this park anyway?* Cissy wondered.

Lindy looked down at the lily that was lying next to her and picked it up. She had not noticed it before.

Cissy continued with her questions. "You come up here to hear the drummers?"

"Just for a little while. I have to go now," Lindy responded as she glanced at her watch and realized that it was time to meet Betty Goldstein. Walking away from the bench and Cissy, Lindy smelled the lily and felt an overpowering feeling of love and peace.

The Florida Avenue Grill was small and very popular. It was known for its chitterlings, collard greens, fried chicken, corn bread and sweet potato pie. Lindy had been there plenty of times with Nick over the last year. He loved the place, said it reminded him of his mother's cooking. Lindy arrived before Betty Goldstein and managed to get a booth in the back. She was looking over the menu when she glanced up to see Betty coming in the door.

Betty Goldstein walked in and all heads, including those of the women, turned to look at her. She was stunning, with a larger-than-life brownish-blond Afro, and large breasts accentuated by a small waist and hips. Several gold bangle bracelets encircled her arm and a two-carat diamond ring covered her finger. As she made her way to the booth, she stopped several times to greet people and hollered at the waitress, "my usual!" Lindy noticed that she had this air about her, sexy but sophisticated. She reminded Lindy of Foxy Brown, a black female superhero in the movies.

"Hi," she smiled at Lindy. "Have you ordered yet?"

"No, I just got here. I was looking over the menu. I am not that hungry," responded Lindy feeling a little in awe of this woman.

"Nonsense, you can't come to the Florida Avenue Grill and not eat. At least get a piece of the corn bread or sweet potato pie."

"The pie is my favorite."

Betty's "usual" turned out to be fried chicken, potato salad, collard greens, yams and rolls. Lindy decided to order a turkey sandwich and the pie. They made small talk as they ate their food. Lindy could hardly stuff down the sandwich, hoping that Betty would tell her something that would shed some light on her situation.

"Betty, do you know something about the woman that was at your house?" Lindy asked as her eyes turned a deeper violet.

The changing of Lindy's eyes didn't go unnoticed by Betty. In time, Betty knew, Lindy's beauty would be striking. She looked liked a plain Jane now, but with some makeup, a new hair style, and some meat on her bones, she was going to be a knockout. The outfit she'd worn to the party the other night was hip but tasteless. The wig was all wrong, too. The girl had possibilities.

"The woman that you described, I saw her not the other night, but many years ago," Betty said. "I was about your age."

"Are you sure?"

"Yes. Her name was Mary, she was dressed in a white robe, and the robe was gathered around her waist by a gold belt. The clasp on the belt was formed by the heads of two snakes. She was just as you described her. That is why I asked you to repeat what she was wearing. And that's why I left the room, not to ask other guests if they had seen her because I knew they hadn't, but to get myself together."

"Tell me who she is," Lindy asked excitedly. "Tell me about your experience with her."

"While I was in college, I met a man who was a Muslim. I became involved with him and converted to Islam. I wore the traditional women's clothes, I prayed five times a day, and I shared him with his other wives."

"How many wives?" Lindy's mouth dropped opened.

"I was number three. After a year of trying to get pregnant, I could not. The other three wives either had children or were pregnant by him. To save face, he got rid of me. I was devastated. I loved this man. He just told me to get out as if I was nothing. I totally lost it. I couldn't stop crying, I couldn't eat, my weight dropped to a hundred pounds. I looked like a walking skeleton. Then it started. The dreams. I kept seeing this woman next to my bed. She looked exactly like the woman you described. She didn't talk, but we communicated. Do you know what I mean?"

"Yes." Lindy thought about her own experiences with Mary.

"I went back home, and my mom and dad helped me to get through this difficult period. I never told anyone, not even my mother. I was already on the edge, and I didn't want them to commit me. It was that bad. My doctor prescribed Valium for me. What a trip! I was high all the time."

"What did she tell you?" Lindy pressed her, trying to keep the conversation on track.

"She kept reciting this Bible verse to me, Luke 8: 1-3."

"The one where Jesus drove the demons out of Mary and the other women?" Lindy stated.

"Your grandfather would be proud of you. You know your Bible."

"Why did she recite this particular verse to you?" Lindy's curiosity really had the best of her.

"It had something to do with what she called my 'soul's mission.'"

"Soul's mission?" Lindy repeated, feeling a chill.

"I'm getting there," Betty promised, searching in her purse for a pack of Kools and lighting up.

"I had this dream," she went on at last. "The woman in white was in it. I was lost in a forest or jungle, I don't remember all the details, but she appeared in the dream and led me out of the forest. When we got to the edge, she said an opportunity was going to come my way and for me to take it. I asked her name, and she looked at me and said, 'Don't you know who I am? When are you going to wake up out of this illusion?'"

Betty took a couple of drags on the Kool before she continued.

"Soon after that my aunt, who was very religious, was traveling to the Holy Land for a conference, and she asked me to go with her. My parents didn't want me to go, and I still wasn't interested in anything. I just wanted to take my Valium and float away. But I remembered the dream about the opportunity, and said yes. The trip changed my life. In Jerusalem, I felt like I had come home.

"My aunt was busy with her conference, and I spent my days wandering the streets of Jerusalem. I had the feeling that I had walked upon that soil before. My aunt's conference was for a week, but she was offered the chance to stay for the summer on a special project. I decided to stay with her.

"To occupy my time, I learned Hebrew and studied world religions. It was at the university that I met Harvey Goldstein. He became my friend and lover. When I came back to the States, we kept in contact. He encouraged me to return to college and go to law school. He immigrated to the States and got a position at Georgetown, and we were married soon after he got here."

"Do you love him?" Lindy wasn't sure why she asked that.

"What's love, Lindy?"

Lindy thought about herself and Nick. What did she know about love?

"You still haven't told me about the soul's mission," she said.

"Each soul has something that he or she must do in this incarnation," Betty replied.

"What's yours?" Lindy tried not to show how excited she was when Betty used the term "incarnation."

"I am still trying to figure that out. I know that it has something to do with religion. I was raised a Baptist, but I don't go to church, or, for that matter, practice any religion. I do believe in God and Jesus. My father and mother have tried for years to get me to go back to church. The hell and damnation sermons don't do anything for me. Moreover, most religions exclude women from being priests, rabbi, and ministers. Am I stepping on your toes?"

"To be truthful, I am so mixed up I don't know what to believe," Lindy answered. "Sometimes I think I am crazy. I had two other experiences with Mary since your party."

"Speak, child, you are holding out on me!" Betty teased.

Lindy quickly told Betty about everything. How she saw the eye colors, could sense illnesses in others, how Mary told her how to heal her grandfather, and her encounter with Mary in the park.

"What you call 'eye colors' is the person's aura," Betty explained.

Lindy pressed her body against the table, leaned over as far as she could and whispered to Betty, "Aura? What is it, and can you see it?"

Betty could see how difficult it was for Lindy to talk about this. She wanted to reassure her that she was not hallucinating or imagining that she had been seeing things all these years.

"The aura is the energy field around living matter, specifically, the physical body. You are what we call a psychic. God, if only I could see and do what you can do!"

"You make it sound as if it is a gift instead of curse."

"It is a gift, a gift from God to help you with your soul mission."

Lindy didn't respond. She just looked at Betty as if to say, *I am not buying this; maybe you're the one who's crazy.* Sensing Lindy's ambivalence, Betty decided to go one step further.

"Do you really believe that you had these encounters with Mary, or do you think your mind is conjuring or playing games with you?"

"To be truthful, I don't know. I go back and forth. When I am experiencing the encounters, I believe. Once they are over, and I am going over them in my mind, I think I am crazy. My mother and grandfather told me that people just don't go around seeing colors around others, and that it's not right to think you know what ails a person."

"There are plenty of people who can do what you do, Lindy, and even more."

"Yeah, where are they? At Howard, I was known as weird. I promised my grandfather that I would let it go, but I can't help myself. For example, I was listening to the radio before coming here. I hear the DJ say 'wake up' and the name Mary. To me that was a sign or message. I went to the park, and Mary was there. I don't think anyone else could see her."

"I saw her," Betty responded.

"How do I know you are telling me the truth?"

"You don't, but it's no coincidence that we met. There is a meeting on Saturday that I think you should come to that will help clear up some of your doubt. It helped me." Betty wrote down the time and place and passed it to Lindy.

Lindy looked at the address and said, "I don't know, Betty. My grandfather is upset with me. I don't want to cause him any more trouble. I think I'd better cool it."

"All I am asking is that you think about it," Betty said sincerely, resting her hand on Lindy's on the table. "Pray on it and follow your heart. It is the doubt that keeps you confused to the truth."

Lindy stared at her and said, "Those are almost the same exact words that Mary said to me."

"You are special, Lindy," Betty told her. "You see auras and spirits, and you can heal. This is no time to doubt yourself. You will meet others at the meeting who have had paranormal experiences. Come and you will find out that there are others like you. I think this group will point you in the right direction to learn how to develop your gift."

"I'll let you know," Lindy said, getting up from the table.

They walked out of the Grill together into the high levels of pollen and humidity of the afternoon. Betty reached into her bag and pulled out her sunglasses and a book.

"Read this." She handed it to Lindy. "I think it will help you."

The title of the book was *There Is a River*.

CHAPTER ELEVEN

Nick got up early Monday morning. He hadn't slept the night before, after Diana dropped her little bomb on him. The first thing he did upon arising was to call the professor. Betty Goldstein had already left for her office when Nick arrived in Georgetown. This time he had to catch the bus then walk a few blocks to the professor's house. Nick tried not to look conspicuous in this neighborhood, but he stood out like a sore thumb. Blacks shopped in Georgetown, but they didn't live there.

The Harvey Goldstein was waiting for him. He had known by the sound of Nick's voice on the other end of the phone that something was wrong. Nick didn't want to discuss it over the phone. He was hoping that it didn't have anything to do with their arrangement. Maybe he just needed money.

The professor led Nick to the garden, where he offered him a large glass of iced tea. Nick would have preferred to stay indoors, but the professor was working outside and wanted to finish doing his planting before midday. Nick didn't waste any time telling the professor about his dilemma.

"Is she going to have the baby?"

"She hinted that she would," Nick replied.

"And what do you want?"

"I don't love Diana, and I don't want a baby!" Nick threw up his arms as he walked back and forth along the brick-lined path. The Goldsteins had had their garden designed by one of the leading landscapers in the country. It had won a number of awards, and their house was listed on the Georgetown Tour.

The professor was dressed in shorts and sandals. His chest was bare. His curly red hair, white around the edges, was almost as thick as Nick's. He had a habit of pulling on his beard, which Nick thought was in serious need of a trim. Whenever the professor looked at him, his blue eyes had a twinkle in them.

"So, what are you going to do about it?"

"What can I do?" Nick shook his head as the professor offered him a drag on a joint. Nick declined. He wanted to keep his head clear. He was meeting Diana later that day.

"You could try talking her out of it," the professor suggested.

"You mean get her to have an abortion."

"Why not? Let's be realistic here. You have your future ahead of you. Nick, going to the University of Paris will open doors for you. You don't need any excess baggage. But I might be talking out of turn. Are you sure you don't love her?"

"Hell, I definitely don't love her. We just had a thing and, I thought, an agreement."

"Then do what you have to."

"I don't know anyone who can do it."

"Check around first, though I think I may be able to help you. You have to think of your future, Nick. You have your life ahead of you. The opportunity to go to Paris to study art doesn't come every day. You can't let this one get away."

"I know, I know. But even if she decided to have an abortion, I don't have the money to pay for one."

"Don't worry about that. I have been meaning to talk to you about a friend of mine who owns a private school. He likes your work and wants you to do a mural for the school. Here's his number." He wrote the number on a piece of paper and gave it to Nick. "If you get the assignment, the fee should be able to carry you for the summer, and pay for the abortion."

"You make it sound so easy. I want this thing over as quickly as possible," Nick responded as he got ready to leave. He had taken up enough of his mentor's time.

The rest of the morning passed slowly for Nick. He kept going over and over in his mind what he planned to say to Diana. He had called her late Sunday night and convinced her to meet him after her doctor's appointment on Monday. He could tell by her voice that this was going to be an uphill battle. She was supposed to meet him at his apartment by noon.

It was now two. He was worried that she would not show up. Then he heard that knock on the door. Nick jumped off the bed and two leaps later he was opening the door.

"I thought you were going to be here by noon?" Nick said testily. His nerves from waiting had made him edgy.

"The doctor's office was crowded. I had to wait my turn," Diana said as she sat on the bed. She had decided to wait as long as possible before confronting him. She had almost decided not to come. She had vomited twice that morning. The nausea made her feel lightheaded.

"What happened?" Nick demanded as he looked at her with disgust. He felt that she had deliberately kept him waiting. He had to get a grip on himself or he would mess up everything.

"I told you, Nicky, I am six weeks pregnant. What else is there to tell? We are going to have a baby," Diana responded. She was trying to be brave, when all she wanted to do was cry. She didn't want him to see her crying.

Nick pulled up a chair and sat directly in front of her. He pulled up close enough so that one of his legs was in between her legs.

"Diana…" he stopped, took her hands into his and looked into her eyes. "You have another year in school, and I have the scholarship for art school in Paris—"

"Don't finish that thought, Nicky. I know what you are thinking, and I am not going to let some doctor butcher me up and kill my baby." The tears that she had tried to hold back began to flow freely down her dark brown skin.

Nick stood up and pulled her up to him. He held her in his arms.

"I wouldn't let any one hurt you, Diana. It's not legal, but there are doctors who perform these things. We have to think of our future. Or how about its future? How would we take care of it?"

"Stop calling her an it!" Diana shouted. "I can't do it, Nicky. It is against my religious beliefs. I don't believe in killing helpless babies. I already told my mother, and she told me to come home, and she will help me."

"You did what? You told your mother? Shit! You have it all worked out, don't you? What about my feelings?"

"What about your feelings, Nicky? Was I just a good lay for you all these years? I guess I don't count. Ms. High Yellow is the princess of your life."

"Leave her out of this. I thought we had an arrangement. You dated other guys. Hell, how do I know that it is really mine?" Nick's voice shook with anger. The phone was ringing. He just looked at it.

"Because I am telling you it's yours. Just because I dated other guys don't mean I slept with them. I don't want anything from you, Nicky. Go to Paris, and marry your little princess. I am getting out of here!" Diana slammed the door behind her.

Tears were still streaming down her face as she walked up Odgen Street to 14th Street to catch the bus. She wanted to scream. It hurt so badly. She had always loved him, even though she knew about Lindy. She had hoped that he would come to his senses and see that Lindy would eventually drop him for one of her own kind. But he had started seeing more of Lindy and less and less of Diana. She could feel him pulling away from her. Diana knew that she was just a piece of ass to him. She'd been so preoccupied that she forgot to take her birth control pills for a couple of days. Or did she forget?

She'd thought about having an abortion, but only for a brief second. She was going to have Nicky's baby. She would give him time. Once he saw the baby, she knew he would come around. He was ambitious, but under all that "I want to get ahead" was a sweet gentle guy that she planned to spend the rest of her life with. The problem wasn't Nicky. It was that blue, green, whatever color-eyed girl who lived on 16th Street and had everything.

CHAPTER TWELVE

Lindy stopped at a phone booth to call Nick; she didn't get an answer. She decided to drive up 14th Street and use Odgen to connect with 16th. Maybe she would see Nick walking in the neighborhood. As she made a left turn onto Odgen at the small triangle, Lindy slowed the Beetle down to a crawl. Sometimes Nick hung out with the neighborhood guys, or block boys as the Howardites called them, at the strip of land that formed a triangle. Lindy hit the brakes as a young girl crossed in front of the car. She had almost hit her. The girl looked familiar to Lindy. She was crying. Lindy only got a glance at her, but she thought she had seen her on Howard's campus. As she cruised down Odgen Street, Lindy never gave the girl another thought; her mind was on looking out for Nick. She pulled up in front of his apartment. She thought she could wait for him, but that might be forever. She looked around for a parking space and didn't see any. She pointed the Beetle toward 16th Street.

Margaret was waiting for her when she returned to the house. She could hardly get in the door before her mother started in on her. Lindy just wanted to go to her room and shut the rest of the world out. She knew that this conversation was coming and decided she might as well bear it now rather than later.

"Papa is waiting to talk to you. He is in his study. Don't get him riled up. He's not out of the woods yet. All of your foolishness this weekend has really put a strain on him. I told you the other day he wasn't feeling well, and what do you go and do but upset him with your nonsense?"

Lindy stood there without uttering a word. She knew that if she tried to explain, Margaret would cut her off and continue to rant at her. She always saw it her way, and her way was always the right way.

"I'd like to know where you got that clown outfit you were wearing the other night. You of all people, the minister's granddaughter, walking around the streets of DC looking like a—I might as well say it—a whore."

Lindy shifted her weight from one leg to the other. Her head was hurting from the heat and she wanted to scream, "Leave me alone!"

"Don't you have any shame? What I want to know is, who was that driving your car? The car, not incidentally, which I pay the notes on, young lady."

Lindy maintained her silence.

"You gone deaf on me or something? I said who was driving your car?"

"Enough, Margaret!" Neither one of the women had heard the door of the study open. Lindy saw how frail her grandfather still looked. *He should be in bed,* she thought.

"Lindy, come in here. I want to talk to you, alone." Rev turned and went back into his study.

Margaret folded her arms and turned to go back to the kitchen.

Rev eased down into his chair, and Lindy sat across from him. Neither said a word. Rev finally took a couple of sips from a glass of lemonade and placed it back on the table.

"I know young people like to have fun," he began. "You're young, and you want to have fun with your friends. I'm glad to see you getting out and enjoying yourself."

Lindy was surprised at the way the conversation was going. Had something else happened in that hospital that she was not aware of?

"I am not getting any younger, Lindy. I pray that I get a chance to see you through medical school, and married to a good Christian man with a family of your own."

Here it comes, thought Lindy.

"I always told you it is not easy being the minister's daughter or granddaughter. You are the sheep right behind the shepherd. I need you and your mother to set the example for the rest of the flock. There are some bad sheep out there, Lindy, that will try to get you to follow them. That's where I come in. I am the Reminder of God's will. The devil is always at work, night and day. There is only one way in this world, Lindy—the Christian way. With this way comes certain rules that sinners have trouble abiding by. I don't have to tell you what they are. You know.

"Those hippies, Black Power people, whatever you want to call them, are up to no good. There is a justice. God will reward the good and punish the sinners. Don't let them lead you to hell. Who is he?"

Rev's question took Lindy by surprise. She looked at her grandfather and knew she could not lie to him.

"His name is Nick Lewis. He's not involved in the movement."

"People can fool you. What do you know about him?"

Lindy told her grandfather how she had met Nick, and what she knew about him. She left out the part about their afternoons at his apartment.

"Why haven't we met him?"

Lindy shrugged her shoulders. "I don't know."

"Then invite him to church and dinner on next Sunday. It's time we met Mr. Lewis."

That night, Lindy tried to call Nick for the third time. Still there was no answer. She ached to see him. Unable to sleep, she picked up the book Betty had given her earlier that day. She didn't close it until 2 AM.

CHAPTER THIRTEEN

The address Betty Goldstein had given Lindy was located in Chevy Chase, Maryland, an upscale middle-class white neighborhood. It really wasn't that far from where Lindy lived. The houses were large, with well-kept yards. Lindy found the house she was looking for with no problem. It stood out among the others because of its purple door, with an interlocking triangle prominently displayed in the center.

Odd, Lindy thought, *why would they do that?* Then she remembered that the interlocking triangle represented the symbol of the Jewish faith. Betty was married to Harvey Goldstein, a Jew. Was this a ploy on Betty's part to get Lindy involved in Judaism, by pretending to know about the mysterious Mary, and about eye colors or auras? Why would Betty deceive her? Lindy felt apprehensive about taking those steps to go inside the purple door.

A knock on the passenger side window of her car interrupted her thoughts. An elderly white woman stood there looking at her. She motioned Lindy to follow her as she took hold of the arm of the man standing next to her. The couple made their way to the steps of the front porch. The elderly lady, again, looked back at Lindy and, again, made the motion for her to follow.

Lindy just sat motionless in the car as the couple disappeared into the house. She took a glance at herself in the mirror and frowned. Margaret had thrown away her makeup kit, and she didn't have any money to buy any more. Cinderella had turned back into a pumpkin.

As she stepped out of the car, she pinched her cheeks to give them some color and wished she had some lipstick. The couple waiting on the porch looked harmless enough to her. Could these people actually see auras, or eyes colors, as she liked to call them? The book, *There Is a River*, which Betty had given her, told the amazing story of how Edgar

Cayce, a psychic, prophet, and healer, could see auras. He could also put himself into a trance and accurately diagnose people's illnesses. Then he would recommend cures. *This is what I want to do, heal others*, Lindy thought.

A sign on the door said "Come in." Lindy hesitated for a brief second before turning the doorknob. Fear gripped her. She felt her stomach tighten up. Was she doing the right thing? Lindy felt that if she walked through that door her life would be forever changed. She stood there thinking about how devastated her grandfather and mother would be if they knew she was about to attend this meeting. It was against the Christian way. She remembered the promise she had made to grandfather to stay away from what he called the devil's work.

Lindy did what she always did when she was indecisive. She prayed and asked God what to do. She felt a gentle breeze touch her face, and it sounded as if it said "Doubt and fear keep you from the truth." She turned the knob and walked through the door.

She could hear music, and followed the sound until it led her to a room that she thought was the living room. It didn't have the typical living room décor. About ten to thirteen people were sitting in folding chairs in a circle. In the center of the circle were several large, jagged transparent rocks. Lindy had never seen anything like them before. The curtains were drawn and twelve white candles gave off a warm glow. The walls were adorned with photos of geographic places that she didn't recognize, except for the pyramids of Egypt.

Betty was already there. She wore a plain white cotton dress and a large six-pointed pendant with a purple stone in the center that was breathtaking. She came over and greeted Lindy with a kiss on both cheeks.

"Let me introduce you to the members," she said.

"Before you do that, I need to know something."

The girl looks petrified! Betty thought. "What's wrong?" she said. "Tell me."

"Is this—" Lindy pointed to Betty's pendant, "—part of some cult or Jewish ceremony? If it is, I am going to have to leave. I don't have anything against Judaism, but—"

"Hold on," Betty interrupted her. "What you will experience today has nothing to do with any religious group. Trust me. Where did you get that idea, anyway?"

"The interlocking triangles on the door. Doesn't it stand for Judaism?"

Betty put her arm around Lindy. "There is nothing for you to fear, Lindy. No one is going to force any ideas, practices, or beliefs on you. You are free to go anytime you feel uncomfortable. You are right; the interlocking triangles do represent the Jewish faith, but they are also ancient Egyptian symbols that mean the union between lower and higher consciousness. And that's what they represent for us. There is much for you to learn if you desire or, better still, if your consciousness is ready to wake up."

Betty introduced her to the elderly couple that had entered just before she did. They were Peter and Ruth. Ruth took Lindy's hand and held it for a few seconds. Lindy could not help but notice the unique silver ring that Ruth wore on her right hand. The top of it was in the shape of a pyramid with a blue stone in the center. Ruth smiled, patted Lindy's hand and said, "The High Priestess."

Lindy had no idea what she meant. Before she could ask her to explain, Betty introduced her to the next person, Matthew. He just nodded his head and said, "Welcome." The owner of the house was Mark, who gave Lindy a kiss on both cheeks. The last person was Thomas, an older, distinguished-looking black man. Lindy noticed that all the members were dressed in white.

Several other people were scattered throughout the rooms. Betty explained that this was their first time attending the meeting also. Betty introduced Lindy to each of them. Koto Omo from Ghana was working on a doctorate degree in philosophy at American University. He told the group that when he was a young boy the shaman of his village had told his parents that he was marked with a special gift, and that one day he would be a great leader of his people because of this gift.

Lindy wanted to ask him what gift, but Betty moved on to the next guest, Lin Lee. Lin Lee was a third generation Chinese-American. Her family owned a restaurant in Chinatown, where she worked. People would come to the restaurant not only for the food, but to talk to Lin Lee. She was better than a fortune cookie.

Betty took Lindy by the arm and led her to the crystal room, where three of the guests were walking around admiring the crystals. Betty explained to her that crystals were gifts from the earth in that they store, transform, transfer, and amplify energy. They were used by people of ancient cultures such as the Atlanteans and Egyptians for power and for healing purposes. Lindy picked up one of the stones.

"Interesting that you picked that one." Betty looked at the stone. "It is a moonstone, used for soothing and balancing the emotions. It also helps to eliminate fear and aid in bringing peace and harmony to psychic abilities."

"It's beautiful," Lindy stated as she put the stone back on the shelf.

"No, keep it," Betty said. "Evidently you are resonating to it."

Matthew, an Arabian man, and a Hispanic woman were speaking in Spanish when the two women approached them. Abdul immediately introduced himself. He was from Saudi Arabia, and now working as an interpreter for the State Department. Maria tapped her feet together and twirled around them. She taught dance lessons at a local dance studio, she explained.

Betty pointed out the last member, an older Jewish woman named Barbara Einstein, who was talking to Ruth in the library adjacent to the crystal room.

The most pleasant sound of chimes and bells infiltrated the atmosphere. Betty indicated that they had to return to the main room; the meeting was about to start. The members began to take their seats, and the newcomers followed suit. Betty sat next to Lindy in the circle.

"We would like to welcome you," Mark began. "Each of you is here by invitation from one of the members. There is no coincidence that they met you and extended this invitation to you today. They connected with you on a soul's level, recognized your special talents." He paused and looked around the circle at the guests.

"We are a non-profit group that promotes, preserves, and disseminates the ageless wisdom and carries forth the Divine Plan of God, the ageless wisdom being the accumulated knowledge or sacred scriptures of the world. We are not a cult; neither do we have religious, political, or social affiliations. I know that you have plenty of questions, and we will allow a period of questions and answers. But first, all of our sessions start with a meditation to connect to the divine source and relax our minds and bodies. Clear everything off your laps, and place your feet on the floor. Do not cross your ankles; it blocks the flow of the energy. Just follow along the best you can. Eventually, things will get clearer."

Lindy looked around; the group was sitting with their eyes closed, and their hands were in their laps with the palms facing up. For a few seconds the room was quiet, then the members made the sound A-U-M. The sound permeated the room.

I've heard that sound, she thought. But where?

The word AUM flooded back into her consciousness. Mary had told her to use that word during the healing of her grandfather.

The group then began to chant, "I AM the Alpha and the Omega, the Great White Light." They said it repeatedly until Lindy thought they would never stop.

Finally, the soft, gentle sounds of a harp and flute filled the room.

One of the members began to speak, Lindy didn't know which one, but he had the most incredible voice. It was strong but soothing. "Close your eyes and breathe deeply of God's gift of life. With each breath that you take, you renew your divine connection to God."

Lindy quickly stole a look around the room; everyone's eyes were closed. The sound of the speaker's voice helped her to relax. Soon she could not hold her head up. Her chin kept falling on her chest. She tried to focus on what the speaker was saying.

"Let go of all that is not in harmony with you. Take another deep breath and relax. I am going to count down from the number ten, and at each level you will go deeper and deeper into consciousness."

Lindy tried to maintain consciousness, but the music and the sweet smell of incense made her feel peaceful and relaxed. By the number seven, she realized that she wasn't quite asleep, but neither was she fully conscious.

The last thing that she remembered the speaker saying was "...number one. You are now at a deep level of consciousness where you will connect with the God Force."

Lindy's awareness was pulled to the area between her two eyes, in the center of her forehead. A picture card appeared. On the card, a woman dressed in a blue-white robe sat on a high-backed chair placed between a white pillar that had the letter J written on it and a black one with the letter B. Lindy stared closer at the card. The woman had a large cross in the middle of her chest. A round ball that looked like the full moon was in the center of the crown she wore on her head. She had in her hands what seemed to Lindy to be a scroll. There were words written on the scroll, but Lindy could not read them. At the very bottom of the card were the words: High Priestess.

Before Lindy could react to the words, two other cards appeared. Lindy read the words written at the bottom of each: The King of Cups and The Empress. A hand appeared and placed the King of Cups over the Empress. The High Priestess was placed beneath them. To the right of the cards were placed two others, The Queen of Swords and The Hierophant.

"What does this mean?" Lindy mumbled. Instantly the cards were gone. Her eyes opened. Everyone was staring at her. How long had she been out?

She dismissed the cards from her mind when Mark started talking. "If you decide to join us, you will be paired with a mentor. Your mentor will work with you on a special assignment that will be given to you in order that you fully learn and understand the laws of the universe. Additionally, you will participate in a group assignment. Included in the package we will give you is a bibliography of titles that we recommend you read. We have our own library, and you can borrow books from it. Some of the other titles you can find at Yes Bookstore in Georgetown."

"How does one join?" a middle-aged lady asked.

"'Join' is not quite the right term," Mark explained. "There are no official papers or procedures to follow. You either choose or don't choose to follow this particular path to truth."

Then Betty spoke to the group. "You are the fortunate ones. You have the gift of accessing higher consciousness through your paranormal abilities, and you will soon have the knowledge to understand the universe and mankind. Most of humanity is in a dream state. We call them sleepers. They live in a world of illusion or *maya*. They see the events of their lives as solely good or bad luck. They get caught up in the collective consciousness beliefs of the moment, whether they be illnesses, poverty, sexual diseases, wars or racial issues. You will learn that these events are not real."

"What are you called?' a voice asked from the back of the room. Lindy turned to see who had asked the question. The darkest eyes she had ever seen stared back at her. He looked about her age. He was extremely handsome, with olive skin and straight black hair that he wore pulled back in a ponytail. He looked Native American to Lindy. She bowed her head as if she was reading. He must have come in during the meditation; she didn't remember seeing him in the circle earlier.

"Awakeners," Mark answered back. "You could say that we act as guides on your spiritual journey, pointing the way to reality. An awakening can be very exciting, but also it can be very stressful. Your family and friends will try to put doubt in your minds. They will accuse us of brainwashing you with satanic dogma and occult practices. Some will even turn against you or try to get you to turn against us. If you choose to remain, you will embark upon a path that will be difficult but spiritually rewarding.

"If you look into the package that was placed on your chair, you will find a list of decrees or the twelve principles that we adhere too. I think this will help to clarify what we are about. Today we will just read them, but if you choose to stay, you will spend many hours learning in depth what each of these decrees means."

The group followed along as Mark read each one aloud.

"We believe in God, the omniscient, omnipresent, and omnipotent.

"We believe that we are one with the Mother/Father God.

"We believe we are made in the image of the Mother/Father God.

"We believe that we co-create with God.

"We believe we are Spirits with a soul and body.

"We believe that the body is a temple that we use for each incarnation.

"We believe that the soul/spirit is eternal and indestructible.

"We believe that life continues after death.

"We believe in reincarnation.

"We believe that love heals.

"We believe in the Will of the Mother/Father God.

"We believe in God's Plan for humanity."

Before anyone else could speak, Ruth stood up and began to speak. Lindy looked at the tiny woman. She could not be over four feet tall. What she lacked in height, she had in voice. Her voice was deep and distinctive.

"We know that you have a lot of questions about the decrees. Nevertheless, we want you to hold them for now. Your mentor will select one or two of the decrees to work with you on a special assignment. However, the first three decrees we will work together as a group: We believe in God, the Omniscient, Omnipresent, and Omnipotent. We believe that we are one with the Mother/Father God. We believe we are made in the image of the Mother/Father God. First, you have to make a decision." Ruth looked around the circle at the newcomers. "No one will ever pressure you to stay on this path. You can stop, change, or do whatever you want to at any time. All we ask is that you follow your soul and heart. We will take a short break; you may stay or leave at this time. It is up to you."

No one moved. Lindy looked around the room. The other students seemed to be as mesmerized as she was with the Awakeners, except for one. The young man who had caught Lindy's eyes earlier seemed quite lucid, whereas the rest of the group looked mystified. There was something about him that was different. She felt that he belonged with the guides and not the students. Perhaps he didn't belong here at all.

A bell sounded. Lindy looked toward the direction of the sound. Mark was striking a large crystal bowl. Betty touched Lindy on the shoulder and gestured for her to follow her.

"Have you made up your mind?" Betty asked, looking at Lindy.

"I feel as if I am torn between two worlds," Lindy answered. "I fear that if I stay, I am not being faithful to God and to my family, but at the same time, my heart and soul tell me to seek the truth for myself. Plus I have a lot of curiosity, so here I am."

Betty reached over and hugged Lindy. "Seeking the truth is seeking God. One day you will realize that you made the right decision. I am your assigned mentor," Betty said with pride.

Lindy was glad that Betty was her mentor. She would have had a difficult time explaining if one of the others called her house.

"We are going to work on the following two decrees: We believe that life continues after death and we believe in reincarnation." Betty handed Lindy an envelope. "Inside is your assignment. Read it later and we will discuss it. Let's go eat, and then walk around the garden to get grounded."

Later when Lindy returned to her seat, she found that a deck of cards had been placed on it. She picked them up. She looked around, but no one seemed to be paying any attention to her. Lindy opened the deck and turned the first card over to face her. It was the devil. She let out a little gasp.

"Don't be frightened, child."

Lindy looked at the diminutive woman who stood there in front of her with that same smile she had given Lindy earlier, urging her to come into the house.

"It scared me. The devil is not a good card; at least I know that."

"Sometimes it is. When we face our fears, we learn our greatest lessons." Ruth turned and started toward her seat across from Lindy.

Before she could ask Ruth about the other cards that she had seen during the meditation, Mark was striking the crystal bowl again. Lindy looked around. No one had left the circle. The Awakeners continued with the meeting as if they knew what was going to happen.

Thomas, the older black male of the Awakeners, stood behind his chair and called the meeting to order. Lindy noticed that the Awakeners didn't give last names or, for that matter, reveal much about themselves.

- "Earlier, Mark talked about the extraordinary talents that we all possess. But the truth is, everyone has these abilities, but only some can recognize them. You are not special or weird. Those who criticize you or make fun of you are ignorant to the knowledge or truth." Thomas paused as if to let the information sink in. "You are fortunate that your third eye is open. What you need to learn is why it is open, how it operates, and how it operates for you. There is a difference between the last two.

"We have not always been in the body form that we now have," he went on. "Souls were first in astral form, then animal, more human than animal, and lastly human. However, not the human body of today. At one time, the third eye was the only eyes we had. It was our link to our divine connection. As souls got more involved with materialism, the body changed. The third eye closed and so did our divine connection. We relied on the two physical eyes to perceive our world.

"We began to work out of our lower center, called the solar plexus. That is how we came up with the expression 'I have a gut feeling.' The ability to use your third eye is a higher level of skill to access sacred knowledge. It is your divine connection.

"Science refers to your abilities as ESP, extrasensory perception. ESP is what they call the sixth sense, bringing a person information about events that can take place either in the present, past or future. This information is perceived by the person beyond the means of using his or her five senses.

"Psychical research supports the concept that everyone has the capacity for ESP. How well it is developed depends on the individual. Some people will have ESP experiences throughout their lives and ignore them. Others will have one or two and can make a big fuss about them. Edgar Cayce's abilities developed after an illness. Others have paranormal experiences as young children that get stronger as they get older. ESP can manifest itself in individuals in many different ways. It does not follow manmade time boundaries; ESP covers telepathy and clairvoyance."

Thomas stopped for a moment and looked at the group. "Comments or questions? Please stop me at any time. I am giving you this background so that you can understand that on your path you will be faced with the challenge of differentiating between your talents and your spiritual journey. "

"It is comforting to know that I was not going off the deep end when I started seeing dead people and then angels," Maria, the dancer, said. "They would be just standing at bus stops, or in hospitals, banks, anywhere. I could not shake them. Then they started talking to me."

"Maria, you have astral clairvoyance, where you have a perception of the astral and etheric planes and the inhabitants, such as spirits, angels, devas and demons," Thomas explained.

"I know exactly how you feel, Maria." The African scholar sitting next to Lindy starting talking. "For years my family and friends have been telling me that I was special because I could hold or touch something that belonged to someone and tell them all sorts of things about the owner of the object."

"The technical name for what you can do is ESP, Extrasensory Perception," Thomas explained. "ESP can be divided into telepathy, which is mind-to-mind communication of thoughts, ideas, feelings, sensations, and mental images, and clairvoyance, which is the internal seeing of symbolic images that must be interpreted. There is also clairaudience, where you hear sounds from other dimensions, or sounds, music, and voices not audible to normal hearing. What you will learn here or with your mentor is how to work with your abilities to reach your maximum potential."

"That's me!" Lin Lee hollered out, she was so excited. "When I give someone a fortune cookie, I hear other things that are not written in the fortune cookie. I am able to tell them things about their lives."

"I travel to other places," Abdul volunteered. "I haven't left my house, but I am able to go to other places and come back and describe what the place looks like and what was happening. What is this called?"

"You are having an out-of-body experience or astral traveling. Sometimes you can even go to other dimensions," Thomas answered.

Lindy decided that she might as well join the group, although she had a better understanding of her abilities after talking to Betty and reading about Edgar Cayce. "I see eye colors—I mean the aura around people. I can also tell if someone is sick."

"One of the highest levels of clairvoyance is seeing the auric field surrounding all living things and the ability to see diseases and illnesses in the human body," Thomas said. He had had many years of teaching and, looking at the faces of the students he knew that he needed to clarify the term "auric field."

"An auric field is the energy field that radiates around everything in nature. This includes humans, animals, plants, and minerals. The aura is not visible to the human eye. Those with the gift see it as a circle of light in colors. Is this how you see it, Lindy?"

"I see colors bouncing off people, or next to some part of their body. Before my grandfather's heart attack, I could see a darkness over his chest."

"Why don't you share with the group what happened in the hospital?" Betty asked her.

Lindy hesitated for a moment, and then she related her encounters with Mary and the healing of her grandfather. She felt a sense of relief to have shared her story. The others sympathized with her about her grandfather but asked many questions about Mary and the healing technique. Lindy was never criticized or told that she was doing the devil's work. She realized that it was safe to talk to this group. She had only one regret—that Nick was not there with her. She missed him terribly. They had not seen each other all week. She had finally been able to call him. He had seemed distant and preoccupied, but he promised to come to church and dinner on Sunday.

As much as Margaret wanted to see what Nick was all about, she dreaded meeting him. The night he drove Lindy home, she got a quick look at him, and she didn't like what she saw. For most of Saturday morning, Margaret remained in her room. She could hear Lindy and her father moving about in the house. When she heard the front door shut, Margaret peeped out of her window and watched as Lindy got in her car. Margaret sat on her bed rocking back and forth wondering where Lindy had gone. By the afternoon, she walked quietly down the hallway to Lindy's room. She opened Lindy's door and closed it behind her.

Margaret walked around the room pulling out drawers looking in them for anything that might reveal Lindy's whereabouts. Not finding anything, she went into Lindy's bathroom and stood in front of the medicine cabinet mirror. She was too scared to look into the mirror. The voice kept telling her to do something with her big, ugly nose. Margaret finally looked in the mirror. "Why," she asked herself, "do I have to have my nose spread across my face?" "Pinch it, pinch it!" The voice said. Margaret did as she always did and grabbed her nose between her fingers and squeezed it several times. Turning from side to side, she looked at it again. *Maybe,* she thought, *it is getting more like Lindy's. Papa will see that I also look like that woman.* She couldn't bring herself to say, her mother.

Margaret reached into the pocket of her dress and found Lindy's makeup case that she had taken from her. She opened it and found the red lipstick. She took the lipstick and put three small smears of it on each cheek. Rubbing it in, her cheeks turned into two red circles. Then she covered her lips with it. Margaret let out a weird laugh. She couldn't stop. She never heard the door of Lindy's room open.

Rev stood there not believing what he saw. He quietly closed the door behind him and said, "Lord, help us."

Lindy looked at her watch. It was getting late. Little conversations had sprung up among the students. Thomas cleared his throat and the students focused back on him. "We would like you to write down the history of your talent. When it first started, what types of things you can do, what triggers it or how you can induce it, and any significant events. You must be comfortable with your talents by practicing them to reach your maximum potential, as I mentioned before. The more proficient you are, the easier it will be for you to establish a divine connection."

Thomas took a sip of water and then looked at Ruth, who made some type of signal with her fingers.

"Thank you, Dr. Thomas." Ruth took over the group. This time she remained sitting. "As you walk the path, you will face challenges with your gifts." She waved her hand in the air. "Not like the ones you are facing now, where your family and friends think that you are unusual. In the next decades, with the changing of the planetary energies, many souls will start to awaken to their psychic abilities. They will be obsessed with the occult.

"This is the infantile stage of psychic development. Fortune-telling will be replaced by something called psychic readings. They will be offered over the television, on the phone, and electronically for a fee. Should you be caught up in this materialism, you will be working from your lower center, the solar plexus, and not the *ajna* center, the third eye. When you work through the *ajna* center, you will be able to establish your divine connection and use your talents to help others in their spiritual evolution."

Koto, sitting next to Lindy, asked, "Could you elaborate more on divine connection?"

Ruth brought her hands in front of her in prayer fashion. "Divine connection to other dimensions provides pathways to higher worlds of light. You will be able to access the akashic records. These records, written on the etheric plane, contain everything—actions, thoughts, and emotions—about every soul. They are a record of the spiritual progress of souls. When Edgar Cayce was in a trance, he could access these records to get information about his clients to diagnose their illnesses and recommend healing. You will be able to do this and more. The time is coming in which the world will need spiritual agents to work with the World Order to help mankind.

"It is getting late, and I know we have given you a lot to think about and to do. Nevertheless, we must do one more important thing. My question to you is, who or what is God?"

The room remained quiet.

"Don't everyone speak up at once." Ruth laughed. "Any Catholics in the group? I like to pick on them."

"God is the Father, the Son, and the Holy Ghost," Maria replied as she made the sign of the cross.

"God is YAHWEH," the Jewish woman remarked. She had been quiet most of the day.

Ruth looked around and said, "No other brave souls out there, huh?"

Lindy remembered the scripture, John 4:24. She meekly raised her hand and, as all eyes turned to her, she said, "God is a Spirit. No one has ever seen Him, but He has been described as having wooly hair and eyes of fire. I was also brought up to believe that God is the Father who lives beyond the sky, in heaven, who determines everything in our lives whether it is good or bad."

Lin spoke up. "I am a Buddhist. We do not believe in a personal God, but we believe that we can attain Nirvana."

"The answer to your question is in the Qur'an. There you will find Allah," Abdul spoke with authority. "No vision can grasp Him, but His grasp is over all visions. He is above all comprehension, yet is acquainted with all things."

Ruth turned to the young man with the dark eyes and said, "Do you want to take a stab at this?"

He smiled and replied, "Wakan Tanka is indescribable."

Ruth then looked at all of them with such intensity that Lindy wondered what was going to happen next. "To understand who you are, you must first understand who God is. You must establish a personal relationship with your God. Next time we will delve into more. In the meantime, read, talk, live and experience God." She ended just like that.

Interesting, Lindy thought. *Ruth never told us whether we were right or wrong; neither did she give us her answer to who is God.* Before leaving the center, Lindy asked Betty why Ruth just didn't tell them the answer to the question, "Who is God?" Betty responded that the teaching method they used was to get the student to think for his or herself and not to prove that someone was right or wrong, which was judgmental. It was not their intention to convince anyone to go against his or her religious beliefs. It was through spiritual growing that the person would understand and know God. She further explained that to know God was to know yourself and your mission. Lindy found more truth in her words than in a lifetime of Bible studies.

CHAPTER FOURTEEN

As Lindy was leaving, the young man with the intense eyes stopped her at the door.

"Did you just graduate from Howard?" he asked somewhat abruptly.

Startled, Lindy answered, "Yeah, how did you know that?"

"I was in your year. I've seen you on campus."

"I'm Lindy." She couldn't remember seeing him on campus. How could she have missed him? He was even better looking close up. But not her type. He was a pretty-boy, and probably had dozens of women waiting in line for him.

"My name is Paul."

They stood by her car talking until Lindy realized that she had to go.

Driving home, she reminisced about what he had told her. He planned to go to India for six weeks then return in the fall to attend Howard's Divinity School. For the last two years, he had worked part-time doing a variety of jobs, one that included working for Peter and Ruth. He did research for their book. When that was finished, he had worked in Betty Goldstein's law firm as a mail clerk. Ruth and Betty had both invited him today, but Ruth was his mentor.

Lindy told him how she had grown up suppressing her gifts, about her plans to go to medical school in the fall, and about her uneasy feelings before the meeting. She deliberately omitted that her grandfather was the minister of one of the biggest Baptist Churches in DC. Paul was easy to talk to and seemed to hang on her every word. She had given him her phone number, but could not figure out after the fact why she had done that. Why hadn't she told him about Nick? She didn't plan to have anything to do with him except when they met with the Awakeners. However, the Awakeners never mentioned when the next meeting would take place. Ruth had simply said, "read, talk, live and experience God. Establish a personal relationship with God."

Lindy believed that she already had a personal relationship with God. She prayed every day, lived and grew up in the church. Ruth couldn't be talking about her, or was she? Lindy realized that she had never questioned or doubted what Rev and her mother had taught her about God or the Bible. Rev said that questioning the Bible was the way the devil tempted Christians. Lindy had always accepted that the Bible is the living Word.

After today and the events of the last couple of weeks, though, she was not so sure about that way of thinking. Lindy realized that the Awakeners were asking her to expand her consciousness and not accept religious doctrine based on blind fate. This concept went along with something she had recently read; that blind faith keeps people stuck in limited awareness. Lindy felt that her whole life had been lived in limited awareness. Since the beginning of the summer, a floodgate had opened up, and she was caught up in a whirlwind that she had no control over.

Lindy stole a quick glance at the book on world religions she had borrowed from the library of the Awakeners' center. She knew that she would read about the different religions and sacred scriptures with an open mind.

Even though it had been a long day full of so much information, Lindy still felt her heart racing and the adrenaline moving through her veins. She glanced at the dashboard clock. It was only five o'clock. Still early as far as she was concerned, although she had been gone most of the day. For once she could hope that Margaret wouldn't question her about her whereabouts. The household was not completely back to normal, but at least they all were making an effort to smooth things out. Margaret had started talking to her again. Grandfather looked better as the week wore on. This gave Lindy a little bit of freedom. She had one more stop to make.

The park was as lively as ever. The musicians were there, and a crowd had circled the drummers. Several women were dancing to the music. Vendors were selling jewelry, dashikis, incense and food. Lindy looked around and didn't see anyone she knew. She made her way through the gathering until she got to the bench where she'd seen Mary. Once again, Mary was there.

Mary had her back to her as before. Before Lindy approached the bench, she heard Mary's voice in her head say, "I have been waiting for you child." Lindy just sat down next to her. The woman looked at her, smiled, and then kissed her on both cheeks.

"You are getting stronger. You felt me calling you."

"Yes, I had a strong urge to come here."

"And you followed that inner feeling. That is good. Let this be a lesson for you. It is your Higher Self, your soul advising you to do a particular thing because it is part of your soul's mission and will be good for you. Always follow that inner voice."

Mary went on to say, "For your mission in this incarnation, it is important that you remember who you are and the powers that you possess."

"Mary, who is God?" Lindy asked suddenly, looking at Mary with begging eyes.

"I cannot tell you that, child. You must decide who God is for you."

"Why can't you just tell me?" asked Lindy

"Because it would not have the same impact. I can only share with you enough information to get you started along your path. In order for you to fully comprehend who God is and who you are, you must experience God."

"So that's my mission, to find out about God?" Lindy asked, looking a little perplexed.

"We all have the mission to find out, experience, share and use what we have found to serve others," Mary replied.

Before Lindy could ask Mary another question, Mary put her two forefingers on the space between Lindy's two eyes. It was the same place where Lindy had seen the Tarot cards earlier. Lindy now knew from the lecture that Thomas had given that this was her third eye or the ajna center.

She felt a warm feeling embrace her. She could hear the drums in the background, and the smell of lilies was back. The beat of the drums made her heart race. She felt like she wanted to dance. Then a picture flashed in the space where Mary was touching her. Lindy was in a circle with others, dancing to the beat of the drums. She could not see the faces of the others, but their bodies moved with hers in time with the drums. They urged her to make her sound, a sound that belonged only to her. She threw back her head, and a strange noise came out of her, resonating from her heart. The more she repeated it, the more powerful she felt.

She felt safe in the circle. Whoever these people were, they accepted her for who she was. The sound that she continued to make came from deep inside of her. She was no longer dancing. Her feet were planted firmly on the ground with her legs not quite arm length apart, and her arms were extended in front of her.

She thought she heard Mary say "Breathe, breathe in the gift of life. You are awakening to who you are. In time you will remember. You can only be given what your vibration can handle. If you are given too much too soon, you will not be able to handle it. You need time to absorb and understand the teachings. Remember not to push yourself too fast. As you are given a teaching or principle, you will experience it on four levels: physical, emotional, mental and spiritual. You will be given signs to follow if you choose. Always remember who you are."

Lindy inhaled a large gulp of air and felt her body relax. The tension from before was gone. Her body felt light, and her mind was at peace. The drums were getting loud again. Lindy opened her violet eyes to the landscape of Meridian Hill Park. She was on her knees in the center of the circle of drummers and dancers. In her right hand was a lily. Lindy looked up into the faces of a crowd of people who had gathered for the dancing. They were pointing at her and shouting for more.

Lindy quickly got up and made her way through the crowd. They patted her on the shoulder as a way of acknowledging how well she had done. Lindy looked over at the bench for Mary. She was gone.

As Lindy made her way to her car, she realized that she had no recollection of how she wound up dancing in the middle of the circle. At this moment she didn't care; she had never felt so peaceful and close to God. It was as if she had released something inside of her that she had been holding onto all her life. *Is this what Ruth meant by establishing a personal relationship with God?* she mused.

She didn't see Cissy, the booster, standing amongst the crowd, giving thanks to God that she was in the right place at the right time to witness Lindy's wild, abandoned dancing. Cissy thought Lindy's behavior was downright vulgar, and she would make sure that the right people found out about it.

CHAPTER FIFTEEN

Rev didn't particularly like it that the Reverend Alan Pierce was preaching this Sunday morning. Margaret and Deacon Coleman had convinced him that it was too soon for him to get up there. He protested that he felt fine. The first couple of days he was home, he had felt a little light-headed, but that soon passed. Still, he had to admit to himself that Pierce was a good man. Margaret liked him. Rev was hoping that they would get together. She needed a man; maybe if she settled down, some of that nonsense of hers would go away.

After his little talk with Lindy, she seemed to settle down, too. He had warned Margaret to ease up on her. He knew that what Lindy had done was serious. He had no doubt that a two-legged devil was behind all of it. He just had to flush him out in the open. Nevertheless, Rev was confident that he could rein his granddaughter in.

"Give her some room," he'd told Margaret. "The girl is twenty-two, getting ready to leave home for medical school. She's an adult now."

Margaret, as usual, accused him of siding with Lindy. It wasn't that he was siding with her, he was just being cautious. Rev was determined that he wasn't going to lose Lindy the way he'd lost Amanda.

And speaking of the two-legged devil, Rev looked over at Lindy and her friend Nicholas Lewis sitting in the front pew. Rev immediately pegged Nicholas as a lady's man. It took one to know one, he laughed to himself. This one must be a real charmer, because he sure as hell didn't look like anything. Margaret had been beside herself earlier when she first met Nick. She'd cornered Rev in his office just before the service started.

"Papa, did you see him? She is doing this deliberately to get back at us. Look at him, Papa. I'm not going to have any black, nappy-headed, broad-nosed babies in this family. I just won't have it!"

"Now, Margaret, she's not going to marry him. Just calm yourself. I don't want you getting yourself all upset. I'll take care of this. Service is starting. We will talk about this later."

Rev sat there staring out at the congregation, thinking how could his granddaughter had gotten mixed up with this snake charmer? He was not good enough for Lindy. He had nothing to offer her. What did women see in these types of men? This one had even tried charming Rev himself earlier when Lindy introduced them.

"Good morning, Reverend Johnson. Thanks for inviting me. I have been wanting to visit the church for some time now." He'd smiled.

Hell, Rev silently mumbled to himself, this country boy surely didn't want to meet me!

"What kept you from coming sooner?" Rev asked, playing along.

"Um, I work some Sundays," Nick had lied.

Rev looked at the young man with his big Afro, wearing a suit that looked too small for him. The cuffs of his shirtsleeves were worn. *This boy doesn't have a pot to piss in!*

"Was your car in the shop the other day?" he probed him, still with a smile on his face. "Is that why my granddaughter was out late at night dropping you off at home?"

Before Nick could reply, Rev saw Deacon Coleman and Reverend Pierce beckoning him to join them. The service was getting ready to start.

Rev knew that his reference to the car had put the charmer on notice. I am nice to you in front of my granddaughter, he was saying, even though you are not good enough to even look at her. My mentioning the car is my way of letting you know that I am on to your game.

Rev caught Nick's eyes for a moment. Nick quickly looked away. *Just as I thought*, Rev congratulated himself. *He's no match for me.* Rev relaxed; he knew this one was no threat. No, there was someone or something else out there working on Lindy.

Later that day, they sat around the dining room table and ate in silence, except for polite conversation. Rev had invited Reverend Pierce to join them. Margaret and some of the church sisters had prepared collard greens and cabbage, fried chicken, yams, rice and gravy, and hot rolls. For desert, they had peach cobbler and ice cream. The charmer kept complimenting Margaret on the meal, but she wasn't buying any of it. She barely said two words to him. She would just grunt or mutter a thank you. Finally, after eating a healthy portion of the peach cobbler and ice cream, Reverend Johnson looked at Nick as if he was seeing him for the first time.

"Lindy tells us you from Alabama," he stated rather than asked.

"Yes, sir, Tuscaloosa County," Nick replied wiping his mouth with the linen napkin.

"I know some Baileys from down there. Reverend Joe Bailey, pastor of New Shiloh Baptist. Do you know him?"

"I don't know him personally, sir. But some of his grandchildren went to school with me."

"You're Baptist, or what?' Rev asked.

"We are Pentecostals, Reverend," Nick quietly lied. Well, he told himself, he'd only told a half of a lie. When his parents went to church, they did attend the Pentecostal services, however seldom that was.

"Pentecostal," Rev remarked. "What type of work does your father do?"

"We own some land. My father is a farmer." *Farmer sounds better than sharecropper*, Nick thought. "My mother works in the hospital." Nick was feeling anxious. He didn't like to talk about his humble beginnings, especially to these people. He knew that Rev was putting him down in a cunning way, and there was nothing he could do about it.

"Any other sisters and brothers?" the Reverend asked as he pushed the empty dessert dish away.

Here it comes, Nick thought. No sense in lying about this. "Yes, sir. I have six brothers and five sisters."

"Whoo, now that's a big family!" Rev remarked. "Twelve of you."

"I come from a big family, too. There are nine of us," Reverend

Pierce interjected. "And your oldest brother is a doctor, four of your sisters are teachers, and isn't one of them working on a doctorate degree?" Everyone turned and looked at Margaret. She had finally joined the conversation.

Reverend Pierce shifted uncomfortably in his seat and remained quiet.

"That's right," was all he said.

"You attended Howard on a scholarship?" Rev continued questioning Nick.

"Yes, sir. I received an academic scholarship, and I worked part-time to help put myself through school."

"Now that you have graduated, what are your plans?"

Nick wanted to say, "to make some money, Reverend." Instead, he stuck to his plan to present himself as a nice college graduate just trying to get ahead. "I plan to go to graduate school and get a masters in art education. Then to teach art on the college level."

Nick didn't share with him his plans to become one of the greatest black artists of the 20th century. His paintings would be part of the Smithsonian collections as well as those of private art collectors. One day he would own not one but several large houses with servants for each one. He'd see if Reverend Johnson looked down on him then.

Right now Reverend Johnson looked at his granddaughter and said, "My granddaughter has a brilliant career laid out for her. She is going to Meharry Medical School in Tennessee. Did she tell you her father was a doctor?"

Before Nick could answer, Rev continued talking. "Ever since she was a child, she has wanted to heal people. She even thought she could heal them by touching them. We had to convince her that she really couldn't heal people. She was only doing child's play."

Nick knew that Reverend Johnson was trying to pull him into a conversation about Lindy's gift. He also caught how the Reverend emphasized the sentence about Lindy's going to medical school.

"Lindy will make a great doctor," was all Nick said. At this point, he wanted to get out of there. Lindy's mother hardly looked at him, and when she did, it was with disgust. The grandfather's line of questions wasn't bad; it was the tone of his voice and body language that sent the real message to him: You're not good enough for her!

Nick knew he had to get out of there. He was beginning to feel trapped. He wanted to get out of these clothes or at least unbutton the top button of the shirt and take the tie off. His hands were beginning to sweat. He looked at his watch and motioned to Lindy, who had been sitting there like a puppet all afternoon.

Margaret had gone to the kitchen and was just returning to the dining room with coffee when she heard her father mention Lindy's going to medical school. She knew that her father was sending Nick a subtle but strong message that Lindy's future was not with him.

"Coffee?" she asked him.

"No thanks, ma'am." Nick was surprised that Margaret was now going to acknowledge him. "It's late, and Lindy and I had better be going if we want to get to the movies on time."

"What you think of that Black Power Movement?" Rev asked, as if neither Nick nor Margaret had spoken.

Nick toyed with his fork and then looked at Rev with an expression that said, *I am tired of your bullshit, old man!* "It has its merits and disadvantages."

Rev saw the expression on Nick's face and read it clearly. "What merits would those be?"

"Grandfather, please, no politics today. Nick and I are going to the movies." Lindy pushed back her chair. "Let's go, Nick."

They scurried out of the house before Margaret had a shot at him.

Once in the car, Nick kissed her as if he had not seen her for a year instead of only a week.

"Your grandfather doesn't like me. Neither does your mother." Nick looked at her as he loosened the tie and pulled it off.

"I love you." She reached over and kissed him again.

"It's because of how I look."

"Stop it, Nick! I don't want to spoil our evening together. All parents give boyfriends a hard time. Besides, you're black and beautiful to me."

"See the truth, Lindy. Your parents are into that high yellow crap."

"But I'm not, and that's what counts."

Nick's face was distorted, and he had a wild look in his eyes. He could read between the lines. He started mimicking her grandfather. "Where's your car? What do your daddy and mama do? They don't think I am good enough for you."

"Nicky, stop it! What's wrong with you?"

"What did you call me?"

"Nicky. For some reason, it just came into my mind."

"Don't ever call me that. I can't stand that name." *Shit*, he thought, *maybe she really is psychic.*

"OK. I will repeat my question. What's wrong with you?"

"You're so psychic, why don't you tell me?"

Lindy was lost for words. She didn't know how to respond to Nick. She had never seen him so edgy and angry. She decided to be quiet and just drop the subject for the rest of the ride to the theater. His mood didn't improve any when they drove past the theater and saw the long line. Then they had a difficult time finding a parking space. The U Street corridor was a popular area for Negroes because of the restaurants, stores and three movie theaters. But at last they found a spot, and for the next two hours, at least, everything was fine.

Hours later when they left the movies, Nick seemed to feel better. He put his arm around Lindy as they walked a few blocks to her car.

"I have some good news to tell you," he said.

"What?"

"I got the fellowship to the University of Paris. This little black boy from Alabama is going to Paree."

"Oh, Nick, that's great. I am so happy for you!" She hugged and kissed him. "Why didn't you tell my grandfather?"

"It wouldn't have made a difference, Lindy. In their eyes, I will never be right for you, because of who I am."

"Don't say that, Nick. Besides it is what I want, and I want you."

Ignoring her last words, he continued. "You'll be in Tennessee dissecting frogs and cadavers, anyway. Besides, they want you to marry a doctor like your father."

Lindy knew he was right about a lot of things. The thought of not seeing him for a year was too much for her to think about. Even if she was in medical school, she thought that he could come down to see her and they would see each other on school breaks, but Paris—

"I thought we could celebrate today. I guess I am a little uptight about this work project that I have to do," Nick admitted. "Let's get some Chinese food like we planned."

"I have some news to share with you also," Lindy said.

"Talk, baby, talk." Nick sounded more like himself.

Lindy told him about going to the center and her meetings with Mary.

"Who are these people, Lindy?"

"Friends of Betty Goldstein, the professor's wife."

Those two don't need to be together, Nick thought. Betty knew too much about him. She had met Diana. Diana had gone with him several times to drop off the professor's grass.

"I don't care if they are friends of hers," he said. "There are lots of crazy folks out there doing weird things these days. Look at those hippies in San Francisco. Baby, you've got to be careful of what you are getting into. You haven't been around a lot. I mean you've been sheltered and all."

Lindy was surprised at his reaction to what she thought was her good news. Nick had always been so supportive of her gifts. "They are nice people," she protested.

"That's just what I am talking about. There you go thinking that they are nice without any evidence to back it up. Because the professor's wife invited you, it's OK. What do you know about her and this group?"

"Not a lot."

"All I am saying is, don't go jumping into anything. Check them out before you get all involved. And stay away from Meridian Hill Park. It's not the type of place you should frequent."

"But there's where I meet Mary."

"Lindy, if Mary is a spirit then she can meet you anywhere. Why does she always have to meet you in the park?"

"I don't know." Tears surfaced in Lindy's eyes. Why was Nick being so mean to her?

"You sure you are not still hallucinating from that grass?" he suggested.

"Maybe I should ask you what was in it," she snapped back.

"I don't mean to upset you, baby. It's not everyday a man's girlfriend tells him that she meets a spirit in a public park that no one else can see. I guess I am worried that something will happen to you, and I wouldn't want that to happen." He put his free hand over hers.

"Oh, Nick, I am sorry. I guess it does sound crazy. Maybe something was in that grass. Take me to Paris with you, and then you won't have to worry about me," she teased.

Nick abruptly steered the car over to a parking space in front of the movie theatre on Park Road. He looked at her and said, "That's it! Come with me? We'll be together. You could get a job. I'll get one, too. The University prohibits fellows from working, but I'll figure a way around that. You always wanted to get away from your family and live on your own."

Lindy could see the excitement in his eyes. It shocked her. Nick wanted her to come to Paris with him. "Oh, Nick, yes. I'll go with you."

"What about medical school?" he asked her, a little nervous.

"I can go when we return in a year."

"You don't mind putting your studies on hold for a year?"

"Nick, I want to be with you." They both started laughing and kissing.

"Let's go to my place. We have plans to make, and other things to do," he said as he ran his hand up her skirt.

"*Oui, mon ami,*" Lindy whispered.

Nick headed for his little efficiency apartment. He felt elated. Lindy could come with him. Why didn't he think of this before? He laughed to himself. *Lock horns with me, you old bastard. I'll show you and your high-yellow daughter!* Why couldn't Lindy be pregnant instead of Diana? As he thought of Diana, his happiness was short-lived. The thought brought him down. *I have to get Diana out of my mind. I don't want to spoil the rest of the evening.*

CHAPTER SIXTEEN

Rosenbloom, Moore & Goldstein was a prestigious law firm located in the heart of DC. The partners, one Jewish, one Irish and one black, were all women. They had made a name for themselves by handling cases involving civil rights and women's issues. Betty Goldstein and Judith Rosenbloom had attended Georgetown Law School together, and Betty's husband and Judith's father were friends. The two men supported the women and gave them the seed money for their law practice several years ago. Their investment had paid off.

Lindy sat in the conference room waiting to see Betty Goldstein. She had lain in bed the night before thinking of ways to get money so that she could be with Nick in Paris. She remembered that Paul, the guy she'd met at the Awakeners' meeting, had said that he was a mailroom clerk in Betty's office. Perhaps Betty would give Lindy a job or recommend her to someone else.

She called Betty's office the first thing Monday morning. Two hours later she was waiting to see Betty, who was busy with a client.

Before leaving home, Lindy had stopped in the church office to see if Mrs. Banks, the church secretary, needed help with anything. She had promised her mother that she would assist Mrs. Banks in preparing for the upcoming church revival in August. A few items needed to be dealt with, but were not time-consuming. Although Mt. Olive Baptist Church sponsored the event, several other churches participated. This revival was special because the church was also celebrating its 40th anniversary.

Revivals were a time that people were healed and they rededicated their lives to Jesus Christ. The ministers had been contacted and letters of confirmation had been received. The District of Columbia had issued the church a permit to use the public land behind the church.

Lindy remembered how excited she would get as a little girl whenever the large tent was erected. Now that she was an active part of it, she made sure that everything was in order.

Before Lindy could get comfortable in her seat, the receptionist returned and gave her a package. Inside was a book and a short note from Betty: "I am going to be tied up for another twenty minutes; I thought this book would keep your company, if you care to wait in the library."

The receptionist escorted Lindy into a room that had several free-standing bookcases and others that lined the walls of the room. There were several small tables and an area to make coffee or tea. One of the cabinet doors was ajar, and behind it Lindy could see a wet bar. No one was in the library, so she had her pick of the tables. She sat at one that faced K Street. She could see that the street was still filled with traffic.

At one time, Lindy had thought about going to law school as an alternative to medical school. She liked law and government. However, her mother had impressed upon her that most lawyers were just as cor-rupt as the people they defended. Unless you were lucky enough to be accepted by a large firm, it was difficult to become successful. Lindy had dropped the idea.

She glanced at the book Betty had given her. It was titled, *The Finding of the Third Eye* by Vera Stanley Alder. Betty had placed sever-al small bookmarkers throughout the book. The first one was placed at the preface.

The preface was written by a woman named Alice Bailey. Reading it, Lindy felt as though Mary was talking to her. It said the same thing Mary had told her about the knowledge. Bailey called the knowledge the Ageless Wisdom, which included many different forms such as occultism, esoteric psychology, astrology, numerology, theosophical doctrines, Kabbalisitic lore, Rosicrucian truth, comparative religion, and symbolism.

Lindy moved on to the next bookmark, where Betty had high-lighted the fourth paragraph on the page, which said:

"Many of us are asked to believe in Church teaching and the Bible, both of them containing a mass of contradictions which no one attempts to explain. For example, Christ asked His disciples to carry on the work as He had done, saying: 'He that believeth in me, the works that I do shall he do also; and greater works than these shall he do.' (St. John 14:12) These works referred to healing, prophesying and clairaudience, which, with the gift of tongues (power to be understood by all nationalities), the power to work miracles, to interpret dreams and symbols, and to have wisdom, were the seven gifts of the Holy Ghost. Yet the State, which supports the Church's teachings, may imprison one for prophesying, and the clergy, who should be cultivating these gifts, leave them mostly in the hands of those whom they consider ignorant and superstitious."

Lindy smiled. She now knew why Betty had given her this book to read. Betty, her mentor, wanted her to see how the church teachings and the Bible can easily be interpreted wrongly or interpreted to suit those in power. *We Christians*, she thought, *interpret these works literally*. Betty and the others saw a hidden meaning in the text. *Who is right?* The text also reminded her of something Ruth had said earlier about the future: There will come a time in which mankind will wake up to their gift of prophesy. They will be at the infantile stage and use them wrongly.

Lindy put the book aside, bowed her head, and folded her hands. She decided right then and there that she would pray and ask God never to let her stray and use her gifts wrongly, but to see that she would always use them to help others. The receptionist, returning to the library for the young visitor, found her on her knees in front of the window.

The first thing Lindy noticed as she entered Betty's office was the expensive décor of the room. Egyptian art and statues stood out among the many artifacts placed around the office. Betty came around from behind her large chrome and glass desk and gave Lindy a hug, motioning her to sit at the small conference table that matched the desk, where a lunch had been brought in for the two of them.

The only things out of place were the law books and Betty's personal books that cluttered the table. Betty moved them aside to create space for them to eat.

"I hope that you are hungry," is how Betty opened the conversation as she unwrapped a tuna fish sandwich and took a bite.

"I'm famished," Lindy replied, biting into a ham and cheese sandwich.

She finished eating quickly and got right to the point. She knew that Betty was busy and could not spend too much time with her.

"I need a job. Do you have anything open? I can file, and type 60 words per minute."

"You want something until you leave for medical school in August?"

"I'm not going to medical school." Lindy decided to be honest with Betty.

"What happened?" Lindy could see the concern and disbelief on Betty's face.

"My boyfriend Nick was awarded a fellowship to the University of Paris. He will be leaving in August, and I am either leaving with him then or I will join him later."

Betty was instantly alarmed when Lindy mentioned Nick's name. The professor had told her about Nick's predicament with his other girlfriend being pregnant. Betty wanted to choose her words carefully; a lot was at stake. She waited a second and composed her thoughts before speaking.

"Are you sure you want to do this, Lindy? You will be giving up a lot."

Lindy couldn't look Betty in the eyes as she spoke. "I know. I thought about this all night. I wish that I could go to medical school, be with Nick, and of course continue my sessions with the Awakeners. I know I can't have it all. But I love Nick, and I want to be with him."

"What do you really know about him?" Betty asked carefully.

"You are beginning to sound like my grandfather. Nick attended church with me yesterday and had dinner with my family. My grandfather drilled him. It was awful."

"I'm not talking about his background as much as about who he is as a person," Betty pointed out.

"Nick loves me," Lindy said. "He has helped me so much this last year. He supports my gifts." She decided that his remarks last night about Betty and the Awakeners didn't count because he was upset.

"Aren't you leaving one prison for another?"

"What do you mean?"

"You depend on your family for everything. Aren't you just substituting Nick for your family?"

"That's not true. That's why I am here looking for a job. I want my own money, and when I get to Paris, I plan to work."

"So you are ready to give up your future for love. And where do the Awakeners fit in?"

"Nick is my future." Lindy remembered what Nick had said about Mary. "Mary is spirit. She will be in Paris with me. As far as the Awakeners, you said no one would ever pressure me to take part in the group. I could join now, leave and come back. I will work with the group for as long as I am here."

Betty knew that if she tried to convince Lindy not to go with Nick, it would only push her more to go with him. The group had recognized the potential in Lindy. As much as she wanted to tell her a million reasons she should not go with Nick, Betty knew she could not interfere with Lindy's free will.

"You can work here this summer as my clerk," she said finally. "My secretary and the legal assistants can always use some help in filing and typing. I will speak to them, and you can start tomorrow."

CHAPTER SEVENTEEN

Margaret walked around the grounds of the church and house inspecting the lawn. She didn't like the way the gardener had trimmed the hedges or cut the grass. She made a mental note to herself to have a talk with him. Her father and Deacon Coleman had their heads together. She often wondered what in the world they could be talking about everyday. Deacon Coleman spent more time with her father than with his wife.

While she was at the bank depositing the Sunday service collection, Lindy had managed to get out the house before she returned. She did leave a message with Mrs. Banks that she had gone on a job interview. *Job interview?* Margaret thought. *What is she up to now?*

First she brings home this boy who came from nothing, looked like nothing, and had nothing, and now this. Margaret had told her father that she was not going to have it. Lindy had crossed the line in more ways than one.

After they left for the movies yesterday, Margaret resumed her talk with her father about Lindy's companion.

"Do you know how serious this is, Papa?"

"Margaret, you are overreacting." *As usual,* he thought.

"We need to get her away from him. Papa, she could get pregnant and our dream for her to be a doctor would be destroyed. I know this might sound harsh, but I have to be honest with you. I cannot, and I repeat, I cannot, have him or any children that look like him in this family. They would not be accepted in the right families," Margaret cried.

"Calm down, Margaret. I know what you are talking about, but Lindy will be leaving for medical school in a few weeks. I don't think that he is going to follow her to Tennessee. She'll meet one of those

Meharry Medical School men and forget all about this one."

"We have to break if off now. We can't wait until August," Margaret insisted.

"If you push her, she might do something crazy," Rev warned his daughter.

Ignoring him, Margaret continued. "Papa, I am going to be quite honest with you; I am worried that he is into drugs and trying, if he hasn't succeeded already, to get Lindy hooked."

"Why do you say that?' Reverend Johnson looked puzzled.

"Her behavior that night she came home with those awful clothes on. She had a strange look in her eyes, as if she really wasn't here. She's fooling around with that supernatural mess again."

Rev looked at his daughter with renewed interested.

"I never told you this, but when you were in the hospital, Lindy was alone with you. Your heart monitor went off. We found her with her hands on your chest," Margaret confided to her father. "God knows what she was doing to you in there."

Rev got up from the dining table and left without saying another word to her. Margaret sighed. Over the years, she had become accustomed to Rev's quick departure whenever he didn't want to face something.

She knew exactly what she was going to do—pay Mr. Nick Lewis a visit.

Margaret stopped in her father's office to see if he wanted anything before she went to the sitting room that she also used for an office. He was arguing or debating with Deacon Coleman about whether or not Dr. King should somehow join forces with Malcolm X. Her father was against this union, as she was. Deacon was taking the stand that all Negroes needed to ban together. Margaret closed the door behind her, knowing that neither would win that discussion, and they would be back at it tomorrow.

Margaret looked at her watch; she had about twenty minutes before her guest would arrive. *Some guest!* she thought. She opened the church books and began to review them for any errors. The money collected for the revival was a separate account that they had begun collecting on the first of the year in order to have sufficient funds for the event. They had to rent tables, chairs, the tent, lighting, and the sound system. Money also had to be set aside for the food committee. Margaret was happy to see that they would have more than enough for the revival.

If her calculations were right, they even had some extra. Margaret counted out several hundred dollars for herself. She didn't note this deduction in the church financial records. After all, she rationalized, she had to be paid for all the work she did for the church. She put four hundred dollars in her small fireproof cash box and the rest in her dress pocket to pay Cissy. When the doorbell rang, Margaret pushed the cash box back into the lower desk drawer. She glanced in the mirror and smoothed down a hair that was out of place. She took her time going to the door; she knew that Cissy would wait until she got there. Neither her father nor Deacon Coleman ever opened the door or did anything else around the house.

Margaret opened the door and gave Cissy her biggest and best grin. She looked at the woman and tried not to show how much she really despised her. *Cissy and Nick Lewis belong together,* she thought. They both were big, black and ugly. If it were up to her, she wouldn't even let Cissy and her kind in the main door of the church. They would have to use the side door and sit in the back. Of course, she knew that Papa would not have any of that. He always said we have to live with everyone whether we like it or not.

Cissy was a long-standing member of the church, and she was not one to tangle with. She knew just about all the major players in DC because of what she did. Cissy was a booster. She stole and sold expensive clothes. Margaret had heard gossip about her also selling drugs, but she had decided to ignore those rumors. Cissy had what Margaret wanted, clothes and information. And she paid her dearly for both. Somehow Margaret knew that she had to find out about Nick without Cissy getting too suspicious, and that was not going to be easy. Cissy had a nose like a greyhound; she could smell out anything.

Cissy followed Margaret as they made their way downstairs. Margaret didn't want her smelling up the house. Cissy always smelled like fried chicken, onions, and some other sweet scent that Margaret didn't recognize.

Margaret was trying on a baby-blue Ralph Lauren two-piece suit when Cissy opened up the very subject that Margaret had been deliberating on how to approach.

"I saw Lindy and that young fellow Nick in church on Sunday. They looked pretty good together." Cissy knew that this remark would upset Margaret. She was shocked, as was the rest of the church, that Lindy was dating a darkey, much less that Rev and Miss Margaret had allowed him to court their princess.

"Lindy tutored him during the year, and we were so thankful that he made it; that is, graduated from Howard. We thought it was only Christian to invite him to worship with us," Margaret said solemnly.

"Quite an artist I hear." Cissy pulled out a Chanel suit.

Margaret grabbed the suit and started pulling off the Ralph Lauren. "He's a nice young man from a nice Southern family."

So you want to play games! Cissy thought. *Well then, I will play with you.* "Is it serious? I see them together all the time."

"Where did you see them?" Margaret asked, trying not to show that she was upset.

"Hanging out in Meridian Hill Park with the drummers. I hear that it is one of Nick's favorite hangouts. Lot of stuff going on there. I warned Ms. Lindy to be careful that time I saw her there dancing and prancing around with the drummers. Personally, I don't think it is a good place for a lady to be."

"Excuse me for a minute, Cissy," Margaret said suddenly. "I need to run into the bathroom."

Cissy smiled to herself. She wanted to bring Ms. High and Mighty down a peg or two. Margaret acted as if she and her daughter were better than the rest of the women in church. Hell, wait until she told her about Nick and his other girl! But this wasn't the time. Cissy wasn't going to play her ace card until she had to.

Margaret closed the bathroom door and leaned her back against it. Her face was in contortions. She wanted to scream. She splashed cold water on her face to calm herself. Lindy in Meridian Hill Park with the drug addicts and other low class people! She was probably the laughingstock of the church. How could she keep bringing shame on them?

"You've got to stop her," the voice in her head told her. "But first you have to take care of the one waiting for you." Margaret flushed the toilet. *That is what I am going to do right now.* She opened the bathroom door and gave Cissy a big smile.

"I'll take both of these suits. How much do I owe you?" she asked, keeping her composure.

"Gimme three hundred. I got some more coming in next week. Want me to stop by?"

"Of course. I am looking for a couple of white suits for both Lindy and myself for the revival. Oh, and Nick may need one, too."

"Nick?"

"Lindy's young man. He's coming to the revival. Papa wants him to sit up front with the family. You know I want him to dress like the rest of us. I want to get the suit as a surprise for him. He can't afford the kind of suits you sell." Margaret smiled sweetly at Cissy.

Cissy's antennae, as she called them, were sticking way out. This didn't sound like the Margaret she knew. "I got to get his size. Maybe I'll stop by his place."

"You can't tell him what it's for," Margaret protested. "It's a surprise. Do you have to go out of your way to get to his place? I don't want to put you through any trouble."

"No trouble; he lives in those apartments on Ogden Street."

Thank you, God! Margaret thought.

"Cissy, don't go there, because he will be asking you a lot of questions. I'm going to let Lindy figure out how to get his size."

Cissy's antennae told her something didn't smell good. It was rotten. But she smiled, took her money, and followed Margaret back upstairs.

CHAPTER EIGHTEEN

The idea of Lindy working for a law firm didn't sit right with Margaret. Rev was not too pleased with it, either. They thought she should continue to help in the church office during the day. Rev had decided he would increase her allowance for gas and spending money. Margaret bought her clothes. She didn't have to pay rent, buy food, or anything for that matter. Rev figured that she didn't need a lot of money. Working outside of the church and the home was a part of this counter-revolution that was going on with the young people. He didn't approve.

Margaret was still fussing and fretting about it a few days later when the doorbell rang. She had to catch her breath when she looked at the stranger standing in front of her. He was drop-dead gorgeous. There were no other words to describe him. He was not quite six feet, a little darker than Lindy, with hair that was straight and pulled back into a ponytail. Margaret didn't particularly like that look on a man, but on him it looked great. His eyes had a mischievous look in them. He was exotic-looking, perhaps of Latino or some other mixed heritage. Margaret couldn't put her finger on it.

He asked to see Lindy. He said his name was Paul, he was a friend of Lindy's from Howard, and they now worked together at the law firm where he had gotten her address. Margaret invited him in and introduced him to Rev while she went to get Lindy. Then the questions started. Rev asked him the same questions he'd asked Nick, but he left out the part about the car. He instantly liked this young man. To Rev he seemed mature for his age and seemed to have a head on him. Paul moved the subject into politics, stating that he didn't support the war, or for that matter any type of violence. He talked about the horrors of war and the devastation that it left behind. He told Rev he was on his way to India.

Lindy was surprised to see Paul sitting in her grandfather's office talking as if they had been friends for a very long time. Lindy's first instinct was to get Paul away from her family as quickly as possible. They didn't know about the Awakeners' meeting she had gone to the other day, and she wanted to keep it that way. However, Rev liked talking to Paul and wasn't ready for the conversation to end.

He proceeded with his questions. "You met Lindy at Howard?"

Lindy froze. Paul smiled and answered the question. "We probably ran into each other several times, but were never introduced formally."

"It was different when I was there," Rev stated. "Lot of mess going on at the campus now. Young folks don't respect their elders. They don't care about anything or anyone. What they need it God. What do you think?"

Paul smiled at Lindy, as if to say, "Don't worry. I have this under control."

"I agree. They need to know God," was all Paul said. Lindy breathed a sigh of relief.

"That's what I am talking about, young man. What church do you attend?"

"I have been visiting Howard's Rankin Chapel and a few other churches since attending Howard."

"Then you have to visit our church. We need young people like you in here."

"Lindy, where have you been keeping this young man?" Margaret demanded, sailing into the room and looking at her daughter. For the first time in months, Lindy saw a gleam of light in her mother's eyes.

Paul answered for her. "In her heart," he said, and winked at Lindy.

"A poet, too," Margaret marveled then somewhat abruptly she demanded, "You're mixed with something, aren't you? Latin or what?"

Paul didn't seem offended by the question. "I think of myself as a rainbow of colors. You name it, I've probably got some of everything in me." He laughed.

"Are you from around here?" Margaret asked.

"Yes and no. My family are like gypsies, always moving from one place to another."

"Service. Your dad is in the military."

"No, not the military. He has his own business, which keeps him very busy."

"On that note, I am going to take Paul out to the garden," Lindy announced. "He is going to fill me in on work." She took hold of Paul's hand and led him downstairs, through the back door to the garden.

It was a perfect summer afternoon, the kind that people in DC prayed for. No humidity. They sat under the weeping willow tree that shadowed them from the brilliant sunlight. It was perfect. Before and after church, members would come out to sit at the small pond, watch the goldfish, and listen to the waterfall from the fountain. One member had described it as a piece of heaven.

Paul preferred to sit on the ground than on one of the benches placed around the garden. He pulled his shoes and socks off and dug his toes into the green grass. Lindy followed suit by slipping off her sandals. The cool grass felt good to her feet.

Paul found a spot on the grass for the lemonade and coconut cake that Margaret had prepared for them, but they knew it would not last long because of the ants. Paul kept moving the lemonade from spot to spot, as the ants seemed to multiply out of nowhere. He told Lindy that he didn't believe in killing of any kind.

Lindy looked at him as if she was seeing him for the first time. He was very handsome, but definitely not her type. Yet, there was something gentle and good about him that attracted her to him. He intrigued her and she liked talking to him. He startled her when he said, "You have a very nice family. Your mom is very personable. I love talking to your grandfather."

Lindy looked at him in disbelief. "Are you talking about my family? They're crazy."

"Why do you say that?"

"Because you are not seeing the real them. They were nice to you because you're the right color." She pointed to his skin. "My mother judges people by the color of their skin. You have to be the same complexion as her or lighter or you don't pass."

"I have heard of this, but this is my first time experiencing it."

"It doesn't end there. Your hair has to be straight or of wavy texture." Then Lindy pinched her already small, narrow nose. "You must have a keen nose." She tried to talk while holding her nose.

They both laughed at the absurdity of it all.

Paul moved the glasses again. He caught Lindy by surprise with his remarks, "They don't know any better. It is a part of their belief system. They are locked

into the color-struck lesson."

"Why do you call it a lesson?"

"Because that is what it is. Every soul, person, has lessons to learn. Think of

life as a series of lessons. The lessons are personal, universal or both. The color-struck lesson is both."

"What do you mean?"

"On a personal level, your mom has to learn to love who she is, and on the universal level she has to learn to love everyone because we are all part of the One. When she discriminates against another, she is just discriminating against herself."

"I wonder how this discrimination based on color started."

"Eons ago. It is about power and control over others."

"Power and control," she repeated the words.

"Yes, this didn't start with slavery. The color-struck lesson started when souls took on physical bodies of a rainbow of colors. The seven basic colors of mankind originated from the seven root races. The root race in power has control over the other root races. Let me just mention this right now, but I don't want to get into a lengthy discussion on it.

"The universe exists according to its cyclical nature. Therefore the root races, you could say, take turns at the power and control lesson. Each race is given the chance to learn love and not fear. Unfortunately, I don't think we are doing too good a job in that area. The races continue to instill fear in the form of discriminating against each other based on color. Do you understand?"

"Yes. However, let me just reiterate what you said. This is a universal lesson on love. Each root race is put in power to learn how to love the other races because we are all part of God. The white root race is in power. Instead of teaching love they are teaching fear in the form of using skin color to accept or not accept the other races. They brainwash people into thinking that the color dark is negative and white is positive. In this way they maintain power and control."

"The other part to that is, whatever race is in power will actually lose the very

thing they are trying to hold onto because they are going against the universal laws. As the wheel of life turns, they lose their chance and fall from grace until the next time."

"Paul, what about on a personal level, like with my mom?"

"Let's pretend your mom just arrived from Africa."

Lindy started laughing. "My mom from Africa? You must want to start a war. She disassociates herself from anyone or anything dealing with Africa."

"This is my story, so she is from Africa, where the color of her beautiful ebony skin was never questioned. She is stolen from her tribe and is brought to this country against her will. Now, the color of her skin determines how she will fare in the new country. She is repeatedly raped by the master of the plantation and her children are now light, if not as light as the master's. The children that she has by another slave are dark. The fair-skinned children are treated differently than the dark ones. They are raised in the house, educated, and eventually given their freedom. They have a better life.

"The belief is never spoken, but it is implanted in her subconscious that the lighter your skin the better your life. This belief is handed down from generation to generation. The white root race believes that they can stay in power by controlling the people through influencing them to believe that white is right. This culture perpetuates this through the media, movies, music, education, and jobs, you name it.

And, of course, everyone wants to be right."

"You know," Lindy said thoughtfully, "I remember a story that my mother once told me that she had gotten from my great grandmother. One of great-great-grandmother's sisters gave birth to a dark-skinned child. When the baby was around six months old, one of her brothers tried to change her color by putting her in a tub of water filled with bleach."

"What does this story tell you?"

"It tells me that these people were sick if they tried to bleach a child to change the color of its skin."

"First there is the belief," Paul said gently. "Then people act according to that belief. That man was trying to make it better for the child with dark skin. Although now we know how wrong his behavior was."

"He could have seriously hurt the child."

"It shows you the depth of what people will do to adhere to the belief that white is better."

"It's wrong."

"Yes, it is. Nevertheless, this belief is buried deep into the subconscious of humans. After thousands of years of conditioning, it is part of the human psyche now, no matter what color you are. I believe that groups such as the Awakeners are helping to bring out the truth," Paul said as he finished his lemonade.

"How are they doing that?"

"By making us aware of these beliefs. Once we are aware, we can do something about them."

"Paul, be serious! My mom is aware that she is discriminating against her own kind."

"Are you sure about that?"

"Yes, I am. She is an educated woman."

"She is not aware of it on the universal level. Neither is she aware that she is discriminating against herself when she discriminates against others."

Lindy took a deep breath. How did he know all of this?

"So you are saying that discrimination takes place because the person doesn't love himself. In the case of our ancestors, they were stripped of their beliefs through I guess you could say, brainwashing through physical, mental, and emotional abuse. Then the belief that white skin is better was instituted as a form of control over them."

"You're getting it. Through the centuries this belief is reinforced by the others in order to keep the control. It even goes farther. Remember in class the other day, Ruth said in order to understand who we are we first have to understand who or what God is? Have you given any thought to that question?"

"That's all I have been doing, thinking and thinking about who God is. I have to tell you that I have been questioning what I was brought up to believe."

"That bothers you?"

"I feel I am going against the teachings of my grandfather and the church." Lindy looked at him with remorse in her eyes.

"Think about it as becoming aware of your beliefs, and not as going against anyone or anything. First there is awareness, then learning."

"You could say that I am evolving."

"We are all evolving. The universe is either evolving or revolving. Things are never as they seem."

Lindy looked at Paul not as her contemporary but as someone much older and wiser.

The two remained under the tree laughing and talking until dusk. She told him about her encounter with Mary after the Awakener's meeting, and about the dance to discover her special sound. He reacted neither favorably nor negatively. He just accepted what she told him. He told her Mary was her spirit guide and, he believed, a very powerful one.

She was sad to hear that he would be leaving for India very soon and would not return until the fall. She felt as though she had found another friend, and here she was losing him already. She was not interested in him as a lover. He was so different from Nick. Nick was rugged, whereas Paul was gentle. *Not my type*, she told herself again. *He's too*…Before Lindy could finish the thought, she realized that she was discriminating against him because of how he looked. How could she judge her mom when she was doing the same thing?

From inside the house, Margaret would steal a look at them periodically. She invited Paul to stay for dinner, but he declined. When he left, Lindy felt a strange longing for him. They had spent an entire afternoon together, and she still didn't know anything about him. She had even forgotten to ask him why he was going to India.

CHAPTER NINETEEN

Within weeks, Lindy had learned who all the employees in the law firm were. Besides the three partners, the firm had several legal assistants, secretaries and a receptionist. Paul and a couple of other students did odd jobs for the firm. In the beginning, Lindy felt awkward because she really didn't have a lot of work to do. She realized that Betty had created a job for her. She was given a desk in the office of one of the legal assistants. She would help the file clerks or type one or two documents for the secretaries. It was as if she was the invisible person in the office. No one bothered her, and this suited her fine.

Most of her time was spent recording her meetings with Mary, reading metaphysical books, taking notes in one of the several books that Betty had given her, and talking to Paul. She looked forward to their lunch hour every day. He became her second mentor, teaching her about the ageless wisdom.

Mostly she enjoyed the work he did with her to help her develop her gifts. He encouraged her to trust her intuition and discern the colors she saw around people. She used the people in the firm as her subjects without their knowledge. Betty was her main guinea pig. Lindy found Paul hard to read; even the color surrounding him mostly stayed the same, a pale blue. She asked him about it, and he told her he had learned how to control his lower nature. Lindy just looked at him and blushed. She mistook his use of the term lower nature to mean sexuality, but Paul was referring to the esoteric meaning that denotes ego or personality.

Lindy realized that she never mentioned Paul to Nick. She knew he would not understand their relationship. Besides, she told herself, she and Paul were only friends. However, it seemed as if they had been friends forever. She dreaded the fact that he would be leaving for India.

Lindy had become close to him in such a short time. Paul told her it was because they had been soul mates in another lifetime, and that family members and friends usually reincarnated together. Lindy would smile at him, but she didn't quite understand or believe all that he told her about reincarnation.

She asked him again about the power and control lesson. He explained that it was the ageless battle between good and evil. He referred to the evil forces as the dark ones who were always tempting the individual in order to keep the soul enmeshed in matter or materialism. They wanted to control the universe. Lindy told him it sounded very much like what her grandfather had been preaching for years, only he would say the devil and the devil workers were after you.

Sometimes Betty would join them, and they would stay late into the evening discussing the principles and laws of the universe. Betty had given Lindy an assignment to write down all of her paranormal experiences since childhood, as well as her encounters with Mary, and to find out as much as she could about Mary. Lindy felt as though she had two earth guides in Betty and Paul. She felt as if this was the best time of her life, except for one thing. She missed Nick. She wanted to see him so badly and to feel his body next to hers. She would console herself with the thought of their being together in Paris.

She would talk to him each day by phone, but each time she tried to see him, he would give her some excuse why they couldn't get together. He promised that they would be together soon. The days turned into weeks, and before Lindy knew it, July was almost over.

She was daydreaming about Paris when Betty summoned her to her office. Betty was busy reading the first set of papers Lindy had given her about her gifts and meetings with Mary. She motioned Lindy to take the seat across from her at the conference table. Papers and books were still piled high on one end of the desk. Lindy sat quietly as Betty read. Her thoughts drifted to Paul. She hadn't seen him all morning. Usually, he arrived in the office before her. Glancing at her watch, Lindy realized that it was near lunchtime. She wanted to ask Paul more about reincarnation and soul mates. Lindy wanted to know if she and Nick had had a past life together.

Betty finally looked up and said, "This is wonderful." She waved the papers back and forth in front of her before continuing. "Do you realize how fortunate you are to have contact with your spirit guide?"

Lindy tried to speak, but Betty put up her hand and said, "Let me finish. You are the bridge between the two worlds—spiritual and physical. Ruth called you the High Priestess because you are in contact with the spiritual world and able to receive information. There is so much for you to learn." Betty had gotten up from the table and was walking around the room as if she was in the courtroom. Lindy had never seen her so agitated or stressed.

"I really feel overwhelmed," Lindy said tentatively. "To be truthful, I still don't know what to believe. Sometimes, I ask myself am I dreaming. Is this real? Normal people don't go around seeing and talking to spirits from another world. If I told someone this, they would laugh at me or think that I was crazy."

"This is not the time to share your gift with others because they don't understand," Betty told her seriously. "We are in the Piscean Age of secrecy and uncertainty. What you have to do now is study, develop your skills and trust in yourself."

"Paul mentioned to me once that the universe revolves through different zodiac time periods, but he didn't explain. What is the Piscean age?"

"It is one of the astrological ages, named after one of the twelve constellations of the solar system," Betty explained. "Each planetary age lasts about 2,000 years and has particular characteristics associated with it that influence the evolution of the universe and mankind. This age is also called the Christian era. The universe will be moving into the Age of Aquarius, a period of time which embodies the world's dream of a golden age."

"Will that be the end of the Christian era?" Lindy looked horrified.

Recognizing that Lindy was still very imbued with her Christian teachings, Betty tried to be tactful. "Religion as we know it today will not be the same. Those hidden doctrines that impede mankind's spiritual evolution will be exposed and fall away. More and more people who are not involved in any metaphysical movements will have spiritual encounters such as the ones you are having now. The veil between the spiritual and physical worlds will be thinner, allowing increased interaction between the two. They will become believers in the unseen and ageless wisdom."

"I wish we were in this Age of Aquarius now," Lindy said.

"There is one more thing I must tell you," Betty warned her. "People like us are a threat to those who want to control the world through fear. They will try to stop us. Roadblocks will be put in our paths to impede our progress, and to make us doubt ourselves."

"Who are these people?"

"The sleepers, the ones who walk the path of materiality. In time you will be able to recognize and know them."

Betty handed Lindy three sheets of legal-size paper. "This is my account of how I got involved with the Awakeners and everything that we have experienced together. I felt that it was important for me as well as for you to write these details down. Read them later. You must find out how we are connected and what we must do together."

"I'll try. Do you think Paul could help us? He seems to be so knowledgeable about so many things. I want to ask him so much before he leaves."

"I am afraid that it is too late," Betty said. "He's already gone. He came by my house last night. He said that he had an emergency and had to leave earlier than he expected. So yesterday was his last day."

Lindy's face showed her disappointment. "He didn't even say good-bye."

"He left you this card." Betty reached into her middle desk drawer, pulled out a white envelope, and handed it to Lindy.

Lindy tore open the sealed envelope and looked at the card. On the front was a lily. She opened the card, looked up at Betty and started reading it aloud.

"Dear Lindy,

I am sorry that I didn't get a chance to formally say farewell to you before I left. I cherish our friendship and look forward to seeing you in the fall. Remember that life is never as it seems.

Shanti,

Paul"

Lindy thought about how she would not be there when he returned. Why did that thought fill her with pain?

CHAPTER TWENTY

The weeks went by quickly for Nick. He had started the new job painting a mural on the wall of a private daycare center in Anacostia. The center, not far from the Frederick Douglass home, was new to the community. Children between the ages of two and five attended the center, run by an all-black staff. The owner wanted a mural that depicted the history of black people, as well as something that would instill pride in the young ones.

First Nick did a rough rendition of the concept he planned. The colorful painting showed the capture of a young African male and female from their country, the trials and tribulations they experienced in slavery, and the progress of the black race through the Civil Rights Movement. The owner was so pleased with the preliminary model that he increased Nick's payment.

Nick knew what he had to do with the money. It was his ticket out of DC to follow his dream. If he budgeted right, he could make it through the summer and buy Lindy's ticket as well. He decided that he was not going to take the chance and leave Lindy behind. As far as he was concerned, she was too vulnerable. Anyone could talk her out of joining him in Paris. She had to leave with him.

The wild card was Diana. What was she going to do? Abortions cost money and babies even more.

Nick was glad that Lindy was working, because it kept her occupied and out of his hair. He couldn't deal with Lindy right now; he had too much on his plate. After all, he would be living with her for a whole year. Right now he was juggling both Diana and his French tutor. Besides, he had to admit to himself that Lindy frightened him with her psychic ability. He didn't want her getting into his head. Calling him "Nicky" the night they went out to the movies was enough to convince him to block his thoughts when he was around her.

He couldn't wait until they were both in Paris. They had talked about all the things they planned to do once they were there. Nick imagined them living in a loft on the Left Bank. He planned to paint endless pictures of Lindy in the nude. She would be his Mona Lisa. This was his dream, and he wasn't going to let anything or anyone get in the way of it.

Diana had agreed to meet him on Thursday afternoon in front of the Quad, one of the four dormitories of Howard. She had been lucky enough to get a room in Baldwin Hall for the summer.

In his mind, Nick had rehearsed what he planned to say to Diana. The main thing was to remain calm, concerned but firm. He must convince her that she was throwing away her life. The strategy was to focus on her life and the future.

When he arrived at the Quad, Diana was sitting with several other students on the small wall that ran parallel to the building. The guys would drive up and down 4th Street checking out who was sitting on the wall. Diana was dressed in a white shirt with Delta Sigma Theta written across the top in bold red letters. Nick found that interesting, because most of the time Diana ignored the sisterhood. She had told him that her sorority line had almost been kicked off campus because of hazing activities the previous year.

After pledging, she had strayed away from the sorority, getting more involved with the Black Power Movement. She hadn't even supported the Delta's candidate running for homecoming queen the previous year. Instead, she voted for the independent candidate, who won the race with a landslide. The new homecoming queen reflected the mood of the time. Her skin was a beautiful coffee brown, and her hair was as wide as a sombrero.

Nick gave Diana a peck on the lips and helped her get down off the wall. He suggested that instead of going to the canteen as they had originally planned, they walk around the reservoir and talk. He grabbed her hand and intertwined her fingers with his.

They walked in silence for a few minutes before beginning any conversation.

Diana looked up into his face, and he seemed different to her. Perhaps he was coming around to the idea of the baby.

"You're wearing a Delta shirt," he said just to make conversation. "What's going on with that?"

"I found it in the back of my drawer when I was cleaning things out to send home. I decided to wear it. I am a Delta girl, you know."

"Yeah, but I didn't think you were gung-ho into that sorority thing," he responded as he swung their arms back and forth. *Easy*, he kept telling himself. *Stay cool! Don't get her upset. Let her know how supportive you are of her.*

"Last night I was talking to some of my sorors, and I realized how much I missed being involved with them," Diana explained. "They don't know that I didn't vote for their homecoming queen candidate. When I graduate from here, I might need them to help me get a job or whatever."

She couldn't believe that she was walking along 4th Street in broad daylight holding Nicky Lewis' hand. Did he break up with Lindy when he found out about the baby? Diana was too scared to ask him.

Nick wanted to let go of her hand so badly, but he knew that would be a bad move. He just hoped no one would see them. He had to take his chances. It was a big gamble.

He stopped walking for a moment and looked into the eyes of the girl who held his life in her hands and said, "You still want to finish school?"

"Of course, I have come too far not to. I will be the first college graduate in my family. If I don't finish I will disappoint my parents and grandmother."

"It's the same with me. I am the first graduate. I will also be first in my family to go and live in another country." Nick realized too late that he had touched a sore point.

"That means you are going, huh?"

"I've got to go, Diana, an opportunity like this doesn't come all the time."

They started walking again. Neither knew what to say next. Nick broke the silence.

"What does your mom want you to do?" Nick still could not bring himself to say the words "have a baby." Somehow saying those words made it too real to him.

Here we go, thought Diana. She had not been entirely honest with Nicky about her parent's reaction. Her parents didn't know. They were Pentecostals. They didn't believe in pre-marital sex or abortions. They only thing that she had told them was that Nicky and she were thinking about getting married. She promised that before they did anything, she would call them. She had lied to her parents and to Nicky.

"They're not getting any younger, and are looking forward to having a grandchild. You know my sister Brenda has been married for three years now and is still not pregnant. Daddy says that Mom and him could have another child by the time Brenda has one," she laughed.

Nick, ignoring her humor asked, "Let me get this straight. After summer school, you will go home and sit out the next year?"

Diana was beginning to perspire a little around the forehead. The sun was beaming down on them and the sweatshirt was hot. That morning she had vomited twice before going to class and had to leave the classroom once more to throw up.

"Nicky, I am feeling a little woozy. Let's cross over to Drew Hall so I can use the bathroom."

Nick put his arm around her so that he could support her better as they crossed the street. He looked down 4th Street and saw a couple of cars approaching, but he figured they had enough time to cross over to the other side of the street. They had barely made it when the cars sped by.

Nick heard the screech of tires from one of the passing cars. From his peripheral vision, he got a glance of what he thought was a little black car. For a moment his heart stopped beating; he thought that it was Lindy's car. That's impossible, he assured himself. Lindy was at work.

Once in the lobby of the men's dorm where she could get a drink of water, Diana started to feel better. They sat there on the couch for a while until Diana didn't look as pale. She told Nick that she needed to eat. She had emptied most of her breakfast. He let her lean on him as they walked up to Kenyon's Bar and Grill. Nick acknowledged the bartender and a few of the regulars as they took a seat in the back.

"You didn't answer my question about what you plan to do about school," Nick commented as he lifted up his cool draft beer.

"Like I said, I have to finish school or it will break my family's heart. It's just going to take a little longer than I planned. I probably will have to work part-time. I don't know, Nicky. I haven't thought that far."

"I know, and that's what I'm worried about. Just hear me out for a moment." He leaned across the table and looked her in the eye. "You have your life ahead of you. You have your dreams, and the dreams of your folks for you to succeed in life. Having a baby is a big responsibility. Are you ready for that?" Before Diana could answer, Nick continued to talk while he still had the edge. "You have one more year left, and then you wanted to go to law school? If you have this baby," Nick took a deep breath as he said the word "baby" again, "chances are you will not complete school. You will have to go to work, and look at the burden you will be putting on your folks. Think about what type of life you will be offering the baby."

Diana began to cry softly. She knew what Nick was saying made sense. Her parents really couldn't afford to help her that much. She had a younger sister and brother at home. They would be so ashamed of her. She really didn't have anywhere to go. She needed him to help her. If only they would get married. He could still go to Paris. She would go with him. Her baby would be born in Paris. She could get a job, and next year return to school. She would not have to give up her dream to be a civil rights lawyer. She felt as though she was between a rock and a hard place. She was a Pentecostal; they didn't believe in taking a life, and that included abortions. As much as she wanted to be a lawyer, she could not take her baby's life. This was God's way of punishing her for not abiding by the Holy Scripture. Besides, the thought of giving up

Nicky and her baby made her heart ache.

"It's our baby, Nicky," she said. "If I do what you're suggesting, I would be killing her. You talk as if you're not going to have anything to do with her. Besides, it is God's will, and we are only being punished for our sins."

For the first time, Nick now understood what this was all about. How could he have forgotten that she was Pentecostal? They didn't believe in going to the movies, dancing, sex before marriage or abortion. Some of their women didn't even wear make up or jewelry. *Shit, shit!* he thought. Diana had broken all the rules, and now she was having a guilt trip at his expense.

"Diana, listen to me," said Nick as he waved to the waitress for another beer. "How far gone are you?"

"Nine and a half weeks," she responded, her voice a little cautious, for she didn't know where he was coming from with this line of questioning.

"Nine weeks, hmm. That's not a baby. It's just a bunch of cells. At nine weeks it's not that developed."

"You don't know what you are talking about!" She started getting a little agitated. "At nine and a half weeks a baby has just about everything in place," she snapped back at him.

"God, Diana, it isn't even called a baby, but an embryo or something like that. I know that much!" Nick glared at her. Then he realized that he was losing it again. He had to remain calm and focused.

"That's the medical terminology. To me it's a baby." Diana glared back at him.

Nick could sense that this line of reasoning was not going anywhere. He would have to change tactics again.

"When would you finish school?"

Diana felt uncomfortable talking about any future plans. She had not figured out her present predicament. "I don't know. I hope that in a year or two I can come back here or transfer my credits to a school at home."

"How are you going to take care of a baby and go to school?"

"Maybe if you stop thinking about yourself and start thinking about the baby, you could help me. We could get married, you know." Diana looked at him with pleading eyes. "We could go to Paris together. I could get a job while you are in school. When you finish, I could then complete my degree. Nicky, it could work." Her eyes were glittering.

Nick now felt as if he was going to black out. He felt hot all over. He drank down the beer the waitress had brought him without coming up for air. He waved to her to bring him another one. He looked at Diana as she was telling him about going to Paris with him and how they could get married. She was trying to trap him into marriage, Nick thought. Marriage? Hell, marriage was out of the question. He wasn't ready to marry anyone. He liked being a free agent. However, Lindy was special and maybe one day they would do the thing, but not right now. If those French girls were anything like his French tutor, he couldn't wait to get to Paris. He just had to be careful around Lindy; she wasn't as open as Diana.

"You got this all figured out," Nick said with a slur in his voice. The beer was now talking. The calmness was gone. He didn't care what she thought or felt. "You're trying to trap me into marriage. I am not sure this baby, as you call it, is even mine." He looked at her angrily.

Diana knew she had let the cat out of the bag just when he was warming up to her. She had to get him to understand how much she loved him.

"Nicky, now you listen to me. What's wrong with me thinking about marriage? I am carrying your baby. I love you and I love our baby." Diana softened her voice to emphasize those words. "This child is just as much your responsibility as mine. If you don't want to help me, then I will do it by myself. I am sorry I even told you." Tears were surfacing in her eyes.

I wish you hadn't! Nick thought. "If you really love me then you will get rid of this problem," he told her. "We can go on with our lives and no one gets hurt. You can come to Paris during the winter break."

Diana's eyes got larger for a quick second. Nick saw the flicker in her eyes and that gave him encouragement to continue in that vein. "You could finish school and be the first graduate in your family. We can have a baby later."

Diana wiped her eyes and asked, "You want me to come to Paris for Christmas?" She was too scared to even mention his last statement.

Nick knew he had finally hit the right chord. "We have a life ahead of us. Paris is a beautiful city. You could come back after graduation and spend the summer before you go to law school. We'll do some traveling. How would you like to see England and Spain?"

Tears slowly flowed down Diana's face. The few people in the Grill were beginning to stare. She didn't care. She felt so torn. She wanted the baby. How was she going to commit such a big sin as killing her baby? But what she really wanted was Nicky. She looked at Nicky and said, "How would I get rid of it? I don't know any doctors that would do it, if I decided to get one."

Nick was on his fifth beer now. He was feeling in control and on top of the world. "I'll take care of the doctor and his fee. You don't have to worry about anything. I'll get in touch with you with the details."

"I didn't say I would definitely do it. I have to think about this. You don't understand. I am going against God's will."

Nick started waving his hands and shouted, "Stop this bullshit about being punished and going against God's will! Why do you think God made a way to get rid of problems like this?"

"It was not God's way, but man's. It's against the church and the law! We are killing a human being, and abortions are not legal," Diana whispered back at him, wishing he would keep his voice down.

"You can come to Paris with me or you can have your baby. It is up to you. I am not going to argue with you about the moral aspects of this, because we will never agree. I'm going to Paris. I'll let you know when I have things lined up. You can come, or you can have this baby. You can't do both. Let's get out of here."

After dropping Diana off at the dorm, Nick made his way to 15th Street. He felt jubilant not only from the beer but because he knew that Diana was at her breaking point. She kept talking about Paris and how, being a language major, she always wanted to travel abroad. Nick thought this couldn't be the same girl that an hour ago was sickly and crying about having an abortion. Now she was planning what clothes to take with her. *Damn, sometimes women could be so fickle!*

Nick entered Meridian Hill Park from the 15th Street entrance and walked over to where a group of Howard students were listening to the drummers. They were sitting around shooting the breeze about Stokely Carmichael and the Panthers. He joined the conversation for a while until he saw his contact enter the park. As usual, she was weighed down with bags. He watched her work the crowd, going from group to group pulling clothes out of her bag and probably other things. He was in no hurry, so he could just wait until she came over to him.

Nick stretched out on the grass under a tree and looked up at the sky. The day was beautiful even if it was hot. He must have dozed off for a few minutes when he felt someone nudging him in the ribs. He opened his eyes, but the glare of the sun was too strong. He put a hand over his eyes like a sun visor to block out the glare so he could see who it was. It was Cissy.

Cissy flopped her bags down next to him. "You're getting as bad as your little sweet girlfriend, sleeping and hanging out in the park," she said with a sly grin on her face.

Nick sat up, looked up at Cissy with bewilderment, and asked, "Who are you talking about?"

"Come on, Nick, who else would I be talking about, but Lindy? This is her hangout. If she's not nodding off on the bench," Cissy pointed to the bench in the far northeast corner of the park, "she's talking to herself. Have you been giving her more than this weed?" She handed him a small bag that was covered by a T-shirt.

By now Nick was standing up looking at Cissy, wondering what she was up to. "Naw," he answered. "Lindy is not into that type of stuff."

"Well, you could have fooled me. Ask Muhammad how she per-formed the other day. I didn't know she had it in her. That girl shook her booty all over the place. I have to admit she's hot. I thought she was ready to get it on right here in the park."

Nick couldn't believe his ears. Was Cissy really talking about Lindy? As he handed her back the T-shirt, he slipped her a fifty. "Are you sure it was Lindy?"

"I told you, nigger, it was her. Ask Muhammad, the drummer, if you don't believe me," she dared him.

"No, it couldn't have been Lindy. She's been under a lot of pressure lately, getting ready for medical school, and now she's working for the first time," he replied. "She wouldn't be doing that kind of thing."

"Sure," Cissy said, her voice full of sarcasm .

Nick decided to change the subject and vowed that he would get to the bottom of this. "Look, Cissy, I need your help. A friend of mine is in trouble. He knocked up his girlfriend and they need to get it taken care of. You know anyone can do the job?"

"Is that what's wrong with that girl, Nick? You done gone and knocked Ms. Margaret's daughter up?" Cissy started hollering and laughing.

"Shut up!" Nick shouted. But Cissy couldn't stop hollering. "You got everything ass-backwards as usual. No, it is not Lindy. I told you it's a friend of mine. Now, can you help me or not?" He was losing his patience with Cissy.

"Yeah, yeah. There's this guy who was a resident at Georgetown medical school. He was kicked out or he dropped out of the program, and he does them on the side," Cissy replied, now looking seriously at Nick. She knew he was upset.

"Is he safe?"

"I never used him, so I don't know. I have referred girls to him twice before, and I never heard anything bad from anyone."

"How do I get in touch with him?" Nick asked.

"I'll have him call you. He doesn't like to give out any numbers.

You know what I mean?"

"OK, as soon as possible. My friend wants to get this thing taken care of." Nick walked away from Cissy. The sky didn't look as beautiful to him any more. He pushed the thought of Lindy in the park out of his head. He decided he would deal with that later when he saw her. Right now he had a lesson with his French tutor. She was teaching him French, and he was teaching her about French kissing the American way.

CHAPTER TWENTY-ONE

Cissy headed toward U Street. She was meeting one of her regular customers at the fish place. She also needed to use the phone and the bathroom and get something to eat. Cissy could not believe what she had just found out. Lindy was pregnant by Nick. She walked as quickly as she could with all the bags of clothes she was carrying. As she went to cross Florida Avenue and 16th Street, a black and white cut her off. Two of DC's finest got out of the car.

"Well, well what do we have here?" the first officer asked. "What's in those bags, Cissy?"

"Just some old clothes. I can't leave my things in my room. People steal stuff. Why are you hassling me? Go and find some real crooks!" Cissy said with her hands on her hips. This was not the first time she had been hassled. Usually they let her go after they played with her for a while. They were probably bored. Cissy was praying that a call would come through and they would move on. But no such luck; they started going through her bags and pulled out not clothes but several ounces of grass.

"That's not mine!" she protested. "I don't know how that got into my bag. One of those junkies put it in there when I wasn't looking."

The second officer pulled out a pair of cuffs, put Cissy's hands behind her back and helped her into the squad car. Cissy was already thinking who she could call before the car had even taken off.

Two hours later, Margaret answered the phone in her most regal tone. "Hello, the Johnson/Lee residence."

"Ms. Margaret, this is Cissy."

"Oh, Cissy, you are just the person I need to talk to. I was hoping that you'd call," Margaret lied.

"Ms. Margaret," Cissy said before Margaret could say anything further, "I have run into a little bit of trouble and need your help."

Margaret had helped Cissy out of other predicaments before by advancing her money. She knew she had to stop this. "Help you how, Cissy? I really don't have any extra cash right now."

"It's not that, ma'am. I've been locked up."

"Locked up? Why, what happened? You didn't give them my name, did you?" Margaret's mind was racing. Papa would have a fit if he thought she brought any disgrace to the family. It was bad enough with Lindy disgracing them, but Margaret was supposed to be above reproach.

"No, ma'am. I didn't give anyone's name. I am entitled to one phone call. Can you come bail me out?"

"Bail you out? How much does it cost?" Margaret had regained her composure. She had to think.

"Five hundred dollars, ma'am."

Margaret screamed into the phone. "Five hundred dollars? Why so much? What are you in for?" By now she knew that she didn't want to have anything to do with Cissy. She had to get off the phone. She was not going to pay $500 to bail this woman out of jail when she probably belonged there.

"Someone planted some drugs in my bags. I swear I don't have anything to do with that kind of stuff. I was in the park talking to Nick Lewis. He went through my bags looking for a T-shirt. I'm not saying he did it, ma'am, but the next thing I knew the cops were stopping me and they found that stuff in my bags. I was on my way to the phone to call you. I have something important to tell you about Lindy. She needs help ma'am."

The mention of Lindy's name immediately piqued Margaret's interest.

"Tell me what's going on!"

Cissy knew she had her. "Ma'am, I can tell you everything. I know all about what Nick is up to. But you have to get me out of here. I can help you. I'm at the Fourth Precinct on Georgia Avenue."

"OK," Margaret said, reaching for her car keys. "I will be right there."

She didn't dare tell her father where she was going. He was out with Deacon Coleman again making their rounds, visiting members of the church who had been ill. She quickly changed her clothes to something more presentable to go out. She went to her father's office, opened his desk drawer, and took a check out of the church's checkbook. Her father had authorization to sign church checks, and she often signed his name for him when she paid the church bills.

An hour later, Cissy was sitting next to Margaret as she drove the big Cadillac down 13th Street. Margaret was quiet all the way to Cissy's house. Margaret was thinking, *this had better be good, or else I will make sure she never sells another piece of clothing in this city again!*

Margaret parked in front of Cissy's boarding house, then turned to her and said, "Talk. I want to know everything you know about Nick Lewis and his relationship with my daughter."

Cissy was glad that she had saved her ace in the hole. "Ms. Margaret, that Nick is not good for Lindy. He is playing her."

"Get to the point. What do you know?" Margaret had lost her patience by now. She couldn't believe that she had just bailed out a potential drug dealer. Thank God she hadn't seen anyone that she knew!

"Nick planted those drugs on me, ma'am, and he got Lindy hooked on them, too."

"How do you know this?"

"Lindy has been hanging out at Meridian Hill Park, ma'am. She acts strange. Sometimes she sits on this bench and talks to herself or nods off. I don't know how to tell you, ma'am," Cissy paused in her story.

"Just say whatever you're going to say!" Margaret snapped.

"She was doing this dance where she was bumping and grinding in front of everyone in the park. You can ask the others, ma'am. I can take you there now if you want to. They all seen her pulling up her dress and shaking her boobs in front of the men." Cissy knew that she had exaggerated Lindy's dance, but she didn't care.

Margaret just sat there. Her face was expressionless.

Cissy decided to play her ace card.

"Ms. Margaret, Nick asked me for the name of a doctor."

Looking perplexed, Margaret asked, "Doctor? Is he sick? Oh my God, does he have some awful disease?"

"No, ma'am. He wants a doctor to get rid of something that would come in nine months." Cissy looked directly at Margaret. She didn't want to miss her reaction.

"That's it," Margaret said coldly. "So Lindy is pregnant. No wonder she looks so terrible and couldn't eat the other night." Margaret realized that she had let out too much.

I was right! Cissy thought.

"I have to go now, Cissy," Margaret said abruptly, looking her square in the eye. "I expect you not to say anything to anyone. If I hear about this from anyone else, I will bury you under that jail. Do I make myself clear?"

"Yes, ma'am. You don't have to worry about me. Your secret is safe. I have some new things from New York, if you want to take a quick look."

Margaret looked around to see if anyone was watching them. She was a little paranoid about being seen with Cissy. If the police were watching them, she supposed she could always tell them Cissy was giving her a dress or two as a present.

"Quick, let me see what you have. I don't have all day." Margaret wanted to get away as quickly as possible. She needed time to think. Lindy pregnant and on drugs. Margaret's face turned bright red just thinking about it. She wanted to crush Nick Lewis, and she vowed that she would. How was she going to tell her father?

CHAPTER TWENTY-TWO

Cissy had practically run up the three flights of stairs to get the clothes to show Margaret who turned them all down. Cissy didn't care. It had been quite a day. She was physically and emotionally tired. Now for a second time, Cissy dragged herself up the three flights of stairs to her tiny room and flopped on the bed. She was glad to be home as such as home was. The room was cheap, but it served her purposes. She shared a bathroom with two other tenants. They weren't supposed to cook in the room, but Cissy had a hot plate that she used to heat up coffee and soup.

She didn't like to keep too much food in the room because of the roaches. They were everywhere. She had sprayed her room several times, but they always came back and brought their whole family. Cissy figured she could deal with the roaches, but not with rats. DC was known for rats that grew as big as cats.

One day Cissy planned to walk away from this life with money and a new identity. She was so close to her goal. Another couple of months and she would be able to kiss this city goodbye. She had saved and invested the money she got from selling drugs. Now this bust could put a hold on everything. She couldn't afford to go to jail. Hell, she needed a lawyer. She pulled out her address book from under the bed. She hid it because she used it to write beside each name tidbits of information that always came in handy when she needed them, like what she had just found out about Lindy. She loved to see the high and mighty fall. They all thought they were better than her, Cissy the booster. Well, she would show them. Cissy flipped through her book until she came to the name of Betty Goldstein.

The buzz of the intercom distracted Betty from her work. She picked up the receiver and heard the soft articulate voice of the receptionist saying, "Mrs. Goldstein, line one is for you."

"Did you get a name?"

"Yes, it's a Ms. Cissy Carter," the receptionist replied.

"Tell her I am busy and to call back later," Betty responded in a voice that said *don't bother me!*

Betty replaced the receiver and turned back to her writing and her thoughts when the intercom buzzed again.

"I must tell her to hold all calls for at least another hour…" Betty mumbled to herself as she picked up the receiver again.

"I am sorry, Mrs. Goldstein, but Ms.Carter insists that she speak with you. She said it is a matter of life and death."

"All right, but after this call, hold all calls for another hour unless it's my husband or Lindy."

"No problem."

Betty clicked over to line one. "Cissy, what can I do for you?"

"Thanks for talking to me, ma'am," Cissy answered in the voice she used for her high paying customers.

"Cut the 'ma'am,' Cissy; you know my name," Betty responded, a little irritated that she had to take this call.

"OK, ma'am—I mean Mrs. Goldstein. I need help. I was arrested today."

"For what?" Betty tore off a piece of paper and started writing the date, time, and Cissy's name. This could be serious if it involved Cissy's stealing. She had many prominent clients in the area that would not want to be named as a recipient of stolen goods, and that included Betty herself.

"Someone planted some drugs in my bags that I carry around with me. Then out of nowhere the people showed up and busted me," Cissy said. "And I think I know who did it, too."

"Where are you now?"

"At home."

"Who posted bail for you?"

"A friend who owed me a favor," Cissy replied with caution. She didn't know how much she should reveal to Betty as of yet.

"Look, I don't play games!" Betty said sharply. "If you want my firm to represent you, I have to know what we are dealing with. So answer the question."

"It was Margaret Lee. I don't know if you know her. She is the daughter of Reverend Perlie Johnson of Mt. Olive Baptist Church on 16th Street."

Betty almost dropped the receiver; she was so taken aback. *What was the connection between Lindy's mother Margaret and Cissy? Friends? I doubt that very much!* Betty thought. *Probably Margaret is one of Cissy's main customers and Cissy did some kind of guilt trip on her.*

"What type of drug was in your possession?" Betty asked.

"It wasn't my drugs. Nick Lewis, a guy from Howard University, planted that stuff in my bag. I had just left him earlier today at the park. Ask anyone, there were plenty of people in the park who saw me with him," Cissy told Betty.

First Margaret and now Nick. What in the hell is going on here? Betty wondered. "Just because he was in the park with you and he went through your bag and others saw you with him doesn't mean a thing. You still didn't tell me what type of drugs you were caught with."

"Some weed," Cissy said with remorse in her voice.

"Some?" Betty demanded. "How much is 'some'?"

"Cops said less than a pound."

Betty prided herself on reading the body language of clients whether they were in her presence or on the phone. She knew from the tone of her voice that Cissy was not being truthful.

"Let's do this," she suggested. "I am going to connect you with my secretary for you to make an appointment to see me or one of my associates next week. We will review your case and let you know if we will take it."

"Ok, but ma'am—I mean Mrs. Goldstein, I want you to handle it," Cissy said modestly.

"We'll see; I can't promise you anything. It depends on my caseload and my colleagues'. Hold on." Betty clicked over to the outer offices and told the receptionist to schedule an appointment for Cissy.

Betty pulled out a cigarette from her purse. She looked at it and put it under her nose as if it was a cigar. The aroma from the cigarette smelled so good. She imagined herself taking a puff, then another puff, and then another. *That's the problem* she thought, *one puff always turns into another puff. No*, she put the cigarette back into her gold cigarette case. She would stick to her plan. She was allowed three cigarettes a day: one in the morning, lunch and one before bed. She had been doing well so far. She eliminated the one at lunch. The next steps would be to do away with the morning smoke, then the one before bed. Betty knew the bedtime smoke would be the hardest.

The second hardest thing that faced her was getting her husband to stop using marijuana. He loved it. They argued constantly about his drug habit and his arrangement with Nick, which bothered her. Harvey had even hinted to her that he wanted to try LSD. Betty let him know in no uncertain terms that she would leave him, if he decided to experiment with hallucinogens.

P

Betty cleared her desk and was eating lunch when Lindy walked into her office. Lindy had called earlier and said that she would work the afternoon instead of the morning because she had to do a few errands for the church revival. She looked terrible. Her eyes were red and her face pale.

"You look awful. What happened to you?" Betty asked as she motioned Lindy to take half of her sandwich.

"I just saw Nick with another woman."

"What?"

"They were walking along 4th Street. He was hugging her." Lindy began to cry.

"Did he see you?"

"No, I don't think so. He was too busy looking at her." She could hardly get the words out.

Betty walked around her desk to where the young girl was sitting and put her arms around her.

"You're young yet, Lindy. Maybe it's better that you find out about Nick now rather than later. You deserve someone better than that."

"You sound like my mother. What's wrong with Nick? Do you know something about him that you can make that remark?" Lindy sat straight up in the chair.

Betty knew she couldn't tell her about Nick getting another girl pregnant. Her husband had told her that in confidence.

"He reminds me of my first husband, that's all."

"But I love him."

"I loved my first husband, too. One moment I was on cloud nine, and the next moment I would be down in the dumps. Relationships, or should I say people, come into our lives when we need to learn a particular lesson or we need to receive a message. My relationship with my first husband was not a healthy love relationship. I never adjusted to his culture and religion. I wanted him to give them up for me. Looking back, I realize how much I blamed him for my misery and suffering. I now know that I didn't love myself enough to make good or healthy choices for myself."

"Nick is different," Lindy protested. "At least I thought he was. He has always been there for me. He really wants me to go to Paris with him; at least I thought he did." Lindy continued to cry as she looked at her mentor.

Betty handed her a Kleenex to wipe away the onslaught of tears. Softening her approach, Betty lifted up Lindy's face. "I didn't mean to imply that Nick doesn't care for you. I guess I just don't want you to go through what I went through. Talk to him. I am sure there is an explanation for what you saw. Just don't let anyone sell you a bill of goods." Betty couldn't help but add that last sentence. She didn't mean to just jump out there and cut Nick down, but it infuriated her that he was taking advantage of Lindy. Nevertheless, this was Lindy's path and her choices for her spiritual evolution.

"I'm not. I wish people would stop treating me as if I were so fragile. I am stronger than most people think," Lindy countered through her tears.

"Yes, you are." Betty pulled out a cigarette, but she didn't light it. She just held it between her fingers. It made her feel better.

As Lindy got up to leave, Betty remembered her conversation with Cissy. "Lindy, do you know a woman named Cissy?" she asked.

"Yes," Lindy replied in surprise. "My mom buys clothes from her. She is also known around town as the town gossiper. Cissy knows something about everyone. Lately, I have been seeing her in Meridian Hill Park. Why do you ask?"

Without divulging too much information, Betty explained that Cissy might be a future client of the firm.

"Why did you ask me if I knew her?"

"Cissy mentioned that your mom helped her out of some trouble today."

"Oh, is that all? Mom represents the church, and she is always helping people out of trouble."

Betty knew this was about more than the church helping people out, but she left it at that.

CHAPTER TWENTY-THREE

Margaret returned home to find her father working in his study. He was alone. She wanted badly to tell him everything that Cissy had told her, but she knew she was in no state to share this information now. She needed to mull over it.

Rev was drinking a cup of coffee. The doctor had told him to stay away from coffee, but he insisted on at least one to two cups a day. Margaret got herself a large glass of iced tea and sat opposite her father.

Rev was working on his sermon for Sunday and didn't want to be disturbed. When he finally looked up at his daughter, he could see that she looked agitated. *Oh no,* he thought, *she is going to have another attack.* Her skin was dark and she had a strange look in her eyes.

"Are you all right?" he asked her.

"I have seen better days, Papa. I guess I am so worried about Lindy."

"Did you find out anything about this woman she is working for?"

Margaret tried to remain calm as she answered her father's question. "Yes, Betty Goldstein. She's the attorney Lindy works for."

"You didn't tell me she was working for a Jew!" Rev said with surprise in his voice.

"She is a Negro married to a Jew," Margaret corrected him.

"That's even worse," Rev announced. "Now I think we are on to something. What do you know about her?"

"Nothing."

By now Reverend Johnson was on his feet, walking back and forth. "Lindy is young and can be easily influenced. Someone has gotten to her and is filling her head with this religious heresy. A Negro married to a Jew! I don't like that combination."

"Lindy carried a large satchel of books into her room the other day," Margaret added.

"Books," Rev mused. This was too much like his Amanda. First she got involved with those people, and then all she wanted to do was read those doggone books. "Let's go up and have a look at them." Reverend Johnson followed his daughter up the stairs.

Even though they lived in the same house, he had not stepped foot in either his daughter or granddaughter's room for years. There was no reason for him to do that. The room still looked the same to him as when Lindy was a child. The same white walls, white furniture and scattered rugs. You could see yourself in the hardwood floors. It was like that throughout the house, thanks to Margaret. She had her problems, but she was a meticulous housekeeper.

Papers were piled next to the bed and on the night table. Rev took a quick glance through them. Lindy was writing a story about a Mary. Was it something for her Sunday school class, he wondered.

Margaret interrupted his reading when she hollered out, "Here they are!" She was standing at the edge of Lindy's dresser. Margaret had noticed that the dresser was not quite in place. She pushed it out a little and reach down behind it and pulled out a book and then another. She handed her father two of the books. He looked at the first one, *There Is a River*.

"Trash," he said, and he tossed the book back onto the bed without even opening it. He didn't need to open it. The back cover told him it was about a twentieth century psychic. The other book that he held in his hands, he wished that he had burned it years ago. It was, *The Book of Life* by the Two Adepts. What was in this book that had fascinated first his wife and now his granddaughter?

Reverend Johnson sat down on his granddaughter's bed and opened the book where Lindy had left a bookmark. Margaret watched her father as he squinted his eyes and started shaking his head.

"What's wrong, Papa? Tell me!"

Rev continued to read as if she wasn't in the room. Finally, he put the book down and looked at his daughter and said, "Get rid of these works of Satan. Get them out of the house of the Lord." He got up and left the room, looking twice as old as when he walked in.

Margaret took the books out to the trashcan. As she dumped them, she felt her spirits lift. At last Papa was taking action. It was just like old times… just the two of them.

Rev slowly made his way back downstairs. He stopped to get some coffee and carried it to his study. He needed another cup to soothe his nerves after reading that passage in the book.

How could he explain to Margaret that the section that he read in the book talked about a place that beckoned to him in a dream over and over again. Shamballa. The book described it as the heavenly kingdom where the most sacred spiritual teachings are found.

As he sipped on the hot coffee, Rev recalled the dream that had haunted him for years.

I would hear this buzzing sound, and bells. Yes, after many years, I distinguished the sound of bells, faint, but nevertheless bells. As the buzzing sound got louder and the bells dimmer, I felt as though I was being struck out of my body. I was in complete darkness. Fear gripped me and then these horrible, grotesque faces appeared in front of me. I could not see their bodies, but I sensed that they were trying to pull me down. Just when I thought they were going to devour me, I felt another presence, a light. It was in the distance. Instantaneously, I started moving toward the light. I could still feel the power of the others trying to get me. Whenever fear gripped me, I moved backed toward them. , I felt another presence, a light, in the distance.

*The bells got loud again, and I felt this feeling of love. I tried again to move toward the presence. The presence was Amanda. I saw her arms stretched out, reaching out for me. She was standing at the gateway to a city called Shamballa. I tried calling to her, but no words came out of my mouth. I woke up frightened out of my wits…*Rev got up and walked over to the window facing 16th Street. He stared out at the cars going back and forth. *All my life,* he thought, *I have served the Lord. I have been a good servant to the Lord. I sacrificed the only woman I have ever loved to be faithful to my God.*

As a young man I was on my deathbed, dying of scarlet fever. The doc-

tors had given me up. Papa went to Amanda's mother and begged her to save me. She did, and years later I married her daughter, Amanda. Papa was against the marriage, but I loved her and would not let him talk me out of it.

She kept challenging Papa on everything. I told her to keep it to herself. She had that way about her. Amanda, just like her mother, could heal anything. You would have thought that she had gone to medical school. She could just look at someone and know what was wrong with him, and then use some of those herbs out of the woods to heal him. Papa John told me that Amanda was poisoning my head and those of others in the church with her nonsense about reincarnation and this ageless wisdom.

Papa made her leave me and the baby, family and friends, the church and the place she was born and raised, because she would not give up this mess. Amanda didn't want to give up Margaret. She begged him to let her take the baby with her. Papa said it was her punishment. She didn't deserve the child.

God what does all of this mean? Shamballa—is it real? Was Amanda right all along? Rev walked back to his desk and opened his Bible to II Timothy and started reading. "Yes," he said to himself, "this is what I will discuss in Bible class tonight."

Satan is busy. He almost had me with this Shamballa madness. Making me think that such a place is real and my Amanda is there. No, like Papa John always said, "The devil comes in many disguises, waiting for you to get weak so that he can work his ways into your soul." I couldn't save my Amanda, but I have to stay strong and save Lindy from this evilness. It was only a coincidence that I found that word in that book. Satan was trying to make me doubt the Lord!

CHAPTER TWENTY-FOUR

The members were glad to see Rev was back to being his old self. He was leading the Bible study session that evening. A good-sized crowd always attended these classes. Rev counted at least fifty people. Since many of the members who composed the revival committee were there, Margaret gave a brief report bringing them up to date on the revival activities. Cissy nodded her head in agreement with everything Margaret said. Margaret ignored her. Her mind was racing with the information Cissy had revealed to her about her daughter.

Margaret's head was pounding. She swiped her forehead with her white linen handkerchief and sank her teeth into the inside of her lip so that she wouldn't scream. Every time she looked at Cissy, she wanted to lash out at her. The voice kept saying "black bitch, black bitch…" At that moment Margaret hated Cissy because she knew that Cissy thought she had one up on her. Cissy had probably already told everyone in the church about Lindy. Margaret was sure they were all secretly laughing at her. Here she was standing in front of them, and they were laughing at her. The voice told her that they didn't like her, and they were glad that Lindy had brought shame and disgrace to her.

Margaret looked at her notes and realized that she had finished with her report. She sat down in the front row and wiped the beads of perspiration that had now formed on her upper lip. She looked over at Papa, and he glared at her as if to say, "Don't you dare shout out in here!" Margaret closed her eyes to try to will the voices away. They were getting louder and using more profanities. It was just too much for her to bear.

Lord only knows, she thought, *I tried to protect that girl from the evils of the world. I gave her everything, and this is how she repays me.* Margaret knew that eventually she had to tell her father about Lindy being on drugs and about the pregnancy. For a minute the thought of an abortion flashed through her mind. She knew that was out of the question. She was not going to be part of a murder. *Suppose the baby is damaged from the drugs and is severely handicapped?*

Margaret realized that she had to take control of this matter as soon as possible. Lindy was scheduled to go to medical school in the fall. They could send her away to one of those homes and put the baby up for adoption. They could adopt the baby later, pretending that it belonged to a distant cousin. What if the baby looked like Nick? Then it would definitely have to go up for adoption. Margaret maintained her posture as she tried to focus on the lesson for the night. She looked to the back of the room, and Lindy was sitting in the last row of seats.

Lindy had rushed home from the office to attend the Bible class. Rev didn't like for her to miss his classes. Lindy hadn't been looking forward to tonight. She wished that she could just go to her room, climb in her bed and bury her head under the covers. She could not get her mind off Nick and that girl. They had looked like lovers. The thought of them made her want to cry. All through dinner she could not look at either her mother or her grandfather. After helping her mother with the dishes, she went to her room to freshen up for that night's class.

At first Lindy didn't notice anything odd about her room. It was not until she reached for the books behind the dresser that her hand felt nothing but empty space. She pulled the dresser out and the books were gone. All of them were gone, the books Betty had loaned her, the books she had borrowed from the center, and her grandmother's book. She knew instantly what had happened. They had taken them. Lindy then realized why they had been so quiet at dinner. She had been getting the cold treatment and didn't even know it. Her mind was so occupied with thoughts of Nick.

Her mother was giving her report on the revival when she quietly entered the sanctuary. Margaret had had a room in the church basement restored to accommodate small meetings or the overflow from the Sunday services. Lindy wanted to march up to the front of the small sanctuary and accost her mother and grandfather about the books. Instead, she took a seat in the last row of the pews. She didn't know how much more she could take of them prying into her personal belongings. She was beside herself with anger. They had entered her room and removed her books. She went outside and found them in the trashcan. One by one, she took them out and cleaned them off. They were now piled next to her on an empty chair.

Deacon Coleman was reading the scripture II Timothy 15:17 for the night's studies. "And that from a child thou hast known the holy scriptures, which are able to make thee wise unto salvation through faith, which is Christ Jesus.

"All scripture is given by inspiration of God, and is profitable for doctrine, for reproof, for correction, for instruction in righteousness.

"That the man of God may be perfect, thoroughly furnished unto all good works."

Rev stood up and exclaimed, "I want you," he said to the congregation, "to repeat after me.

"I am a Christian, first because Christians believe the whole Bible, and accept nothing but the Bible as their guide in matters of faith and practice." Rev emphasized the words "Christians", "Bible", "faith" and "practice." The congregation followed suit. Lindy never opened her mouth. She sat there staring at her grandfather.

"If you have forgotten, then, children, I want to remind you tonight that as a Christian, you believe in the gospel to be the power, and no other words. It is your duty as a good Christian to read, search, and study only the Bible. There you will find the answers to your questions. Because the Bible is the living word of God."

"Amen, amen," several people from the audience called out.

"Do you hear me?"

"Yeah, Rev, we hear you." Deacon Coleman was always the one to answer him when he asked questions. Everyone knew that this was his role, although no one had assigned it to him.

"As a Christian in good standing, you attend church regularly, tithe, and do a service. A good Christian is also faithful to the Word of God, which is found in the Bible. We do not accept any other gospel, whether preached by men or angels." Rev picked up his Bible and read, "Galatians 1: 8-9: But though we, or an angel from heaven preach any other gospel unto you than that which we have preached unto you, let him be accursed. As we said before, so say I now again, if any man preach any other gospel unto you than that ye have received, let him be accursed." Rev looked at Lindy. It didn't elude his notice that she was sitting in the back. He knew that he had the devil on the run.

The new parishioner, Matilda Williams, spoke out, "Rev, does this mean we cannot read those pamphlets that the Jehovah Witnesses give us? They come to my home and talk about God and leave me one of their pamphlets." She smiled at him.

Rev decided to go gentle with her because he had a feeling that he was going to get to know her a little better. In a soft, non-threatening voice he said, "You see, Sister Williams, that's exactly what I am talking about. Listen to what I am saying. You read only the scripture that I, as your spiritual leader, give to you. You must come through me and Jesus to get to the Kingdom." He was returning her smile when he heard a sweet angelic voice from the back of the sanctuary. Lindy was standing in front of him just as Amanda had stood in front of his father.

Lindy had gotten up her nerve to approach her grandfather. She was shaking as she stood up and held the books in her arms. "'In my Father's house there are many mansions.' Couldn't this mean there are many paths to God?"

Every head in the room turned to face her. Margaret put her hand to her mouth as she realized Lindy had taken the books out of the trashcan. Cissy smiled.

The question didn't bother Rev. It was seeing Lindy confront him before the church members and her holding those damn books up to him. Margaret was supposed to have gotten rid of them.

"Have you forgotten the scripture, Amanda?" Rev shouted at her. "John 4:24, 'God is Spirit; and they that worship him must worship him in spirit and in truth.'" he declared.

Lindy felt the presence of Mary. She could smell the lilies, and olives, too. It was as if she could hear Mary telling her what to say.

"God is a power that we each have to find for ourselves. In order to find that power, we have to go within to the core of our very being to open us up to the real meaning of life. This invites us to explore, study and understand all types of religions. The more we explore these different religious adventures, the more we will find that everything is interdependent, interconnected and indivisible."

For once Rev was lost for words. Lindy took this opportunity to continue.

"There are the ancient teachings that tell of the nature of being, the origin of the universe, and the spiritual laws of God. Religion was established to wake us up by providing us with different paths to return home to the spiritual world. There is no one or right path to take to return to the heavenly Kingdom. All of the many religions have a purpose and are part of God's divine plan. Each religion gives the soul the opportunity to grow spiritually, for it must seek its own path and experience the lessons for its own spiritual growth."

"Stop this nonsense! Do you hear me?" Margaret jumped up and screamed at her daughter. She could not stand by and let her ridicule Papa in front of the members. "How dare you question Papa?"

"Amanda, you still have the devil in you from forty years ago," Rev added.

Cissy and the rest of the members present that night then turned their heads to see what Lindy would say from the back of the room. *Why was he calling her Amanda,* they wondered. The old man had finally lost it.

Lindy looked at her grandfather and could see the hurt on his face. She picked up the books and rushed from the room. What had gotten into her, to lash out like that? Then she remembered the events of the day and tears streamed down her face.

Rev managed to finish Bible class, but it wasn't easy. He could hardly walk the short distance to the house from the church; he felt as though the wind had been knocked out of him. He wasn't even aware that Margaret had grabbed him by his arm and led him into the house to his office with Deacon Coleman and Reverend Pierce following closely behind them. They sat there in silence for awhile, waiting for their leader to speak. Although it was late, no one was ready to go home. They were too keyed up from what had unfolded earlier during evening. Deacon Coleman only knew what the old man had told him, and Rev Pierce had no idea what was going on. All he knew after tonight was that something terrible was going on inside the senior minister's home.

Finally, Rev spoke. "Well, gentlemen," he acted as if Margaret was not there, "you have seen the devil for yourselves. I have been trying to keep this within my family, but as you can see the devil has made it a church matter. I need your support and prayer." He looked at each of his lieutenants as he spoke to them.

"You can count on me, Rev," Deacon Coleman said.

"Me too, Rev," Reverend Pierce, added.

"I'm going to ask Reverend Pierce to lead us in prayer, " Rev stated as he turned to the his assistant minister. Then he did something that the others had not seen him do in a long time. He knelt on his knees and lifted his head up. The others followed their beloved minister.

Rev closed his eyes and thought about what Lindy had said earlier. This is absolute nonsense! he thought. I have been her spiritual leader all her life. Now she is telling me that she is getting spiritual fulfillment from a bunch of books.

He had to get a grip on this. If his granddaughter could think like that and say what she wanted to in front of the other members, he would lose his control over the congregation.

Now he understood why his father had to send Amanda away. She had begun teaching other members of the old church about her new way of thinking. Amanda had divided the church. She had gone as far as thinking about opening up her own church. What Papa John did to hold the church together was right. Now it was up to his son to make a stand. Rev's heart was full. He swiped away a tear from the corner of his eye. He loved Lindy, and it hurt him to think about what he had to do.

CHAPTER TWENTY-FIVE

The loud ring of the phone on her night table startled Lindy. She didn't want to pick it up. She knew that it was Nick. She let it ring several times before she reached for it. Hearing his voice brought the pain back.

"Hi, beautiful, I have been thinking about you," Nick said in his sexy voice.

"Hi," she responded.

"You have a cold or something?" he asked.

"No."

Nick instantly knew that something was wrong. This was not Lindy's usual upbeat voice. Her tone gave him an uneasy feeling in the pit of his stomach. "Why don't you come over here after work tomorrow?" he suggested.

"OK."

"OK, then, I'll see you around six."

"Around six or six thirty," she said and hung up the phone. She didn't give him time to respond.

Nick lay back on his bed. This was not Lindy. Something had definitely happened, and he was sure it involved him. The hairs on his back were standing up. Tomorrow he would find out what was going on. He didn't like being left in the dark. But in the meantime…he looked at the clock; it was early. He called his French tutor. Several minutes later he was headed out the door. He stuffed two condoms in his wallet. After Diana, he was not taking any chances. The only woman he decided he wouldn't use anything with would be Lindy. However, he would make sure she was on the pill.

❧——❦——❧

The next morning, Nick collected the new paints he needed for the mural. He was running a little late for work. It didn't matter, because no one was checking up on him. He was commissioned to do the job, and the hours he put in were up to him as long as he completed the work on schedule. He had gotten in late the night before. His French tutor had all but worn him out. She never let him come up for air. He hadn't gotten back to his place until 2 A.M. She had wanted him to spend the night, but he didn't want to get that involved with her. A couple of hours a week was all he needed right now.

As he opened the door to his apartment, he got the shock of his life. Margaret Johnson-Lee was standing there in front of his door with her hand in a fist ready to knock. Nick was speechless.

"May I come in?" Margaret pushed past Nick and entered the tiny apartment. She was not surprised at what she saw. Dirty clothes were everywhere. The trashcan had not been emptied. A pile of dirty dishes was in the sink. The place reeked of cigarettes and some other smell that Margaret couldn't put her finger on. She decided to get right to the point of her visit. She didn't know how long she could tolerate being in such filth.

"You do know Cissy, don't you, Nick?" Margaret asked.

"Yes, I know her."

"How do you know her?" Margaret's voice was cold.

Shit, he thought. Where is she going with this?

"Everybody at Howard knows Cissy. She sells clothes to the students."

"Don't you do drug transactions with her in the park?" Margaret asked. Before Nick could answer, she continued, "You met her in the park the other day and planted drugs on her," she accused him.

Nick looked at her in disbelief. "Planted drugs on Cissy. You don't know what you are talking about, lady. Who's telling you these lies? Cissy?"

Margaret could see the veins in his forehead. He looked big, black and ugly to her. Suddenly she was scared. *I'd better get out of here,* she thought, *but not before I do what I came here to do.*

"Stay away from my daughter or I will have you arrested. You are not right for her."

Before Margaret knew it, Nick was an inch away from her. He smelled like cigarettes and cheap cologne.

"'Not right for her.' You mean I am not light enough for her. You could run a train through my nose. Oh yeah, my hair isn't the good stuff that blows with the wind." Nick took his Afro pick out and stuck it in the crown of his head. "Take a good look, lady, because this is what your grandchildren are going to look like."

"No!" Margaret screamed as she ran from the apartment. She sat in her car and cried. *It's true, Lindy is pregnant.*

Nick didn't see Margaret as he made his way up to Georgia Avenue. How did she find out where he lived? She had even gotten past the receptionist. *The woman is crazy,* he thought. Now he understood why Lindy was the way she was. But in a few more weeks it wouldn't matter; they would be out of here.

Lindy kept her sunglasses on most of the day at work. The others in the office didn't disturb her. She told them that her allergies were bothering her and they made her eyes puffy and swollen. Most people who lived in DC long enough suffered with either allergies or sinus problems. It had something to do with DC being below sea level.

Lindy arrived at Nick's place around 6:00 o'clock. She sat outside in her car thinking about how she was going to deal with what was before her. She could still feel the pain. It was not as sharp or piercing as before, but more of a dull ache. She pushed back the tears that were beginning to surface again. Her mind was racing. She could see Nick and the other woman all over again. Each time she remembered a detail, Lindy's face would turn red and the anger welled up inside of her. She wanted to hurt him as badly as he had hurt her.

She heard a voice within her say, "Apply the teachings." Lindy tried to focus on the thought that what she was going through was a lesson for her spiritual growth. But the pain was too deep, and it hurt too badly for her to focus on any lesson. The thought of losing Nick made her break down and cry again. She looked up to the sky and put her hands together.

"O Father, help me. I love Nick and I know that he loves me. Please, Father, take this pain away and make it all right between us again. I ask for your forgiveness for anything I have done wrong to deserve this. I promise, Father, that I will be good…"

She realized that she was praying to a Father in the sky, begging for forgiveness and asking God to spare her from pain. She sat there a little longer, crying softly. She didn't know if she was doing right by praying to God in the sky or if she should try to find God inside her. She took a deep breath through her nose and let it out through her mouth. It felt good. She breathed deeply several more times until the blood that had rushed to her face made it rosy. She continued to take the deep breaths for several minutes until she felt calmer.

Nick heard Lindy's knock on the door. He opened it with a big smile on his face. The smile slowly dissolved as he looked at her. *She looks like hell,* he thought. He grabbed her up in his arms and gently kissed her on the lips, eyes, nose, and lips again. She melted in his arms. The hurt, anger, and lessons all went out of the window.

She started to say something and he muffled her words with more kisses. "I missed you, baby. What's wrong? Talk to me," he said as he pulled her down on his bed.

Lindy sat straight up and looked Nick in the eyes. All she could get out was "I saw you."

Nick paused and replied, a little taken back. "Saw me? What are you talking about?"

"You know, yesterday. I saw you hugging this girl, Nick, and don't deny it. Who is she?" Lindy said in a cold methodical voice. Her face had turned red again. Nick could see the anger in her eyes.

So this is what this is all about, he thought. Then he remembered the screeching of the tires he had heard and the flash of a car in the corner of his eye. *It was Lindy!*

"Look, you got it all wrong. Yes, it was me. I was with my home girl, Diana. I told you about her."

Lindy interrupted him. "You never told me about any home girl." She had pushed him off her, and was standing up looking down at him on the bed.

"I thought I told you about her. Anyway, that's not important. Her boyfriend lives in Drew Hall, so we decided to walk over there to see him. On the way, she felt faint and I grabbed her to help her. Gee, Lindy, you got all bent out of shape for nothing, baby." Nick was standing up now, laughing as he faced Lindy and held her by her shoulders. He planted a kiss on her forehead.

"There is still so much I don't know about you, Nick. You never really shared your friends with me."

"That's because they are not important. I want to spend all my time with you and only you. Diana's only a friend and doesn't mean beans to me," Nick said as he pulled Lindy into his arms. "You are the only one for me, baby, and in a couple of weeks, we will be in gay Paree."

They fell on the bed. They slowly undressed each other. Nick caressed her breasts and gently sucked on each one. She felt his tongue in her ears, on her neck, between her breasts, and then between her legs. Lindy let out a little scream as the feeling overtook her. She felt him enter her. She wrapped her legs around his back and moved with his every thrust. He arched his back and tried to pull out so as not to come inside of her. Lindy tightened her hold on him as they both climaxed together. He shifted his weight to lie on his side, but remained inside of her. His head was on the pillow close to hers. She could feel his breathing, and he gently slept. Nick was now snoring in her ear. She grabbed a lock of his hair and twirled it on her finger. She loved to play with his hair. Then she let her hand stroke his back. *Nick loves me.* She smiled to herself.

Then a picture flashed before her. She was driving, when she almost hit a girl who stepped in front of her car. Lindy bit her lip to keep from crying as the girl had been crying that day. Lindy now knew who the girl was. But why was she crying? Had she been coming from Nick's apartment? Lindy couldn't hold back the tears; they ran down her cheeks. And before she left that night, he told her about her mother's visit.

When Lindy returned home, her grandfather was in his office. Margaret was cleaning off the table. "I guess you're happy now. You have made a spectacle of yourself, and embarrassed me. You had no right to go to Nick's apartment and tell him to stop seeing me. I am an adult."

"And I am your mother, and I know what's best for you," Margaret shouted at her. "You are living under my roof. I pay the bills here. As long as you live here, you will abide by my rules."

"I won't be here much longer, you can bet on that."

"Don't forget I am paying for your living expenses in school."

Lindy then realized that her mother thought she was talking about when she left for medical school.

"You never wanted me to have friends," Lindy went on. "Every time I tried to make friends, you always found something wrong with them. They were either not light enough, their parents didn't make enough money, they lived in the wrong neighborhood, attended the wrong church, they were jealous of me or their parents were jealous of you or they were just not good enough. There was nothing wrong with them. It was all about you. You're crazy!"

The china cups and saucers Margaret was holding fell to the dining room floor. The plates and cups broke into little pieces. Reverend Johnson, hearing the commotion, rushed from his study. He saw Margaret grab Lindy's shoulders and start to shake her.

"How dare you talk to me like that? Who do you think you are? I have done everything to keep you safe and provide a home for you that is fit for a queen. And what do you do but go whoring around with the first ugly black man you can get with. I'm trying to protect you and secure the right future for you. He has no future. I will disown any children you have by him."

"Let her go!" Rev yelled.

Margaret stopped and looked at Lindy, who stood there as if she was paralyzed. She let her go. Lindy quickly ran past her grandfather and stormed up to her room.

Margaret got on her hands and knees, picking up the pieces of china. Her face was distorted and covered with tears. Reverend Johnson helped Margaret to her feet. He sat her down in a chair and tried to calm her down. She was crying uncontrollably. She could not stay in the chair, but rushed out to the kitchen.

As she cleaned the dining room and kitchen she banged the pots and pans, slammed the refrigerator door, the kitchen door. She kept yelling upstairs to Lindy that she knew her secret and that she wasn't going to get away with it. She threatened to go to the police about Nick's selling drugs. Rev retreated to his office and stayed there until the streetlights came on. It was hours before Margaret calmed down. By now Rev had finally reached his boiling point. He was trying to remain calm as he talked to his daughter.

"You have to get help, Margaret." She tried to cut into the conversation. He waved her off and continued. "These outbursts have to stop. You are pushing Lindy away. You are not well."

"There is nothing wrong with me!" Margaret shrieked. "Lindy is the sick one. Even you said that she was possessed by demons. What are you doing about that?" She stared back at him. Her eyes were red. Rev watched his daughter rocking back and forth as she sat on the edge of a kitchen chair.

"What am I doing about it? I have everything under control. Just leave it to me."

CHAPTER TWENTY-SIX

Rev heard the chimes of the doorbell. Usually, Margaret or whoever else was in the house would answer the door. However, today Margaret had stayed in her room, and he hadn't seen Lindy this morning. The chimes kept ringing; he finally made his way to the door.

When he opened the door, the woman standing in front of him took one look at the great Reverend Johnson and wanted to laugh. He reminded her of Dagwood, the Sunday comic paper character. His glasses were perched on his nose, his eyes were red from being up the night before with Margaret, and his hair was disheveled and sticking out from his head on all sides.

"Reverend Johnson, good morning. I'm Betty Goldstein; Lindy works in my office." She extended her hand.

Rev was dumbfounded. All he could think about was how terrible he probably looked to this woman. With his broadest smile he greeted her, "Good morning, Mrs. Goldstein. Please come in. It's a pleasure to meet you. Thank you for giving Lindy a chance to work this summer."

Betty followed him into his study.

"It's been my pleasure. She is an excellent aide, for not having a legal background. She is going to help me do some research today, so I told her I would pick her up, and she wouldn't have to drive." Betty sat in the chair opposite the Rev's desk. From what she could see, the house was tastefully furnished.

Rev paused a moment to collect his thoughts. God had answered his prayers. He had met Nick and he knew that the young man didn't have the kind of influence on Lindy that was causing her to challenge him. This woman was different. She was educated, classy and beautiful. He told himself he had to be careful and not be fooled by her looks. The more he looked at her, the more he realized that she fit the perfect description of what he had warned his members about. She wore her hair in that Afro style, wore big silver earrings and tight slacks. Rev hated slacks because he was a legman and wanted to see them.

"I'm curious, Mrs. Goldstein, where did you meet my grand-daughter?"

"She came to one of my husband's parties," Betty said carefully. "He's a professor at Howard."

She knew what this was about. The great Reverend Johnson planned to find out what she was about before he launched his attack.

"I am glad that we are having this little chat," Rev said pleasantly. "We—that is, my daughter and I—are worried about Lindy. She hasn't been herself lately. We were wondering if the job was too stressful for her. You know she has never worked outside of the church before."

"She's doing just fine," Betty assured him. "I am impressed with her abilities. She would make a great lawyer. In fact, I think Lindy will be great in whatever she chooses to do."

Rev didn't like the tone of her voice. She sounded very authoritarian to him. *I am dealing with one of those feminists who thinks she has balls*, he thought.

"Lindy's mother is concerned that she has gotten involved with the wrong crowd," Rev went on. "You know how easy it is for young people to be influenced by fast-talking slickers. What do you know about Nick Lewis?"

I can't believe he used that word "slicker," Betty thought. "Nick Lewis? Isn't he Lindy's friend?" she deliberately answered with a question.

Just like I thought, she is cunning! Rev thought. "We are both concerned. I'm sure you can understand. We don't want anyone filling her head with things that can eventually hurt her."

"Reverend Johnson, I don't get involved with my employees' personal lives. I suggest that you talk to Lindy. She is of age and will be going off to live on her own soon."

Reverend Johnson listened attentively to what Betty Goldstein was saying. She spoke like an attorney—evasive, never really answering his questions. Something about her was beginning to rub him the wrong way. He detested these feminist women who thought they knew everything and challenged you on every point. *Is she trying to get Lindy to convert to Judaism or something else. Lindy is at an impressionable age. Thank God she only had three to four weeks before she would be going off to medical school!* In the meantime, he had to figure out how to get Lindy away from this woman.

"Goldstein…that's a Jewish name?" Rev asked.

"Yes, my husband is Jewish," Betty answered.

"What church do you attend?" Rev decided to focus on her.

"I attend Unity of Washington, DC."

"Unitarian."

"No, Unity. It's a New Thought Church that meets at the YWCA on K Street."

Rev's mind was racing. New Thought, that's one of those churches that deals with that mess Amanda was involved in. They weren't Christians. They were a cult. This is where Lindy is getting that mess from. Giving her those damn books and filling her head with things that are against Jesus and the Lord. Rev almost fell off his chair. Jesus, she is with working with these people! They are confusing her, probably making her think she has some kind of supernatural abilities.

"What denomination is that?" he persisted.

"It's nondenominational," Betty said patiently.

Rev deliberately changed the conversation. "Do you have children of your own Mrs. Goldstein?"

"No."

Just as he thought. Most of those women didn't have husbands or children. She had to marry someone outside of her race to get a man. That's why she wears her hair in that ridiculous style. White men like that jungle look. She needs to get it pressed straight to look decent, Rev thought. All of a sudden she didn't look so pretty to him.

"Well, let me tell you something as a parent and a grandfather, Mrs. Goldstein. No matter what age your child might be, good parents are always worried about their children. We know how easy it is for them to get in harm's way or mixed up with the wrong folks. It is our duty as parents to keep them on the Christian path. I don't understand the faith you practice Mrs. Goldstein, but in the Christian faith, we don't believe in such nonsense as psychic abilities and paranormal experiences. Our belief is in God, the Almighty." Rev raised his voice a little. "Lindy was raised as a Christian and will remain one if I have anything to do with it."

Betty looked at Rev with indifference. Reverend Johnson sounded exactly like some of the men she encountered in her profession every day. He was putting her down and implying that something was wrong with her because she didn't have children. Betty thought about how much crap she had taken from men all of her life. Now he thought he could lecture to her as if she were a child and had done something wrong. He was being very accusatory, without evidence to back up his accusations. No wonder Lindy wanted to get away from that household.

"What are you afraid of, Reverend Johnson?" Betty came straight to the point.

She was greeted with silence.

"What am I afraid of?" he replied at last. "I am afraid that my granddaughter is being tempted by the devil. I am letting the devil know that I won't be sitting on the sidelines. Not this time. I plan to fight him or her, in whatever disguises the devil is taking, to save the soul of my granddaughter."

Before Betty could respond, they both looked up; Lindy stood in the doorway.

"I didn't hear the doorbell. I see you've met my grandfather. I'm ready." Lindy had heard enough of the conversation to want to get Betty out of there.

"Good luck with your battle," was Betty's parting shot to the Reverend.

As the two women got into the car, Margaret watched from her bedroom window. She opened the draperies just enough to get a good look at Lindy's boss. In an odd way, she thought, Betty and Lindy could pass for mother and daughter.

Margaret pulled the draperies together and just stood there at the window for the longest time deep in thought. *It's all coming together now. They're all in this together. Betty and Nick were plotting against me to help Lindy take Papa and the church away from me. Then I would have nothing.*

She had heard the doorbell ring but refused to leave her room. She was not ready to face the world. This was the only place she felt safe. The draperies were shut tightly, and she had not bothered to turn on any lights. The room was dark and cold from the air conditioner. She liked it that way. Her head hurt and the voices would not stop.

Margaret pulled out the church's financial ledger. She made the switch in funds that she needed to pay for Cissy's bail. This was nothing new. For years she had juggled the church funds around to cover expenses. Who was going to question her? Through the years, some board members had challenged her, but Papa always quashed anything before it even got started. She closed the books, feeling in control of this much, at least.

CHAPTER TWENTY-SEVEN

Once in the car, Lindy also felt safe. She always felt better once she was in the presence of Mary, Paul or Betty. She wished that Paul had returned from his trip and would be at the Awakeners' meeting that was scheduled for later that day. She and Betty were on their way to Yes Bookstore in Georgetown to find some books on reincarnation. She had lied to her grandfather again about where she was going. It was better this way. After the Bible study evening, they had hardly said two words to each other.

Nick had called her before she left the house that morning and told her he missed her. She smiled. She had pushed the pain away for now, even though it had a way of creeping back into her consciousness. She could not shake the picture of Nick and Diana together. She had tried to get him to tell her more about Diana, but he would just clam up.

Betty steered the big Mercedes around the curves in Rock Creek Park. Traffic was heavy when they got to the zoo and the tunnel. Betty wasn't concerned about the traffic as much as about parking. After circling the block several times, she decided to park on the lot. It was expensive. It would have been easier for Lindy to meet her at the bookstore, since she lived five minutes from it. But she wanted to meet the girl's family. Curious that the mother never showed herself.

The entrance of the bookstore was full of announcements and newsletters. Soft soothing music was being piped throughout the store. The two women decided to browse and get the layout of the store. There were books on every metaphysical subject possible. Lindy smiled at Betty and said, "We have struck it rich!"

"You're right about that, my little sister. Let's find some books on reincarnation and religion."

In the main room were benches where one could sit and read.

Lindy sat in one corner and Betty in the other. The women didn't converse until an hour later. Betty had at least six books that she wanted to purchase. Lindy had two. The store offered lectures on Friday nights on a variety of subjects. They vowed to attend some of them when time permitted.

Betty suggested that they find somewhere to eat. It was her treat. They found a restaurant on M Street not far from the bookstore.

"The food is good here," Lindy opened the conversation. She noticed that Betty had not smoked all day.

"Yeah, the professor and I come here often. It reminds me of Mr. Henry on Capitol Hill."

"I've never been there. I feel like I don't even know my own city. I have been living in a shell," Lindy replied.

"You'll be OK. You are young yet, and you have your life ahead of you. Have you decided what you are going to do about medical school?"

"Nick and I made up, and I am still planning to go with him to Paris."

"You are giving up a lot," Betty stressed.

"I love Nick. I don't want to be separated from him. I plan to work while I am over there and save some money." Lindy's voice was anxious.

"I know I probably sound like your mother, but why not think about it some more? That's all I ask."

"You don't like Nick, do you?" Lindy asked.

"It's not that I don't like Nick. I just know how difficult it is for women to get ahead. We are always giving up our dreams to help our men get what they want. Consider visiting him on semester breaks. If he really cares for you, he will want you to fulfill your dreams, too."

"The problem is, I don't know what I want anymore. I always wanted to be a doctor to help others. Now I am not so sure. I feel like there is something else that I am supposed to be doing."

"I know how you feel in that regard. I am seriously thinking about getting a doctorate in theology."

"Will you give up your law practice?" Lindy was glad that the conversation no longer focused on her. Why was everyone against Nick and her being together? she wondered.

"I have no idea. I haven't even discussed this with my husband. I just know that I have a restless feeling inside. It is like something is pushing me also to do something different."

CHAPTER TWENTY-EIGHT

They were the last ones to arrive at the house in Chevy Chase. Lindy looked at the two large crystals in the center of the circle. From her readings, she had discovered that crystals were powerful tools to open gateways, heal, and help with interdimensional communication.

The meeting started the same as before, with a meditation led by Mark. Lindy enjoyed his soothing voice, and as the meditation proceeded, she could feel her shoulders drop and the tension leave the back of her neck. This time she didn't experience anything unusual.

Mark opened the meeting by welcoming them all back. Lindy could not believe that it was already the end of July. In two weeks, she would be leaving for Paris with Nick. A part of her would miss all of this, especially Paul. Lindy looked around the room; all the students had returned except him. Betty told her Paul was still very much part of the group. His assignment involved his going to India. The group had to be composed of exactly seven disciples and seven students.

Mark quickly turned the meeting over to Ruth, saying that they had a lot to cover in a very short time. Ruth seemed even older to Lindy this time. Lindy noticed that she was not really as tiny as she had thought; it was more because she was bent over. There was a hump on her back. She wore her silvery white hair piled on top of her head. Lindy wondered if that was to give her height. Ruth opened the discussion with the question "Who or what is God?"

The eldest of the seven students, Barbara Einstein, immediately raised her hand. Ruth nodded to her to respond. "I have had the weirdest experiences since the last meeting. I have asked several of my friends, co-workers, and family members the question, who or what is God? I found that most of them have difficulty answering the question. They responded the same way we did. It was a toss between God being a man in the sky playing games with our lives or God being the Holy Spirit."

Ruth shook her head as if she agreed, and looked around at the other students for their responses.

Maria spoke out. "I thought I knew who God was until you asked that question, and it really made me think. I was raised as a Catholic, and I realized that I simply believed what my priest told me. We believe in the Trinity—the Father, the Son and the Holy Ghost. Now I am quite frankly confused."

All of the students shook their heads in unison to agree with Maria.

"I am also confused," Lindy spoke up. "The other day I had a crisis in my life. I found myself praying or, better still, begging God in the sky to spare me the pain and forgive me for any sins that I might have committed. Yet I have read that God is within us and not in the sky. God does not punish us; we punish ourselves. We choose to suffer and this life is about suffering. Why did I go back to my old way of praying?"

Ruth looked at them and said, "This is a good sign. Confusion is good. It means that you are thinking. You are open to new ways and not settled on one way. Life's journey is about many ways or paths. It is not about a right way or a wrong way. This is a very important lesson. I asked you who or what is God to start your thinking process. It has been severely damaged by the indoctrination that you have been going through since birth.

"It is through thinking that you can become aware of all this programming. After awareness comes internalization. You will be given lessons and tests. First comes the lesson in the form of a life experience, such as a health challenge, financial difficulty, trouble in your relationships, and inability to get what you want in life. Based on the law of attraction, you pull to you the people, places and things that you need to learn the lesson."

Betty looked at Ruth, and the latter nodded her head.

"Think of life as a school full of different classes. One of the classes you have to take is drama. You play many roles in this drama. You are the director, the various actors, the writer, and the editor. Do you understand?' Betty asked them.

"You mean we create our own life experiences or dramas," Koto Omo answered.

"Yes," the Awakeners all responded as one.

Thomas then got up and stood next to Ruth. She was so short and he was so tall, they looked like Mutt and Jeff. Thomas continued where Ruth left off. "For the next part of this lesson, we need you to clear everything off your laps, and I will lead you in a short meditation. Now I am going to ask you to relax and breathe deeply of God's gift to us, breathe. With each breathe that you take, you will go deeper into consciousness."

Lindy could feel herself again relaxing, but this time she felt as though she was floating through a tunnel. She thought she heard Ruth saying, "There is no right or wrong path. But a path rooted in spiritual knowledge is rich in knowledge and experiences."

Suddenly, Lindy saw an image of a student sitting at the feet of a teacher inside of a temple. The floor of the temple was gold and there was no ceiling, just the brilliance of the sun. For a minute, Lindy thought of Nick and the image faded. She felt a light pressure on the space between her eyes and the scene was restored. Lindy looked closely at the student. It was she, and Mary was the teacher. From outside of herself, Lindy watched and listened.

Student: But I'm so young, why me?

Teacher: It doesn't matter what age you are. It is not important. What is important is that you have lived many lives and have much wisdom within you to share with others.

Student: How it that possible?

Teacher: You are part of the Absolute, the All There Is, the One Mind that is eternal, so therefore you are immortal.

Student: You are saying that the Absolute is God?

Teacher: Yes, God, Brahman, Allah, the Lord, Jehovah and the Infinite Intelligence are titles used to call that which is indescribable by language. God is Spirit. God is Light. God is an intelligent energy force. We are made in the spiritual image of God. It is the Holy Spirit, which is within us. It is all-powerful, It is everywhere, and It knows everything.

Student: So we are intelligent energy force.

Teacher: When God sought self-expression and companionship, It created spirits made in Its own image. We are pure energy, connected to the One Mind to express love and to create all that is good. Another way of saying this is that we are spiritual beings having a human experience governed by universal laws.

Student: How did the spirits become human?

Teacher: The spirits used their creative powers to advance their egos. They became self-centered rather than expressing divine love and goodness for all. Many spirits followed the path of self-indulgence and they became attracted to the third dimensional realm called the physical plane. They descended into matter by taking on a physical body as a way to experience materiality. Many of our myths and folklore tell of the descension of spirits. Soon they forgot that they were spirits and part of the Absolute. They only saw themselves as human.

Student: How could they forget that they were first spirits?

Teacher: When they descended into matter, they used their powers to become more enmeshed in the experiences of the physical plane. They forgot their spiritual attributes and what they could do. Although many spirits chose the materialistic way, others followed the path of divine love and truth. These spirits also descended into matter, but they stayed centered on God to teach and share the ancient teachings with other humankind, to awaken them to their spiritual divinity. The teachings are protected by a body called the Inner Government of the World or the Great White Brotherhood.

The word "White" does not refer to race, but to Light. The Ancient Mystical White Brotherhood is composed of highly evolved spiritual beings that are considered the caretakers of humanity. Often referred to as Ascended Masters, they are considered perfect and no longer bound by the Law of Cause and Effect. The group works on the etheric plane for the welfare of humankind, fostering love, peace and truth.

Buddha, Confucius, Lao-Tze, Abraham, Mohammed and Jesus of Nazareth are all Ascended Masters and teachers of the sacred doctrines who had a hand in the development of the great religions of the world. Unfortunately, many of the religions have been corrupted by those still in darkness and selfishness. For this reason, the Brotherhood selects those souls who through their many lifetimes have demonstrated the desire to learn and teach the knowledge in order to help raise the consciousness of humankind.

Student: This is why I was selected?

Teacher: Yes.

Student: Where do I start?

Teacher: By waking up to who God is and who you are.

Student: How do I do that?

Teacher: You must go on a spiritual journey. Through seeking spiritual knowledge, you actually become a true student on the path. The ancient teachings will help you understand the mysteries of the universe and what, why, and how we evolved to where we are on the spiritual ladder. Most souls are ignorant of how God's laws work, and therefore create havoc in their human experiences. But these experiences are for the soul's spiritual growth.

Student: Where do I start?

Teacher: You will start with life and will end with life.

The last words of the teacher were drowned out as Lindy heard her own name being called. She opened her eyes and Betty was smiling at her.

"Did you go to the temple?" was all she asked.

"Yes," Lindy responded.

Ruth looked at the group of students. "Some of you went to a temple, some didn't quite make the journey. Nevertheless, that's OK. You will all get there in time. Who or what is God?" she asked.

"God is not for only one group of people," she went on. "God is for all of us. We call God by many different names and come to God by many paths, but no matter our varied perspectives, God knows us all as one. Each soul must find God for him or herself."

Ruth put her two hands together in front of her chest as if she was praying and gave a slight bow to Lindy.

"Someone went to the temple," she said.

After a short break, the group broke down into groups of two, disciple and student. Betty took Lindy into the crystal room. She said that the energy was very powerful in the room and that it would help with their assignment. Betty revealed Lindy's assignment to her.

"Your assignment is threefold. To find out about your soul and your soul's mission, to learn how we are connected and what Mary's role is, and who is in your soul's group."

"This soul group?" Lindy asked, not certain she understood.

"You have to identify the group of souls who play a major part in your life or mission. Groups of souls reincarnate together. Sometimes they are in the same family or are friends, co-workers, acquaintances or strangers. Interacting with other souls throughout eons provides a way for each soul to work through karma and learn to love unconditionally."

"OK, I have to be honest here," Lindy said with a grimace. "I am still adjusting to the idea of reincarnation. I don't want to return as an animal. Now you are telling me that we all come back together."

"Although there are some religions that believe that it is possible for the soul to return as an animal, we believe that evolution is always upward. You cannot return to a lower kingdom such as the animal, plant, or mineral kingdoms. You are a soul, your consciousness stays intact after you let go of the physical body."

"I have been taught all my life that once you die, that's it. Either you're saved or you're not. You don't get a second chance at life."

Betty smiled at Lindy and gently tapped her forehead with her index finger. "There is a lot that you have been taught that will conflict with what you are learning now. Only you can decide what to believe. No one will ever force you to accept a belief. When your soul is ready to awaken to the truth, you will know. I believe this is what is happening to you now."

"I'm like the young student in the temple."

"Right. Each student is given an assignment based on his or her level of consciousness."

"You mean we all have different assignments."

"Yes, because each of us perceives life differently and our lessons are centered around this perception."

"My assignment is for me to find out as much as I can about my soul, its mission, and our connection, and identify the group and its mission."

"It's very important that you have a clear understanding of what you must do or you will be going around in circles. You're lucky. No, let me rephrase that. You're blessed. There is no such thing as luck. It is simply God's laws at work."

"Why do you say I'm blessed?"

"Because you have gifts that you are already learning to use. Thomas talked about these gifts at the first meeting."

"But I have no control over them. I can't *make* the colors appear or, for that matter, make Mary appear. It just happens."

"In time you will learn how to control them. You are also blessed because of the family you chose to be born into in this incarnation."

"How can you say that? You sound like Paul."

"Life on this dimension gives the soul a chance to learn valuable lessons to help it on its spiritual journey. You could say the more difficult the lesson, the better it is for the soul's spiritual growth. You know the expression 'God never gives us more than we can handle?' It's true. The soul has free will, so it chooses the lessons it wants to work on and the players. You are responsible for everything that happens in your life."

The gong rang and they ended the discussion. As they walked back to the main room, Lindy thought about what Betty had just said. Lindy realized that she was more confused than before. There was no way that she had created hurt and pain for herself, such as seeing Nick with his home girl. Even though he explained what had happened, Lindy still felt uneasy.

John, the quiet disciple, as Lindy thought of him, spoke to the group for the first time. "We will not meet as a group again for what probably will seem like a very long time to you." Everyone looked surprised. Two of the students immediately raised their hands. John waved them down. "The group sessions are designed for the purpose of getting you started. The number of times that we meet depends on the level of soul awareness of the students. It seems that your group is pretty well advanced.

"The Hierarchy felt that they could no longer wait for souls to wake up on their own. This planet, Earth, is in serious trouble, due to the negative thinking or collective consciousness of mankind. It is spinning out of control. It is pertinent that souls wake up because of the events that will take place over the next four decades and specifically what could happen in 2003 or 2012."

"Will any of us be around in 2003? That's a whole new millennium!" the Jewish grandmother laughed.

"Spiritual work doesn't stop on any one dimension, but continues wherever you go," John said. "Remember, your soul made a covenant with God." Lindy sensed that John was uneasy speaking in front of the group. "Some mentors will set up regular scheduled meetings with you; others will observe your progress and only contact you on an as-needed basis. Spiritual teachers on this plane and from the Hierarchy will watch over you. Some, if they have not already, will appear and disappear from your life. Life itself will be your greatest teacher."

CHAPTER TWENTY-NINE

On Thursday afternoon, Nick waited patiently for Lindy to pick him up from the school. They had talked on Sunday and planned to get together today. He knew she was running late because the traffic coming across the southeast freeway was always heavy at rush hour. He didn't mind because he was putting the finishing touches on the mural. It was coming along nicely. Another few days and the mural would be finished.

The medical student from Georgetown that Cissy had put him in touch with had contacted him, and they set an appointment for the second Friday in August, about two weeks away. Nick realized that was cutting it close to the date Lindy and he would be leaving for Paris. He wished it could be over with now. Diana was getting on his nerves. He was tired of playing up to her like a lovesick puppy. She had to be constantly stroked. Nick knew he couldn't just tell her about the date of the abortion, he had to be very skillful in how he went about it. She was at his place last night.

They were lying across his bed. She wanted to have sex, but the thought of it repulsed him. He didn't want to touch her. He forced himself to rub her back and kiss the back of her neck. He told her he was scared he might hurt her, and it would be better if they delayed sex. He turned her around to face him and kissed her on the lips before she could respond. Nick waited a few minutes before springing on her the reason he really had her to come to the apartment.

"The doctor got in touch with me. It's set for the second Friday of August." He looked intently into her eyes. Diana's eyes got cloudy with tears. He pulled her toward him, put his arm around her shoulders and gently rocked her.

"Nicky, are you sure, I mean real sure we are doing the right thing?

We would be killing our baby." Her eyes pleaded with him.

"We are not going to beat ourselves up discussing this again. We made a decision that is best for all of us. In December you will come to Paris. If I stay over for another year, then you can join me."

"You never told me that you were going to stay over there for another year," she said in a hurt little voice as she snuggled up to him.

"It all depends how this first year goes."

"What about Lindy?"

"What about her?" he asked. Diana had caught him off guard.

"Are you still involved with her?"

"Lindy is going to medical school in the fall," he lied. "I didn't finish telling you about Friday," Nick changed the subject. "You will come to my place around 5 p.m. I will give you a key to get in just in case I'm late getting there because of the traffic. The doctor is going to come between 6 and 7 p.m."

"You're not going to be here?" Diana looked a little scared.

"Yes, Diana, I am going to be there with you through the whole thing. The doc said it takes less than fifteen minutes to do what he has to do. Then you wait a couple of hours. He said you'll start to experience some cramps, and pretty soon it will be over." Nick stopped talking because he could see the distress in her eyes. He pulled her to him and kissed her ear. "Relax, baby. It's going to be all right."

The sound of Lindy's horn brought him back to the task at hand. He put down the paintbrush and went to open the door for her. He watched her get out of the car. She looked good, even in the childish clothes she had gone back to wearing.

Lindy parked the Beetle and came into the school. She wanted to see the mural. It was, as she expected, a work of art. Nick was so gifted. One day he would be famous. She was sure of that.

"Do you think your mom called the police on me?" was Nick's

greeting to her.

"I don't think my mother would do anything like that. Why, what happened?" Lindy asked, a little concerned.

"Two detectives showed up at my apartment. They searched it for drugs. Then they took me to the Fourth Precinct for questioning." Nick finished off a carton of orange juice he had on his worktable. "I was down there most of last evening. Your mom did threaten to have me arrested!"

"Oh, Nick, are you all right?"

"Yeah, yeah, I'm OK," he replied now that the ordeal was over. Lindy looked so scared. "Hey, I am sorry to hit you like that. Come here."

Nick pulled her into an empty classroom where they hugged and kissed for a while before leaving the school.

Lindy sat on the passenger side of the Beetle. Nick always drove when they were together. He said it was a macho thing. It felt strange to have a woman drive him around. She reached over and kissed him on the cheek.

"Yeah, yeah," he said distractedly. "Do you think your passport will come in time? We only have a week and a half." He looked worried.

"I checked, and they said I should get it in a couple of days. I can't believe that in less than two weeks we will be in Paris. I don't know when I am going to tell my family."

"I hate to say this, but after spending some time with your family, I think you need to wait until we are actually in Paris. Your mother will go to any lengths to stop you. Man, that woman hates me!" Nick exclaimed as he blew the horn at a car that had cut in front of them.

Lindy sat there thinking about her mother. Margaret was getting worse. She didn't want to tell Nick about how her mother had man-handled her the other evening. Lindy admitted to herself that her mother was capable of reporting Nick to the authorities.

"Hey, come back here!" Nick said, reaching across to fondle her breast. "Where are you? You're not zoning out on me again, are you?"

"Sorry, I was just thinking about something."

"What, may I ask?"

"My mom is just sick; with what, I don't know. You might be right. I could leave them a letter then call them once we are in Paris."

Sweat was running down Nick's brown face. The traffic jam that they were caught in was not helping matters. "You could have fooled me. You had that crazy look in your eyes. As if you were somewhere else."

"For a moment I was thinking of something Betty Goldstein shared with me."

"Are we going to play twenty questions? What did she share with you?" Nick was getting upset.

"Betty and I have been studying the ageless teachings. She said that everyone in my life, and maybe even others I don't know yet, are part of what is called a soul group."

"I don't know what you mean by ageless teachings and, to be truthful, I don't want to know. Did you tell Betty that you are going to Paris with me?" Nick quickly changed the subject.

"Yes."

"Shit, what in the hell did you do that for?" Nick was shaking his head back and forth.

"What's wrong with that, Nick?" Lindy was getting hot, and not just from the weather.

Taking a quick glance at Lindy, Nick responded, "People talk; that's all. The less people know the better. I don't want anything to happen that could mess up our plans. We are coming down to the deadline. Betty might try and change your mind so that you can stay here and work on this wisdom stuff."

Betty probably knew about Diana, Nick surmised. Thank God she had not told Lindy, but he could not take a chance on that. He had to get Lindy away from her. He had no idea that Betty was involved with this occult thing. She was too much of an influence on Lindy.

"You should stop working soon," he said. "I don't want your family getting suspicious. Pretend that you are getting ready for med school."

"I thought that we needed the money."

"We do need money. I will have enough to get us there and live off for a short time until the fellowship kicks in. Then you will have to work and take care of your old man," he joked.

Once they were in Paris, he hoped that she would forget all of this nonsense about some ageless wisdom, and especially that psychic stuff. He would go along with it here, but not in Paris where they would be starting a new life.

"I'll think about it." Lindy knew that she didn't want to stop working. She didn't have any other way to stay in contact with Betty, her mentor. He was asking her to give up something that was too much a part of her—the teachings. Nick didn't seem quite as supportive about her gifts as when they first met. He didn't ask her what she wanted; he just told her to give up her job.

The evening went by quickly. They made small talk for a while. He was sitting close to her on the sofa bed. She could smell his cologne. The smell of him made her intoxicated. She wanted him so badly. Lindy watched Nick get up and move to the stereo. She heard the sweet sound of Eddie Kendrick's voice fill the tiny apartment. She loved the Temptations.

Nick came over to her and held out his hands. Lindy put her hands into his large ones. He pulled her up into his arms. His arms closed around her waist and she put her arms around his neck. Nick was so romantic. He never just jumped on her. Every pulse in her body wanted him, including her heart. Lindy knew that she loved the ground that this man walked on. Nick kissed her fully on the lips. She could feel his tongue parting her lips. He unzipped her dress and she felt it fall to the floor.

It was her turn now. Lindy slowly unbuttoned his shirt. Underneath he had on a tight white t-shirt that showed the largeness of his chest and biceps. He looked like an Egyptian god. Her hands found the zipper of his pants, and she slowly pulled them down as she used her tongue to caress his skin. Lindy looked up into his eyes and realized how much she loved him. They fell back on the bed and made love as if it was their first time.

Afterwards, she lay with her head on his shoulder, feeling contented and safe. She always felt safe when Nick was around. She wanted to stay, but they agreed it was best for her to return home early to keep the peace in the house.

Lindy smiled to herself as she shifted the Beetle into first gear and headed up 16th Street. It was only 9 o'clock. The night was hot, humid and muggy. Nick would probably hang out at one of his boys' houses, since she was not going to stay with him. Her mind started racing again with the thoughts of Nick and Diana together. The pain was back. She told herself it didn't matter to her anymore. Soon Nick and she would be together forever.

Lindy had hardly opened the front door before her grandfather came hurriedly out of his study. The look on his face told her that something had happened. He motioned her to come into his office. Her mother was sitting there in her usual seat. Lindy remained standing at the door. Her grandfather motioned again for her to come in and sit down. Lindy had not talked to Margaret since Sunday afternoon when they had had words. Margaret never looked up to acknowledge her daughter. Lindy thought, *Oh, the silent treatment.* Rev looked at both women and knew that part of the problem was that two strong-willed women could not live in the same house.

However, since graduation, Lindy's behavior had changed. She was not the soft-spoken child who had grown up in that household. Lindy had become brazen, argumentative, and a know-it-all. Rev had no doubt that Betty and Nick were influencing Lindy, turning her against her family and Faith. What really bothered him was that she questioned his spiritual knowledge and authority in front of his church folks. He was convinced that she had sold her soul to the devil just like his wife, Amanda. This was dangerous. He should have put a stop to this earlier the first time she taunted him. Lindy's actions had triggered a return of Margaret's condition. When she didn't take her medication, anything could set her off. The two of them were driving him to an early grave. He decided to go slow and easy on both women but at the same time restore some order to his kingdom.

"I was hurt the other night by what happened. Especially what you said in front of church members."

"I can explain," Lindy tried to interrupt him.

"Just let me say what I need to say," the old man said sternly. "I should have done this a long time ago. I have been mixing things up a bit. I have always prided myself on the fact that we are one of the most influential families in the District. The church is a pillar of this community. My ministry is well known for its charity and the saving of souls. It would not look good to the community if word got out that I was having trouble in my own household. I can hear the gossip now. 'Old Rev cannot even be the spiritual leader for his family. How can he get up there every Sunday and tell us how to live?'"

Both women sat there quietly. Margaret was still looking down at her shoes. Lindy looked her grandfather dead in the eye. He didn't know which was worse, the one who was ignoring him or the one who was ready to take him on.

"We've got to be a family. More than ever, with the sad state our country is in, the church can play an important part in keeping families together and showing unity. I was pretty much disturbed about what happened in Bible study the other night, and, for that matter, what has been happening in this house for the last several weeks."

Lindy tried to sit there quietly, but she could hardly contain herself. She wanted to shout at him about how she felt being spied on and accused of things by him and her mother. How could her grandfather talk about being a family when they weren't tolerant of each other? How could they be a role model for others when they weren't tolerant of others cultures, religions, and values? They pretended to be, but when they were faced with someone or something that was different from them, it was simply unacceptable.

"You always encouraged me to be tolerant of others religions and lifestyles," Lindy began.

Margaret finally looked up and cut her daughter off. "Not for you to get involved with some two-bit drug dealer who has nothing to offer you. Just look at him."

"You're right, Mom, look at him. The color of his skin is black, he has a broad nose and kinky hair. That is what this is really about. You don't want any darkies in this family," she chided. "If we are Christians, why are you judging Nick by his looks? Jesus didn't judge people." Lindy looked from her mother to her grandfather.

Margaret was on her feet waving her arms. "Lord, what have I done to deserve this?" Her head was pounding and the voices were cussing. She wanted to scream the words out to get them out of her head.

"Margaret, sit down and get yourself together. I'll handle this," Rev admonished her. He turned to Lindy. "Yes, I taught you tolerance and to respect other's right to choose to worship as they please. But that doesn't mean that you have to get all involved with them. You have to be careful out here. The devil has his people out there tempting young Christians to fall off their path. I am not going to let the devil get you like it got your grandmother."

Lindy looked at her grandfather; he looked drawn and defeated.

"I am not on drugs or under the influence of the devil." Lindy could not keep the anger out of her voice.

"I want you to quit this job and help out here in the church," Rev announced. "I talked to Mrs. Banks today. She needs help because of the revival. Besides, I think that Goldstein woman is too much of an influence on you."

"Quit my job." Twice in one night she had been told to leave something that she loved. It was not the job, but Betty and the freedom to pursue her spiritual studies that they were against. "I won't do that. No one is influencing me. I have friends for the first time in my life. They are wonderful people."

"Nick Lewis is a drug dealer, and you call him a friend," Margaret replied as she started rocking back and forth.

"Margaret!" Rev called out to her. He wanted to handle everything.

"Nick's not a drug dealer. How can you call him names when you associate with a woman who steals clothes?" Lindy demanded.

Margaret jumped up from the chair and was in Lindy's face before she knew what happened. "How dare you! Who do you think you are?" She leaned even closer to her daughter and whispered, "I know about your little secret. What are you going to do, kill it? Why don't you tell Papa about that?" Margaret put her hands on her hips and looked at Lindy, "One day you'll be sorry."

"Tell me about what?"

Margaret refused to say anything further.

Lindy did what she had always done in the last weeks. She turned away from her family and left to go to her bedroom. She had never felt so frightened in all her life. For the first time in her life, she locked the door. Hours later, she could still hear her mother laughing and screaming obscenities about her. It hurt so bad. Lindy started praying, but not to a God outside of herself. She prayed to the God within to teach her how to have unconditional love for her family.

CHAPTER THIRTY

Lindy stayed in her room the rest of the evening. She kept trying to call Nick, but he never answered his phone. Her mother was partially right about the drugs. Nick did smoke weed, but he was no drug dealer. She wished he would stop. He told her it was no big thing, that half the country was smoking something. What secret was her mother talking about? Lindy tried to put the pieces together, but too many parts were missing. She needed to talk to Nick. Something was amiss. Did her mother know about her and Nick going away together? Impossible! Who could have told her? And what or who was she supposed to kill? It just didn't make any sense.

Lindy lay on her bed for a long time staring up at the ceiling. She had known for a long time that something was wrong with her mother. She didn't know the medical name for it. Sometimes she could still see those dark circles around her mother's head and heart that took on different shapes. She didn't know what they meant, but it wasn't good. She was sure of that.

Her grandfather was right; she had changed. Through the years she had ignored her mother's behavior. Now she could no longer do that. Either she was less tolerant, or her mother had gotten worse.

Lindy tossed and turned in the bed for what seemed like hours to her. She picked up her grandmother's Bible and tried to read the writing. It was difficult. The pages were old and yellow. The writing was in pencil and had started to fade. Lindy held the Holy Book in her hands and thought about how she had only read the Bible literally or allegorically. Now she knew that the Bible contained a wealth of information that she could get more insight into by reading it metaphysically or understanding the language code.

As she went to put the Bible back on the night table, a small piece of paper fell out of it. Lindy picked up the paper and read, "We have to solve our own mystery. Luke 8:2." She turned to that section of the Bible and it described how Jesus healed Mary Magdalene and other women of the seven demons. "Mary Magdalene," Lindy repeated the name. Could this possibly be her Mary? The one some ministers describe as having a bad reputation.

Lindy held on to the piece of paper as her mind raced with thoughts about Mary. She remembered that Paul had said that Mary was her spirit guide, and a very powerful one at that. Powerful, how could this be? She was at one time possessed by demons, and she had lived an unsavory life. Lindy felt those old feelings of doubt and fear creeping back into her thoughts. Why did Mary choose to be her spirit guide? This she knew was part of the mystery.

Lindy felt her eyelids getting heavy as she closed her eyes. The piece of paper fell out of her hand as she slid down into the bed. She was repeating to herself "Mystery, mystery, mystery…"

Her eyes fluttered as she heard a sound. A dull repetitive noise penetrated her inner ear. Her chest felt heavy, as if someone had put a weight on top of it. She tried to call out, but no sounds came out of her mouth. She tried to wake up and couldn't. She remembered the Lord's Prayer and began to repeat it.

The feelings of anxiety and fear gradually dissipated. The noise pulled her deeper into consciousness. She looked up, and when she looked down, she saw her body lying on the bed. It was not moving. It looked as if she was sleeping peacefully. Instinctively, she knew that she could not focus on the body too long or it would trap her. She heard harps and the sound of Mary's voice calling her.

Mary was sitting on a mountain with other women and men. Lindy was among them, but she was known as Joanna. Betty was there, and her name was Susanna. Lindy heard a voice and immediately turned toward it. It was the voice of Jesus, the Christ. He sat apart from the disciples as His light glowed so brilliantly. He had returned as He had promised to give to his disciples, the women and men, the Truth teachings of the Higher Worlds. Lindy looked around and recognized she was at the Mount of Olives, east of Jerusalem. The place that she knew Jesus loved. A whole flood of memories came back to her. She looked from Mary to Susanna and felt the love, compassion and devotion that they shared for each other and the Master.

She remembered how Jesus came to their towns to tell them about the Kingdom of God. While in the town of Magdala, He saw Mary suffering with the seven demons or evil spirits within her. He knew who she was. With love and compassion, He passed the Light of the Lord through her to set her free of the tormenting demons. Jesus knew that these seven spirits were her negative thinking, which kept her in bondage to punish herself for the great sin that she had committed at the beginning of time. Freed from the satanic bondage, lifted up, and surrounded by Truth, Mary became His devoted disciple.

"Jesus then healed all of us," Mary was saying, "by purging out the inharmonious energy that others called demons and replaced it with the Light of the Lord. At last we too were restored to a peace of mind that none of us had ever experienced before. His love poured out to us and we were never the same, so filled were we with the luminous light of the world.

We women left our towns, husbands and families to follow Him wherever He went to spread his message. Jesus never treated us different than the men. We helped Him with his ministry by providing a way for Him to accomplish his mission. We were emancipated from a life of drudgery and bigotry. Whereas you had a husband, Chuza, I was very devoted to Jesus. His wish was my command."

A thumping noise brought Lindy back to consciousness as the vision rapidly dissipated. She tried to recapture it, but it was gone. The noise that awakened her came from her mother's room.

Lindy turned on the overhead light that was attached to the headboard of her bed. She glanced at the clock; it was 4:44 a.m. Lindy quietly got out of the bed, adjusted the reading glasses that she was still wearing. She found one of her old notebooks from school, and began to write down the dream. A couple of hours later, she lay back down on the bed. The birds were chirping and the sun was rising. She smiled to herself, for she had uncovered a part of her assignment or, better still, resolved part of the mystery.

CHAPTER THIRTY-ONE

Betty had been traveling the same route to work for the last ten years. She would tell herself that if someone wanted to kidnap her he would not have a difficult time tracking her habits. She was a routine person. The only place she allowed herself to be different was in the way she dressed. Some days she would go to work looking like Gypsy Rose Lee and other days a straight-laced high-powered attorney. Today she was in her power mode. The plain blue suit had cost a fortune. She had gotten it and all the accessories when she was in New York a couple of weeks earlier.

Appearance in her business meant a lot. She had learned years ago, when she was a law clerk for one of the superior court judges, that people judge you by how you look, what type of car you drive, where you live, whom you know and how much money you have. Betty knew that those things were part of the illusion that kept a soul trapped in life lessons. The object was not to be attached to them.

She parked in her assigned space in the parking lot across from the law office. Her firm owned the building as well as the lot. Her husband and business partners realized that in years to come the rent on these buildings would escalate. They gambled and bought everything. At last the huge debt was on the downside and profits were up. Betty knew she could afford to go on a sabbatical from the practice and still live better than well.

The office was dark and quiet. It was only six o'clock in the morning. She had decided to leave for work early because of her heavy workload. She had had a restless night, but that didn't bother her. She was better when she had less sleep. It was Cissy's case that had kept her up most of the night. She felt that uneasy feeling that something was amiss. Her instincts never led her wrong.

Betty put her Gucci bag and briefcase on the desk. What she needed was a good cup of hot black coffee. Her secretary had the coffee maker ready to go. All she had to do was walk over to the staff room and turn it on. Once back in her office, she cleared her desk and began to make a list of the things she had to do that day. Where could she fit Lindy into her busy schedule? She needed desperately to talk to her.

The thought of the work they were doing made her alive. She hadn't felt that good since she'd first entered law school. The young naive Betty was going to change the world and make it a better place to live. Twenty years later she realized that the judicial system was not based on truth and justice, but on who can play the game, and who can play to win. The prize was power and money. If you didn't play the game, you would not survive in this field no matter how moral and ethical you were. Through the years she had gotten increasingly dissatisfied with her choice of career. First, she practiced criminal law, then she got disenchanted with that and switched to civil right cases. Betty finally realized that she wanted to save souls, and law was not the way to do it.

The coffee got her juices flowing. Betty started sketching an outline of the events of Cissy's case. Her secretary had put a copy of Cissy's police report on her desk. Cissy was charged with possession of stolen clothes and with possession of drugs. What disturbed Betty was that both the professor and she were recipients of either the clothes or the drugs, and so were a whole lot of powerful people in DC. Cissy could create quite an ugly scandal.

The night before, Nick Lewis had called the professor and told him he had to see him immediately. It was after 2 a.m. when Nick finally arrived at their door. Nick had been held for several hours for questioning by DC detectives. He told them about Cissy's accusations that he planted drugs on her. The detectives had searched his apartment when they picked him up. Nick assured the professor that he didn't incriminate him in any way. He also swore to them that he didn't plant any drugs on Cissy. Instead, she was his supplier.

Betty listened to Nick's story and only asked him a couple of questions. He never mentioned Lindy or her mother. After he left, they discussed Nick's story and the way things were developing. Betty told her husband about Cissy wanting the firm to represent her. At first Betty was going to let one of the junior lawyers handle the case, but with the latest developments, she decided this case needed her touch.

Betty leaned back in her leather chair and smiled as she began to put things together in her mind. The teachings were helping her already. Life is like a play, she thought. Each character has a role that he or she is acting out. Betty listed all the characters. Beside their names she wrote what role she thought each one was playing. *If I didn't know any better,* Betty thought, *I would think that someone up higher was playing games with us.* There was still one piece of the puzzle that she could not answer. Why did Cissy want to take Nick down? What had he done to her?

The law office of Rosenbloom, Moore & Goldstein was humming with activity when Cissy Carter walked into the office. This was not her first time there. She would often stop in and show Betty and a couple of the other women in the firm the latest apparel.

Cissy waited for twenty minutes before Betty could see her. This made her feel uneasy. She hated to wait for anyone or anything. It was as if she was always last on the list. Cissy prided herself on how she looked. Being a big woman with large breasts and broad hips, she had dressed in a plain but expensive two-piece black dress to make her look smaller. Her hair was combed, and she had even put on a little make-up. She didn't want to go overboard with the new look, not yet, but she didn't want to look like a loser, either.

Betty was shocked by Cissy's improved appearance. This was not the same woman who usually wore housedresses, left her hair in disarray and had a peculiar body odor. The woman who sat before her today was neatly groomed, wearing an expensive dress. Her hair—Betty couldn't believe her eyes—was clean and styled.

Cissy told Betty the same story she had related to the police. She pleaded with Betty to represent her. She could not go to jail. She would not make it if she was locked up. Betty let Cissy do all the talking. She knew from experience that later she could go over the conversation in detail and find the inconsistencies in the story.

"Where did you first meet Nick Lewis?" Betty asked, looking attentively at Cissy.

"On the Howard campus," she replied.

"Why would he plant drugs on you?"

"You sound more like the detectives than my lawyer!" Cissy replied as she shifted her huge frame in the soft leather chair.

"The District Attorney will ask you worse questions than these. Why would Nick Lewis plant drugs on you?"

"I thought about it, and the only thing that I could come up with is that the detectives were after him, and he had to get rid of them fast," Cissy answered as her eyes darted back and forth from Betty to the coffee cup.

"Why would they single him out?" Betty asked.

Cissy scooted her chair closer to the desk, leaned forward, and said, "You know Reverend Perlie Johnson, minister of that big church on 16th Street? Well, Nick got his granddaughter Lindy strung out on drugs. She hangs out at Meridian Hill Park. You can go up there anytime and see her sitting on a bench talking to herself. Then the one r day she did this downright disgusting dance in front of everyone. It's the drugs. I think Lindy's mother Margaret sicked the police on Nick. They were probably following Nick that day and saw him go into my bag. They thought I was in cahoots with him."

Betty swore that the woman sitting in front of her had shape-shifted. She had turned into a mean-looking coyote. This was going to be complicated.

CHAPTER THIRTY-TWO

As Cissy got on to the elevator going down, Lindy stepped into the one going up. They missed each other by a second. Lindy rushed into her office, dropped off her personal belongings, and buzzed Betty. Betty told her to come right over. They had a lot to discuss in a short time. Both women were glad to see each other. They embraced and took their usual places at Betty's conference table.

Betty's secretary brought them in some lunch and got instructions from Betty to hold all calls; she was not to be disturbed. The secretary closed the door as she left her boss's office.

She had been with the firm since the beginning. Nothing escaped her eyes. She noticed that her boss was happier than usual, especially when Lindy came around. She had even stopped smoking. The office was buzzing with rumors. Betty had hired this young girl who didn't know anything about law. She also didn't do much work. Betty informed the rest of the staff that Lindy would be working on a special project for her. She never told anyone anything about the project. The secretary didn't know what they discussed behind that closed door. She figured that eventually she would find out, because one thing she had learned quite early in this business was that no one could keep a secret.

"Nick might need a lawyer," Lindy began, reaching for a sandwich. "He was picked up by the police the other evening. They searched his place for drugs. Someone reported that he was selling drugs. This is a bunch of crap."

"There seems to be a lot going on with Nick," Betty responded in between bites. She noticed that Lindy looked radiant regardless of the clothes she had on. There was something about her demeanor.

"My mother accused Nick of selling drugs and giving me drugs. Do you think she reported him to the police?"

Betty then told Lindy about Cissy's arrest for stolen goods and drug possession. She didn't tell her that Cissy had pointed the finger at Nick. Betty decided to be careful. She trusted Lindy, but she knew people talk. She could not afford to have Lindy tell Nick anything she might say about Cissy's case. Nor could she tell Lindy anything about Nick's visit and his arrangement with her husband.

"Nick is no drug dealer. Someone is trying to set him up," Lindy protested. "My mother and Cissy are in this together. My mother wants to break up my relationship with Nick. This is the time I wish I could use my gifts to find out what is really going on."

"Your gifts are not for you to use on these types of things," Betty reminded her. "Remember what Ruth told us. You are not to get caught up in low level psychics or the astral world of fortune telling. Your gift is to access higher wisdom."

"I just don't want anything to happen to Nick. He didn't do anything wrong."

"Don't worry about Nick. He will be fine. Let's get to what we really came together to do," Betty responded as she cleared the table of the lunch debris and pulled out her papers.

"Did you get a chance to work on your assignment?" she asked Lindy.

"I spent yesterday evening in my room reading over some of the materials we bought from Yes Bookstore. I fell asleep," Lindy confessed. Then she thought about it. "No, I wasn't asleep. I left my body and went to another time." Lindy looked at Betty as if to say *Please believe me*.

Reading Lindy's body language, Betty responded, "You had an out-of-body experience. It doesn't surprise me. You are able to do so many different things. I wish my abilities were half as developed as yours. I have visions, but I haven't had them for a long time. Ruth told me that it was because of my job as an attorney. I use my left brain more than my right brain. I need to meditate more and get in touch with my intuition. I think that it has something to do with my smoking. Hopefully, with giving up smoking and clearing my body and mind of pollutants,

I will be able to increase my vibration to have clairvoyant experiences again and do what you can do."

Lindy remembered her experience with smoking pot. She vowed never again to put anything in her body that could harm her.

"Tell me about your OBE?" Betty prompted her excitedly.

"I felt as if I were floating. I could see my body lying in bed. Then all of a sudden, I heard Mary's voice, and I was pulled to this place that I recognized as the Mount of Olives."

"The Mount of Olives where Jesus delivered the Sermon on the Mount?"

"Yes, the same place. We were there Betty, you and me, but not in these bodies. I now know part of the mystery or how we are connected." Lindy had a big smile on her face.

"Right now all I want to know is, did you see Jesus?"

"Why do you think I am beaming today? Yes." Lindy stood up and stretched her arms open. "I am flying. It's not like I saw him as a person. He was a beam of brilliant light. That's the only way I can describe him."

"I was in the dream with you?"

"I can't hold it in any longer," the young girl blurted out. "Our Mary is Mary Magdalene, you're Susanna and I am Joanna. We are the women that Jesus healed of demons."

Betty was silent for a long moment.

"Oh my God," she said at last, "if this is true, then we are back together again. There is definitely something we are supposed to do together in this incarnation."

"What do you mean, if this is true? You are the one always telling me to trust the information."

"I'm sorry, Lindy, I didn't mean it that way. I'm just dumbfounded. I have waited a long time to find out this information. Now that I have it, I am a little dazed."

"Well, wake up, because there is more." Lindy pulled out her notebook and began to read. "While in the town of Magdala, He saw Mary suffering with the seven demons or evil spirits within her. He knew who she was. With love and compassion, He passed the Light of the Lord through her to set her free of the tormenting demons. Jesus knew that these seven spirits were her negative thinking, which kept her in bondage to punish herself for the great sin that she had committed at the beginning of time. Freed from the satanic bondage, lifted up, and surrounded by Truth, Mary became his devoted disciple."

Betty listened attentively to what Lindy was reading before saying, "OK, the key points: Jesus recognized the soul of Mary. He healed her with three things: love, compassion, and the Light of the Lord. The seven spirits were her negative thinking or energy. Finally, she had committed a great sin at the beginning of time. We are on to something."

"If we could only find out what great sin Mary committed," Lindy finished for her.

One of the great things about law, Betty thought, was that it made you analyze every word, thought and action of whomever or whatever you were working with.

"Mary wasn't Mary when she created the sin," Betty suggested. "She was Eve."

"Eve of the Garden of Eden?"

"Yes. You said that she committed the great sin at the beginning of time. Mary is one of Eve's reincarnations. You know that there are no coincidences. I couldn't sleep last night for a variety of reasons. So I started reading some of Edgar Cayce's works." Betty was twirling a pen between her fingers. The twirling of the pen was forming into a habit to replace smoking. "I read that Jesus had several past lives. His first incarnation in a body was as Adam in the Garden of Eden."

Lindy thought about that for a moment. "That's why He recognized Mary."

"God made Eve from the rib of Adam. Eve was the perfect female counterpart to Adam. They were twin souls. One part was male and the other part female. They were equal. God loved both of them equally. You know how Eve was tempted by the devil in the form of the snake to eat the apple from the Tree of Life. She ate the apple and got Adam to eat it, too, angering God. This was the first great sin, which created the Law of Reincarnation, which will allow each soul the opportunity to work out karmic debts until it can overcome the Law of Duality.

"As Mary Magdalene, she was working out her karmic debt?"

"Yes," Betty said with certainty. "However, I feel that there is still something we are missing."

Before Lindy could answer, there was a soft knock at the door, and Betty's secretary stuck her head in.

"I know that you said don't disturb you, but the clerk from Judge Paine's office it on line one. He said that it's urgent that he talk to you before court this afternoon." The secretary looked around to see that there were papers and books everywhere. She was used to Betty's office looking quite cluttered when she was in the midst of a big project.

"Tell him I will be with him in one moment. And then I would like to see you," Betty answered. Then she looked at Lindy and said, "We have to stop here. One day I will have a job where I can think, read, and speak spiritually all day and night if I want to, but for now…"

"Just one last question," Lindy pleaded. "Why isn't this information in the religious doctrines and taught to the people?"

"It's there. The information is hidden for two reasons. The authority figures keep information from us to control us. The enlightened ones have kept the information hidden to protect it. This is why it is important for us to go on a spiritual journey. We must discover the teachings in order to find our way back home. "

"Then why is this information being revealed to us now?"

"You ask a lot of questions, child. I think it is because of the changing of the energies of the planet."

"Paul told me something about that…" Lindy began.

"Go with God," Betty said hastily. "I have work to do."

Betty called secretary into her office before she left for court.

"I need you to type some personal documents for me. You don't have to do it if you don't want to." Betty paused to wait for the nod of agreement that she knew she would get from her old friend. "I will also need you to set up a meeting for next week with the DA handling

Cissy's case."

The woman had been with Betty from the beginning. She ruled the office. The partners called her the real boss of the office. She took the papers out of Betty's hands and said, "Can I do something with the office? It looks like a hurricane went through there."

"I don't know why you are asking me that question. You always do what you want to, anyway."

They both laughed.

CHAPTER THIRTY-THREE

Reverend Johnson felt as if God had returned to his home. It had been quiet ever since they had started preparing for the revival that would start on Thursday. Rev couldn't believe that it was the second week of August already. He was grateful that the house was busy every day with church folks. The sisters of the church were helping Margaret with the cooking and cleaning. The preparations for the revival were going well. They were all working together as a family. Margaret had quieted down. Lindy had not stopped working, but she came home early most days. She was either in her room or helping Mrs. Banks and the ladies. Rev wished that it could remain like this, but he knew that it would not happen. The devil never rest.

For this reason, he had decided to confide in Reverend Lawrence R. Jackson, his good friend and main speaker for the revival, about his problem with Lindy losing her faith and getting involved with devil worshippers. They decided that the prayer circle that Rev had tried to do the day of his heart attack had to be finished. Lindy needed to repent more than ever. Her continued waywardness would allow the members of the congregation to think that Reverend Johnson wasn't in control of his family and church.

Rev thought that he had finally pinpointed the other source of where Lindy was getting her misinformation. It was not the charmer, but the other young man, the one whom he thought had some sense, who showed up at the house unannounced the other day, again looking for Lindy. He had just returned from India. Lindy had just left the house to go shopping with some of the church sisters to purchase food for the revival. Rev ran his hands through his hair and thought about the conversation he had had with Paul that day.

"Vacationing in India?"

"No, sir. I went to stay with my guru in the ashram for a couple of weeks," the young man replied.

They were standing on the front porch. Paul's answer took Rev by surprise. He whirled around to face Paul. "What church did you say you attended?"

"I didn't."

"Well, where do you go to worship?"

"I attend the Science of Mind Center, Divine Science in Georgetown, any of the Catholic, Episcopalian, Baptist or Pentecostal churches, the Buddhist or Muslim temples that are not far from here, and of course the synagogue. Some Sundays I just sit in the park and meditate."

Oh, my God! Rev thought. Here, I thought he was a church-going Christian fellow.

"You're not a Christian?" Rev said with some misgiving.

"I like to think of myself as universal. I don't adhere to any one formal religion. I believe in all religions. I attend all of those different faiths so that I can expand my consciousness. They all lead back to the Source."

"The Source?" Rev wanted to know what Source he was talking about, because he sure wasn't talking about God.

"God. I believe that there is only one God," Paul answered very calmly.

"Do you believe in Jesus, His only Son our Lord?"

"I believe in Jesus and that we are all sons and daughters of God."

Rev had opened the front door then and felt the cool air from the air conditioner. Paul stood in the doorway waiting to be invited in.

"Close the door, we don't want to let the air out." Rev smelled the greens and ham cooking. He beckoned Paul to follow him to his office. He couldn't believe what he had just heard. He shouldn't have invited this stranger in, but for some reason, Rev didn't want to stop talking to him. Paul was different from Deacon Coleman and the rest of the deacons. He was a challenge, a worthy opponent.

"You're one of them, aren't you?" He decided to ask Paul right out.

"One of what, sir?"

He wants to play games, Rev thought, but I don't have time for any of that foolishness.

"One of those nonbelievers, boy. You don't really believe in Jesus, his birth, the resurrection and the Bible as the living word."

"I prefer to say I am a thinker instead of nonbeliever. See, I do believe, Reverend, but I also know that a time will come in which the creeds of Christianity will be questioned because the reality of consciousness has changed, and will change even more dramatically with the new millennium."

"Hell, boy, in twenty, thirty years I will probably be with my Maker. I am concerned about saving souls today, especially my granddaughter. You need some saving, too, young man." Rev laughed. In spite of everything, for some reason Rev realized he liked Paul, and he liked talking to him. For someone so young, he seemed so old. He wasn't like the other nonbelievers who were confrontational. Paul had a quiet, respectful manner about him.

"It still hurts a lot, doesn't it?" Paul looked Rev in the eye.

"My chest is fine. It doesn't hurt anymore." Rev touched his chest to emphasize his statement.

"I don't mean your physical pain, I mean the pain you're carrying around with you from the past."

"Who are you? What do you know about my past?" Rev was getting upset.

"Who I am is not important. You are in a position to also heal others through your ministry. But first you have to heal yourself by letting go of the past. Love and forgiveness are the antecedents of spiritual healing."

"I don't know who you are, but I do know you have no right to come in here to tell me about what I should do!" Rev said heatedly. "I have been a minister for forty years. As a man of the cloth, I am bound to be the spiritual reminder for my church. It is my duty to interpret the living word for my congregation. They are to accept, obey and follow my directions. I think I know something about spiritual healing.

You're the one who has been filling my granddaughter's head with this madness."

"You consider it madness because she is so much like your wife, a gifted psychic and healer."

"I don't want her to think that she has these special powers when she doesn't. She'll be ridiculed and laughed at. People will think that she is crazy. I don't want that for my granddaughter. She is going to be a brilliant physician one day and not some quack. How do you know about Amanda?"

Paul ignored his last question. "People judge and criticize others because they are fearful of what they don't understand. Your wife was gifted, and she healed a lot of people."

"Gifted? She and her mother were the laughingstock of the town."

Rev waited to hear what the young man had to say. He still couldn't get over Paul's reference to Amanda. Paul stood up and walked to the door of Rev's study. Before leaving, he turned and looked at Rev and said, "Until we master the lesson, we will continue to repeat the experience. The experience is the same, but the people and circumstances change. I must leave now, Rev. Tell Lindy I stopped by."

Rev watched the young man walk down the street. He didn't stop at the bus stop but continued walking at a very slow pace down 16^(th) Street. Rev was shaking on the inside. The young man had really upset him. How did he know about Amanda? Lindy must have told him the little she knew. For a minute, he thought Paul was reading his mind. *That's impossible!* he told himself.

His type of thinking was dangerous. No matter how much Rev liked Paul, he realized how serious this matter was. Paul and his kind wanted to destroy Christianity and its leaders. He was poisoning young people's heads, filling them with beliefs that they were more powerful and knowledgeable than their parents, teachers and religious leaders. He was making his granddaughter believe that she had these supernatural powers and that she could perform healing miracles like an anointed one.

These people had to be stopped before others started to think the same way. This rhetoric was dangerous. The church would lose control of the people. Reverend Jackson said he had heard a group of folks out on the West Coast challenging the Christian faith.

Armageddon had started.

CHAPTER THIRTY-FOUR

The sound of the telephone woke Nick up. He peeked at his watch and it was only 6:00 a.m. He wondered who in hell would be calling him that early in the morning. Nick picked up the phone. His voice was hoarse and deep from the DC pollution. He sat straight up in the bed when the caller identified himself as the doctor from Georgetown. *No,* thought Nick, *nothing can go wrong now.* The young med student only confirmed their appointment for the coming Friday night and reminded Nick that he wanted cash. Nick placed the phone back on the receiver and leaned back on the pillows.

Diana was coming to the apartment at 5:00 and the doctor at 7:00. Then he would be free. Everything was in place. He had either sold or given away most of his things. The only furniture he had left was the bed he was lying on and the television. His neighbor who lived underneath him was going to pick those up on Sunday. Nick had decided to give him the furniture in exchange for all the rides he had given him through the years that they had lived in the same building.

He couldn't get back to sleep. Nick wished he had some weed, but after that incident with DC's Finest, he didn't dare keep any joints around. He decided to go for a jog for a few blocks to clear his mind.

Thirty minutes later, returning to his apartment, he could hear the phone ringing as he hurriedly tried to open the door. He caught it on the last ring. It was Lindy.

"Hi, lazy bones, get up!" she laughed.

"Baby, I have been up. I even went out and jogged a few blocks.

What do you have on?"

"My birthday suit." Lindy looked down at the old PJs she was wearing and smiled to herself.

"I'll be right over to give you a nice warm bath and then a spanking."

"Don't take too long now. I'll be waiting for you." She laughed. They always played this game.

"Very soon this will be real. Only I won't be coming over. On Sunday evening we will be flying out of here. Did you get your passport?" Nick asked on a more serious note.

"Yes, they sent it to my office."

"Perfect."

"The church is having its revival starting tomorrow. I'm keeping my promise and helping out with things."

"No problem. But how do you plan to get out of the house with your suitcases?" he asked a little concerned.

"While everyone's in church on Sunday morning, I will put them in the car and bring them to your place. Then you can pick me up later. How is that for a plan?"

"I am scared of you. What happened to little Ms. Lindy of the big house?"

"Boy, she grew up and ran away with one of those field niggers," she teased. "I can't wait to see you," she added.

"Me too, baby. Gotta go. I need to get across town. I have to finish the mural and tidy up some loose ends." He thought about Diana. Lindy's being busy with the revival was a godsend. This gave him the time to spend with Diana. He had given her his silver ring with a panther engraved on the top of it to show that he was for real. The ring had won her over.

Nick headed for the shower, thinking how his nightmare would be over by the weekend.

Margaret, Deaconess Coleman and Sister Williams were sitting at the table drinking coffee when Lindy came down to the kitchen. The women, including her mother, greeted her. They exchanged pleasantries and talked about the upcoming revival that was starting the next evening.

Twenty minutes after Lindy left for work, Margaret left the women in the kitchen cleaning the chicken and greens. Margaret stood at the doorway of Lindy's room and looked back toward the stairs as if Lindy or someone might be watching her. All was quiet. She had not been back into Lindy's room since that day she had removed the books.

She walked into her daughter's room and started searching for anything that might give her a clue about what Lindy might be up to. Margaret quickly looked under the bed and in the dresser drawers. Nothing. She looked over to the partially closed bathroom door and opened it wider. On the counter was a box of sanitary pads. *It can't be,* she said to herself. Leaving the door as she found it, Margaret went to her room and pulled out her personal calendar, where she kept a record of Lindy's cycle. She started counting the days on the calendar; they totaled exactly twenty-eight days.

When Margaret returned to the kitchen the women could not help but notice how happy she seemed. Margaret wanted to, but could not, share with them her joyous news that her daughter was not going to have a black, kinky-headed child by a drug dealer. Now all she had to do was keep him away from Lindy. Who was pregnant? She wondered. Nick had asked Cissy about a doctor. Had Cissy lied about everything? Margaret wouldn't put it past her.

Ordinarily, Lindy would have been at work when Margaret was searching her room. But today the urge to go to Meridian Hill Park was strong. Mary was calling her. She remembered that her grandfather had forbidden her to go to the park, and Nick had told her it was no place for her. Lindy realized that she loved the park. It reminded her of Egyptian architecture. Besides, this time next week she would be in Paris. One more trip to the park wouldn't matter.

Mary embraced her by kissing her on both cheeks.

"Oh, Mary, was I dreaming the other night or did you take me to the Mount of Olives?" Lindy could hardly sit down as she gazed into the face of her spiritual guide.

"Sit here," Mary patted the bench. "Yes, you were really there."

"It's true. You are Mary Magdalene and I am Joanna."

Mary threw her head back and laughed. "You look so serious. Yes, it is true. I don't have much time today and there is something very important that I must share with you." Mary gazed at her pupil with adoration.

"I have so many questions I need to ask you."

"I know, but listen." Mary knew that she was only there as a guide and could only do but so much. "Time is running out for the beloved Earth planet. The Council needs spiritual agents on this planet to help raise the consciousness of those in darkness in order to save the planet.

"Souls who have reincarnated forget who they really are. They are asleep. The shift of the planet's axis and the opening of the grid will create a new period, called the New Age. The funny thing about it is that it is not new. The information revealed during this time will not be new, just forgotten. It will further raise the consciousness of mankind, because some of the secrets of antiquity will be answered.

"As souls awaken, they will take baby steps. They will play with their psychic abilities as if they are toys. Their use of them will be at the lowest astral level of fortune-telling, instead of using them for their soul's growth and evolution." Mary paused and looked at Lindy. The young girl remained quiet.

"The dark side to this period will be the separation between religion and spirituality. Both are part of God's divine plan to help mankind to remember who they are and return home. Their hardest task will be to let go of fear. The dark agents will use everything within their power to keep souls enmeshed in physicality or materialism.

They will promote those with the gift to act as though they are better than those who are still not aware that they too have the same gift. This will create division between souls. False information will be dispersed to keep confusion among the people of the universe."

Again Mary stopped to see how Lindy was absorbing all of the information. Her pupil sat on the bench leaning over with one arm to support her head, all attention. Mary continued.

"You must use your gift to bring the people together, to help awaken them."

"How can you ask me to do that?" Lindy asked. "If my grandfather believes that I am possessed by demons and my mother thinks I am taking drugs, what will others think? I don't know how I will be able to do it. You want me to let others know about my abilities? They will brand me as being crazy." Tears welled up in Lindy's eyes as she looked at Mary.

"There are many ways to look at things, Lindy. Were we not accused in the lifetime we lived almost 2,000 years ago that we had demons? This is your path. You chose this path for your spiritual growth. Remember to look for the lesson in every situation and show compassion."

Mary realized that Lindy needed some encouragement. "You're already off to a good start. You and Betty have already started putting things together."

"It's like a book. That's it, a book," Lindy said. "Gee, do you think it will be a book?" she asked, getting excited.

Mary reached over and touched the space between Lindy's eyes. Lindy thought she saw a flash of white light as Mary withdrew her hand. "Be strong, my little sister, and remember the laws that our Lord Jesus taught us on the Mount." Lindy could see Mary fading away as she said her last words.

Lindy felt this awful pain in her heart, as if she had lost someone she loved very much. She tried to ignore the feeling as she sat there on the hard wooden bench. She realized that she didn't want Mary to go. She still had so much more to ask her, especially about Nick and Paris.

Lindy wondered to herself as she walked back to her car what park would they meet at in Paris. When she opened the car door, a lily lay on the passenger side of the car.

CHAPTER THIRTY-FIVE

Betty sat at her desk reviewing her notes on Cissy's case; she took some deep breaths and put the tip of the pen in her mouth. It was times like now that she wished for a cigarette. Instead, she popped a piece of candy in her mouth. The phone rang. Betty shook her head as if to clear it. She remembered her secretary was out to lunch.

"Betty Goldstein," she answered, a little annoyed. She didn't want to be there. She hadn't wanted to do this job for a long time now.

"Hi, Betty, this is John in the DA's office. I am calling about the Cissy Carter case."

"It's about time you got back to me. What's up?" she asked in his lingo. He referred to Cissy by her full name, as if he knew her personally. She probably sold clothes to him also.

"Since she has no priors, we are willing to drop the shoplifting charge, but the drug charge stays. Because this is her first offense, we're willing to offer one year," he stated.

Betty maintained silence for a moment. She was used to this. She knew this was a good deal. They really didn't have anything to connect Cissy to shoplifting. She had new clothes in her bag with price tags on them, but no store names and no receipts. Hell, that didn't mean anything. The police had been unable to match the items up to any stores. And Cissy had had some nickel and dime bags of marijuana on her. Why were they leaning on her?

"Six months plus probation," Betty shot back at him. "You really don't have anything, John. She only had some nickel and dime bags. Hell, how do you know someone didn't plant it on her?"

"Come on, Betty, we've been watching her. She frequents the park. We've seen her selling. What we really want is her supplier. We will drop the charges if she comes clean."

"Let me talk to her, and I will get back to you."

"OK, but let's wrap this one up quickly, counselor. And if you want to talk over lunch, I am available."

"I'm not. I'll call you." Betty clicked off. She saw her secretary coming back from lunch and pushed the intercom button.

"Get me Cissy Carter on the phone." Betty decided she also wanted to wrap this one up as quickly as possible.

When Cissy answered the phone, Betty could tell she was still asleep. .

"Cissy, it's Betty Goldstein. I just finished talking to the DA's office. This is what they are willing to do…"

Cissy threw the covers off and swung her legs over the side of the bed.

"Can you hold on for one moment?" she asked. Cissy put the phone on the wooden box next to her bed that she used for a night table. She unwrapped the scarf from around her head so that she could hear better. She took a couple of deep breaths and then she picked up the phone and said to Betty, "Mrs. Goldstein, I hope that you have some good news for me."

"Good and bad. What do you want first?" Betty replied. She thought of all the prominent people in DC Cissy could incriminate with her racket of stolen goods. God knows how many others bought more than clothes from her.

"Give me the bad. Let's get that over with." Cissy's voice was barely a whisper.

"The DA is willing to deal. They want names. You know what I mean. They will drop the charges, if you play ball with them. If not, you're looking at one year for the drug charge, and maybe within six months you'll be paroled."

"I can't go to jail. I just can't do that!" Cissy started screaming. Just when she was getting ready to blow this town! She almost had enough money. "Can't you buy me time?"

Betty ignored her last question and said, "The good news is that they are dropping the charge for the stolen clothes. If you decide to go to trial, you will probably get more time. It's a good offer. Within six months you will be back on the streets."

After a few minutes, Cissy said, "Let me think about it. I have a lot of names that they might be interested in."

Hell! Betty said to herself. *This is exactly what I wanted to avoid, dragging in half of DC.* She decided to find out how much she really had by playing what she called attorney poker.

"You mean like Nick Lewis? He was clean, Cissy. The detectives checked him out."

Cissy laughed. "He's a little guy on the pole; I'm talking big names, even a judge or two. Tell them probation or I will blow the lid off this town." Before Betty could reply, Cissy slammed down the phone.

She was tired of playing that Miss Nice Girl with the high and mighty lawyer. She picked up her phone book. She knew what number she was looking for. She had hoped that she wouldn't have to make that call. She was not going to prison for anyone.

The phone rang once. "Yeah?" someone snapped.

"It's me. Did you hear about my troubles?" she asked her supplier.

"Yeah."

"Then what are y'all doing about it? Those fools want to give me a year. I ain't going down."

"Be cool. We'll take care of it. Then you get lost. You get me?" the voice on the other end of the phone chided.

"No problem," Cissy said.

Not an hour later, Betty received a phone call from the DA's office that they had reconsidered Cissy's case. They were willing to give her six months that she would do on the street. Betty hung up the phone. It didn't surprise her. Cissy must have played her ace. Betty had seen this happen too often. If you knew the right people, had the right information or the right money, a deal could be struck. *Law!* She shook her head. It was a crapshoot. All of these criminals, or anyone for that matter who committed a negative act against another person, may think that they were getting away with it, but they were not. A time would come in which they would have to face the law of God, a law that they can't escape.

For the second time that day, Betty called Cissy. Cissy didn't sound surprised. Betty explained that she would have to go before a judge and go through all the formalities. She would get back to her when a court date was set.

"I just have one last question," Betty said. "Why did you finger Nick Lewis?"

"Nick? I don't have anything against him. He would buy some grass every now and then for some rich friend of his. He never told me who. It was his girl and her mother I was trying to get to." Cissy didn't know why she was telling Betty, but it felt good getting it off her chest. "They think that they are so high and mighty with their high-yellow selves. He needs to stay with his own kind. He is so arrogant."

As a little girl, Cissy had been called darkey and tar baby by the fair-skinned children in her neighborhood. Even her brothers who were lighter had teased her. In high school, she wanted to be a cheerleader, but she was too dark to be chosen for the squad. The color of her skin had prohibited her from doing all the things that she dreamt about doing. The hope of being an actress was dashed when she tried out for the school drama team. They hadn't accepted her. Cissy took one look around the room on the day of the tryouts and realized no one else came close to being as dark as her velvety black skin. She hadn't thought of those things for years, but that was then and this was now. Cissy knew that just as soon as her time was up, she was going to blow the Chocolate City.

Betty sighed with relief when she heard that Cissy didn't know that Nick gave his grass to her husband. She also could hear the animosity in Cissy's voice. Betty also knew from experience the color distinctions within the Black race. The closer you were to looking white, fair-skinned with straight hair, the more you were put up front. One thing she could say for her family, her mother and father had taught her not to judge a person by their skin but by their hearts, a rule that she always lived by. Growing up she felt safe with her medium light-brown skin. She was accepted by the fair-skinned crowd as well as the darker ones.

Her thoughts shifted to Lindy. Lindy was oblivious to how she looked. If anything, she wanted to be darker. Was it because her mother wanted her to pass? Anything her mother wanted for her, Lindy was against. Betty pondered on that question for a while. Then she concluded that it was more than just going against her mother's wishes. Betty believed that Lindy didn't judge people because of their skin color. She accepted them based on their personality and now, probably, their souls.

If only the world could understand that all the different skin colors were part of the soul's evolution. Every soul has experienced the different races and nationalities to learn love and tolerance, and to see beyond the physical appearance. *If we could only understand that we all come from the One Mind, the Creator,* Betty thought, *that we are not separate but one. When we focus on our differences, we create separation.* Betty decided that from now on when she looked at others, she would see not only the human being but also the spiritual being.

She picked up the note she had written to Lindy and folded it before putting it in the pocket of her blue mini skirt. The hemline of the skirt stopped midway up her thighs. She tried to pull it down a little as she stood up. It didn't work. She opened the door to the coat closet. It had a full-length mirror. She looked at her body. The short skirt was tight. She had a small waist, hips and butt. However, she knew that her best feature was her big, shapely legs. *I picked the right physical vehicle for this world!* she smiled to herself.

Lindy quickly went through the papers that were left for her to file. She found Betty's note on top of the pile of papers. Betty wanted to meet with her the next evening at Mr. Henry's on Capitol Hill. What surprised her was the news that Paul was back and that he would be joining them. She'd thought he wasn't coming back until September. *What happened?* she wondered. Part of her was happy that he had returned early. She would have a chance to see him before she left for Paris. Another part of her didn't want to see him. She didn't want to tell him about her leaving for Paris with Nick. Why was she concerned about what he would think?

Lindy cleared off her desk so that she could put the typewriter on top of it. The other aide kept it on her desk most of the time. Lindy was glad that she wasn't in today. She had the small office to herself. Ever since she'd left the park that last time, she could almost hear Mary's voice dictating something to her. Lindy put a piece of paper in the typewriter and started typing. She didn't stop until a couple of hours later when her neck and fingers started getting tired.

She picked up the twenty sheets of paper and started reading. She realized that she had no idea what she had typed. Lindy knew that Mary had given her this story. It was incredible. If only she could share it with Betty and Paul now. Thursday seemed so far away. Then it dawned on her—she couldn't be with them on Thursday. The revival would be in full swing on Thursday. Lindy looked at the clock and realized that it was almost three o'clock. She had to go.

It was pouring rain as she raced to her car without an umbrella. She didn't mind, because the city really needed the rain. It hadn't rained for several weeks. This was a real downpour. She was drenched by the time she got into the car. Her hair was plastered to her head, and the blouse that she had ironed that morning was sticking to her skin. As she fumbled with the car keys, Lindy thought about the papers she had in her bag and her dilemma with Thursday evening.

She decided that on Thursday, after everyone was seated in the tent, she would slip out and return before the end of the service around ten. Relieved that she had made up her mind, Lindy eased the little Beetle out into the congested traffic on K Street.

CHAPTER THIRTY-SIX

Nude photos of women adorned the walls of Mr. Henry's. The place was crowded. Lindy was the first to arrive. She got a table and ordered lemonade, then looked to see who was singing. The soulful music of the vocalist made her wish that Nick was there.

Lindy looked around the place; it was a mixed crowd—young, old, white and black. The tables bunched together were round with red polka-dot tablecloth. The waitresses could hardly get by each table, but they managed. The place was too noisy for any serious discussion. Lindy wondered who had picked this place when she looked up into the face of Paul.

Her heart skipped a beat. He was so handsome. His skin was a dark golden tan and his eyes seemed brighter and wiser than before. Paul was no ordinary college graduate, she decided. Perhaps his travels made him wiser and more mature than most people their age. He reached over and kissed her on both cheeks. She could hardly feel the touch of his lips, but her body reacted to his touch. She could feel her nipples getting hard.

"Are you enjoying the show?" he asked as if he had never been away.

"Yes, and I like this place. Was it your idea to meet here? I don't know how we will be able to talk about anything, though. It's too noisy."

"No, it was Betty's idea. But don't worry about it. We won't be here long. I am house sitting for some friends of mine. The house is only a block from here. After we eat, we will go over there."

Betty came in, and heads turned as always. She looked so striking. Paul kissed her the same way he had greeted Lindy. They ate, and Paul told them all about his trip to India. He had returned early because his teacher had an engagement in the United States, and he needed Paul to accompany him as the interpreter. Instead of returning to India, Paul decided to stay here.

Lindy looked at her watch to keep track of the time. She had approximately two and a half hours before she had to return to the revival. As much as the trio wanted to linger in the club listening to the jazz, they made their way back to the townhouse on Capitol Hill.

They were impressed with the house. Like most of the residents of Capitol Hill, the owners had renovated the house. They looked down at the shining hardwood floors and the plush Persian scatter rugs. African prints hung on just about every wall. An off-white leather sectional wrapped around the wall, with an odd-shaped cocktail table in front of it. A piece of marble in the shape of the continent Africa was held up by a base in the form of a dolphin. They also noticed that the base of the dining room table was two old Singer sewing machines.

Betty walked over to the entertainment section that housed an expensive stereo unit bracketed by wall-to-wall albums. The fireplace facing the sofa gave the room a cozy romantic effect. Lindy took a seat on the sofa and kicked off her shoes. The carpet was too plush to wear shoes on. She reached into her bag and pulled out the report she had typed about her out-of-body experience and her meeting with Mary.

"Drinks, anyone?" Paul asked, watching the expression on Betty's face as she gave the place a once-over. Both women declined. He fixed himself a glass of wine and put the bottle and two extra glasses on the table just in case they changed their minds.

"I met with Mary in the park this week," Lindy told them. "I typed up what we discussed, and also a report about my OBE." She handed a copy to each of them.

"Your gifts are getting stronger," Paul remarked.

Lindy sat studying the pair as they read her latest developments. She had a strange feeling in the pit of her stomach as she watched them. Suppose they thought that she made all of this up or that she really was deranged? As the doubtful thoughts took over, Lindy wanted to grab the papers and get out of there as quickly as she could. At that moment

Paul, sensing Lindy's apprehension, reached over and patted her on the hand as if to say, "Calm down, everything is OK. We believe you."

Betty finished first and looked at her young student. The girl's gifts were mind-boggling, and one day she would be a force to reckon with in any field she chose to work. Lindy was able to access information from the higher worlds with such clarity and accuracy, a gift with which she would be able to help others and, to say the least, have a positive impact on world conditions.

Betty knew that the dark agents were aware of Lindy and her abilities. They would try to destroy her, working through her family, her acquaintances, and anyone else to bring about her suppression. Their most powerful method of destruction was to play with the mind and emotions of the person they targeted. Her mind would be consumed with negative thoughts until she could not be a clear channel for information. The information she would receive would be confusing and complex and make her think she was delusional. Betty knew that part of her mission was to guide and protect Lindy.

Looking at Lindy and Paul she said, "Let's look at this from the standpoint of your assignment." She didn't want to appear too excited. "You were to find out as much as you could about your soul, its mission in this incarnation, and our connection, and identify the group and the group's mission. Your soul?"

"I know that I walked this Earth with Jesus," Lindy said calmly. "I was one of his disciples. My name was Joanna." She looked at Paul as if to say something else, but stopped.

Paul put the papers down and looked at the two beautiful women sitting across from him. "There is no coincidence that I have become a part of this group. At first I could not understand why Ruth wanted me to be a part of your group. I now understand that I must have been there with you almost 2000 years ago. " He smiled.

"You were my husband." Lindy looked at him. "We have been together in many lifetimes. You once told me we were soul mates in another lifetime."

"Then you now believe in reincarnation."

"Yes, I believe."

"Good," he replied.

Betty didn't miss the look that passed between the two young people. She continued with her questioning. "You have identified your connection with Paul. Do you know anything else about him in that lifetime?"

Lindy closed her eyes for a moment, and when she opened them she said, "Chuza. During that lifetime, you were a tutor or business manager for Herod."

"Then I was a man of education and position," he stated.

"According to this written account and what you told me the other day, I was also a woman disciple of Jesus?" Betty asked.

"Yes, you were called Susanna, and were one of the women that Jesus healed of demons or infirmities. You, Mary and I were women disciples. We loved Jesus, followed him and ministered to his needs and the needs of the other disciples."

Betty took a tissue from her purse and wiped a tear from her eye. She was so moved. "My middle name is Susan," is all that she said. She reached for a glass and Paul poured her some of the wine.

"Our souls are connected through our work with Jesus," Lindy went on. "I know our soul group mission for this lifetime."

"Then tell us!" Betty exclaimed as the wine made her feel better.

"We are to do exactly as Mary said. We must work together on a project that will aid the Brotherhood in raising the consciousness of mankind."

"You already know what the project is, too." Paul looked at Lindy.

Lindy nodded, thinking, *He reads minds, too.* "We are to take all this information that we have put together and make it into a book. Mary gave me the idea."

"I think you are right," Paul agreed. "We do have a book here. We probably will have to put it out as a fiction. No one would believe it otherwise. I have an idea. Why don't we write this as if one person has written it? We will have to change the names and some other facts to protect our identities."

"Yes, that's a good idea," Betty said earnestly. "People aren't quite ready for this information. It would contain the truth principles under the guise of a work of fiction. It is like Mary said, most people are still asleep."

Lindy reached into her bag and pulled out her grandmother's Bible. "I don't have much time, and I would like to finish that part of Luke 8:13. Mary said we would find out more about our mission there."

Lindy was not the only one keeping track of the time. Margaret glanced at her watch. It was getting late. The first night of the revival and the tent was full, standing room only as they had anticipated. Everything was running smoothly except for one predicament. The granddaughter of the hosting minister was missing. Margaret knew that this wouldn't escape the attention of the church members. Lindy had been gone for most of the revival. She was there in the beginning helping to seat folks. Then it was as if she just disappeared in thin air. Margaret looked for her everywhere. Her car was gone. How could she just leave on such an important night? She couldn't let that happen tomorrow night. Papa and the others had to finish what they started.

Cissy, dressed in a two-piece white suit, looked around the tent. She had gone to the beauty shop for the second time to have her hair pressed and curled. The hairdresser wanted to put that perm stuff in her hair. Cissy told her she wasn't going to let her burn up her hair with that mess. She had heard about how women had gotten that lye put in their hair only to have it fall out right in the sink.

The suit she wore cost more than the one she had sold to Margaret. She saw Margaret starring at her from the corner of her eyes. When Cissy went to speak to her, Margaret intentionally turned her head. Cissy noticed that other people were staring at her also, but seemed to stay away from her.

"Church folks," she mumbled to herself. "A bunch of hypocrites." Had they heard about her troubles? They don't know you when you are in a bad way. "Forget them," she told herself. "I don't care whether they like me or not, especially that yellow bitch; I'll be kissing this town goodbye just as soon as my troubles with the law are over."

What really angered her was all the money she had to pay that lawyer. Betty Goldstein didn't do anything, but almost landed her in jail. Then she found out that Ms. Margaret's princess was working for the firm. Maybe they were setting her up. Cissy looked around the room. "Where is Lindy?" At least, she figured she had squared herself with Nick; she had gotten in touch with the medical student.

Betty took the last sip of her wine. Paul motioned to pour her another glass, but she put her hand over the top of the wine glass. "Let's start with the theory that Mary is the reincarnation of Eve. We have established the fact that Jesus believed in equality among the sexes. In addition to male disciples, he had women disciples to whom he taught the truth principles, too," she said.

Raising his hand as if he was in school, Paul added, "I just thought of something regarding the significance of our trio. Although there were 12 disciples, there were also sets of threes. Jesus's disciples were divided into threes. The male disciples were Peter, John and James and the women were Mary Magdalene, Susanna and Joanna."

"Maybe you could find out some information on the Trinity," Betty suggested.

"I can already tell you something about the number three and the Trinity," Paul said. "As a young boy, I dabbled in numerology, or the science of numbers. In college I studied the esoteric meaning of numbers as they were cited in the Bible. The number three represents the creation of life and the end of dualism. The triune concept is found in each great religion. For example, in Christianity we have the Father,

Mother (Holy Ghost) and Son. The Asian Trinity of God is of Brahma (creator), Vishnu (preserver) and Shiva (destroyer.) We also find the number three in mythology. In Egyptian mythology it consists of Horus, Isis and Osiris. I could go on and on telling you about other triune aspects, such as past, present and future, or body, mind and spirit."

"You are full of surprises, Paul," Lindy remarked with a big smile. "I can't wait to find out what other secrets you are keeping from us!"

"Now where were we?" Betty looked at Lindy as if to say, "Stop flirting!"

"You said the other day there was still a part missing to the mystery." Lindy reminded Betty.

"Let's go over the key points again. Jesus recognized the soul of Mary. He healed her with three things: love, compassion and the Light of the Lord. The seven spirits were her negative thinking or energy. Finally, she had committed the great sin at the beginning of time."

"It's staring us in the face." Paul looked from Lindy to Betty. "What about the relationship between Jesus and Mary? Lindy, you've studied the verse from an intuitive perspective. What did you come up with?'

"As I kept reading the verse repeatedly, and other verses about Mary's relationship with Jesus, one thought remained with me," Lindy said. "It was love and forgiveness. You're right, Paul, the missing part to this mystery is the relationship between Jesus and Mary."

Lindy glanced at her watched. She needed at least 20 minutes to get back up town. She wanted to be there just before the revival ended.

"We have to look at that relationship from both the personal and universal perspectives to fully see the impact on mankind." Paul poured himself some more wine.

"I think we should write this down." Betty pulled out a legal pad.

"Don't worry. I turned on the tape recorder when we started talking," Paul nodded at the machine on the coffee table.

"I never noticed it. Wow, a girl has to be careful around you." Lindy touched his arm.

Betty had never seen Lindy act like this. She was really flirting with Paul. Admittedly, he was good-looking, but they should be talking about more serious things.

"Okay," Lindy said, taking a deep breath. "Here's what I found. They, and I am speaking about Jesus, the man, and Mary Magdalene, loved each other as man and woman. This was not the first time that they had been together as the male and female counterpart. Jesus was the reincarnation of Adam, and Mary was Eve. We know the story of the Garden of Eden. To save time I won't go over that at this time, but I think we need to record it in the book for purposes of clarity."

Lindy's eyes were shimmering as she spoke. They had turned a smoky gray. "When I read the verse, 'She left everything to follow Jesus,' it struck me that she loved Him. He not only freed her from the demons, He forgave her soul for committing the sin of disobeying God."

Lindy was getting really excited now. "In those times, it was considered scandalous for a single woman to follow a man from town to town. Nevertheless, her love for Him was so great that she gave up everything to be with him. This story is better than Romeo and Juliet. It is indeed a true love story. Mary was a highly developed soul. She probably felt trapped in a body and mind that didn't allow her as a woman to express her knowledge, wisdom and autonomy the way she wanted. Mary was not able to express her psychic gifts. When she did, she was said to be possessed with demons. Therefore she had to repress her creativity.

"I am sure at times she didn't know who she was and felt as if she was crazy. I know this is how I felt for a long time. My grandfather is always telling me I am possessed with the devil because of my abilities." Tears began to run down her cheeks.

Betty moved closer on the sofa and put her arm around Lindy. "It's OK, Lindy. You know that's not true now. You are a gifted psychic, but more than that, you know who you are now and what you have to do in this lifetime."

"I'm OK. I just get a little upset when I realize that in thirty years we will be in a new millennium, and we still do not understand what Jesus was preaching when He taught the power of thoughts, words and mind."

"You have a right to be upset. It's OK to release those feelings," Paul said. "However, we have made some progress, but the wheels are turning slowly. This is all the more reason why we have to do what we came here to do. We have to help raise the consciousness of mankind by making them aware of the truth. It is their ignorance of the truth that is keeping us in bondage to problems of crime, prejudice, diseases, wars, poverty, and greed. God, you are right, Lindy, when are we going to wake up?"

Paul picked up the story where Lindy left off. "The seven demons that Jesus freed Mary of symbolically represent the seven sins of greed, lust, anger, hate, envy, pride and spiritual laziness. The act of healing itself was enough to shift her consciousness, and for her to recognize who she really was. With Jesus, she was able to be herself for the first time. This must have been a tremendous relief to her. She was not only free, but with her first love.

"They were again working out karmic debt. By healing her, Jesus forgave her. He forgave her seven times seventy. In turn, she followed him, administering to his every earthly need as a man. Mary and the other women disciples were women of means. They were able to financially support his ministry. He never had to beg for money or worry about such earthly concerns as lodging or food. It must have been a relief to him to know that these things were provided for and therefore he could give his full attention to his mission of preaching, teaching and healing. This was a blessing, because these women were demonstrating the true principle of prosperity that Jesus taught. They gave in abundance unconditionally." Paul took a breath.

"Do you want to stop here, Lindy? It is getting close to the time you have to leave," Betty asked, a little concerned that she might be late getting back to the revival.

"No, I have a few more minutes, and traffic should be light. We must finish this love story. Because this is what it is, the greatest love story in the world. It was pure unconditional love between two souls. His mission became her mission. She didn't question him or doubt him. Mary only had faith in our Lord."

Lindy was not looking at either Betty or Paul, just staring out into space with a glazed look in her eyes. She was thinking about her relationship with Nick. She realized that she was making his mission her mission. Yes, she thought, I love Nick unconditionally. Lindy went on to speak as if she was there actually reliving the events as she was telling them.

"You know from the Bible that Mary was there in Pilate's Hall at the mock trial of Jesus, when Pontius Pilate pronounced the death sentence of crucifixion. Mary's heart must have broken into many tiny pieces at that moment. She had already endured the name-calling and heard the religious leaders begging Pontius to crucify her love. Now it was declared, even though Pontius found no fault in Jesus. Tears poured down her face as she moved among the angry crowd that also screamed for his blood. She followed him each step of the way as he carried the heavy cross to Mount Calvary. She got as close as she could with the other women disciples to comfort Jesus as they heard his painful cries. It was Mary who wept and kissed his bleeding feet."

Lindy paused for a moment to collect her thoughts. Both Betty and Paul recognized that she was in some type of trance. They remained silent as the young girl took up where she had stopped.

"The women disciples knew that their job was not over. It was up to them to care for Jesus in death as they did in life. To show her and the world how much he truly loved her, Jesus permitted Mary to be the first witness of His Resurrection. She mistakenly took him for the gardener at the tomb; he called out to her in the voice that she longed to hear once again. At this point, Mary's soul rose to a higher spiritual level as Jesus bestowed upon her divine wisdom and guidance. Mary transcended her earthly love for Jesus the man to heavenly love for Jesus, the Christ.

"The lesson we all have to learn on this planet is love of the heart and not of the lower nature. Mary Magdalene's life shows how one's life can be transformed through love and the grace of God. She is the female counterpart of the Wayshower.

"One last thing," Lindy said, "Mary wants us to get the truth about earthly love, heavenly love and grace out to the masses. This is why she came."

Lindy stopped at last, looked at the other two and got up to get her things together. "I have to go. I don't want to, but I must."

"We know," Paul said. "There is so much crucial information that we need to discuss. There is always tomorrow. After all, tomorrow is another day." He laughed to lighten the mood.

"I won't be here tomorrow," Lindy blurted out. "I'm going to Paris to be with Nick."

"You're what?" Paul's face and voice showed how shocked he was to hear what she had just said. He looked over at Betty as if to say, "Did you know this?"

"What about all the work we will have to do to write this book?" he asked. "You know, getting the word out about the greatest love story in history?" He was being a little sarcastic with her.

"Take it easy on her, Paul." Betty touched his arm to calm him down. It was the first time she had ever seen him upset. She looked at him, then at Lindy. It was quite evident that he liked Lindy. Betty sensed that Lindy had feelings for him, too.

"I can't stay in that house any longer. I will send you my contributions to the work. I need to get away. I can't live with my mother any longer. You of all people know how they are."

"What about medical school?"

"Next year. Besides, I am not sure any more that I still want to do that."

Paul stared at her and said, "Think about what you are giving up. You have this incredible gift to see illness and heal. Medical school will enhance your natural abilities."

They had reached the front door. "I've got to go," was all Lindy said.

Betty reached over and hugged her. After tomorrow, they would not see each other. They had become so close in a relatively short time. Betty looked Lindy in the eyes as if to say, "We will always be together. Our souls are intertwined." Finally, she released her.

Paul stepped forward and pulled her to him. She could feel the heat from his body as he pressed himself against her. She wanted to pull away, but she felt connected to him. She felt his lips brush her ear, and then he kissed her gently on the mouth. Lindy pulled away from him and ran down the front steps, and hurriedly got into her Beetle and drove away. She brushed the tears away with the back of her hand. She couldn't believe it; she had wanted to kiss him back. How could she be so unfaithful to Nick?

The revival was just ending when Lindy entered the church. No one said anything to her. She stood at the door shaking hands with the congregation and visitors as if she had been there for the entire service. On the outside she might had looked composed, but inside she was shaking. The farewell to two people she had come to love didn't help the situation. For the first time she felt as if she had a life, a life she had been wanting for a long time. She felt torn. She loved Nick and wanted to go with him, but a part of her wanted to be free and on her own. She pinched her bottom lip when she thought about how much she would be giving up. How did one know the difference between earthly love and divine love?

Margaret looked over at Lindy, standing at the door. Tomorrow couldn't come soon enough.

CHAPTER THIRTY-SEVEN

At breakfast the next morning, Reverend Jackson, the featured speaker, and his family ate with them. The two Jackson girls and their mother hardly said a word. Reverend Jackson did all of the talking, between taking bites of ham, bacon, Southern fried potatoes, grits, eggs and biscuits. Lindy could feel his eyes linger on her for a brief second. He had always made her feel uneasy. She sensed pockets of gray areas in his aura.

Tonight was the big night; Reverend Jackson would be addressing the audience, and they looked forward to his lively and inspiring message. Something out of the ordinary always happened when Reverend Jackson was on the stage. The Holy Spirit was strong when he delivered the word. Over the years, he had rebuked the devil and demons out of many people. The telephone had started ringing early. Many people wanted private sessions with him. He was booked up for the weekend.

Reverend Jackson had been ordained as a minister when he turned sixteen years old. At revivals, he always told the story about his calling. He was asleep one night when an angel appeared to him and told him that he had been given the ability to heal others. He took that to mean that he was to heal others through the holy word. His father was a preacher and so was his grandfather, so it was only natural that he be ordained as well. By the age of eighteen he was giving the sermons in his father's church and laying hands on people. They said he was anointed by the Holy Spirit.

What they didn't know was that he liked young girls, the younger the better. He couldn't keep his hands off them. However, he had been careful throughout his ministry and his marriage. He handpicked the girls he would fool with. Most of them were brought to him by their parents for a healing. Once they trusted him, he would have them come to him alone. He always told them that they were special and their healing would go much faster if they obeyed him totally.

One time he came close to being caught. One of the young girls threatened to tell her father. He put his hand on her shoulder and told her that she would fall ill with a fatal disease if she disobeyed him. Just as he could cure illnesses, he said, he could create them. He never heard from her or her family again.

He had watched Reverend Johnson's granddaughter for years. At each revival, he waited to see if the opportunity would present itself for him to have his way with her. But the girl's mother guarded her like a hawk. He was never able to get close enough to her to even touch her. Now the grandfather had come to him with this ridiculous story about the girl being possessed with demons. He decided to go along with it in order to get close to the girl. She was a little old for him now, but even more beautiful than she had been as a teenager.

After tonight's revival, Reverend Jackson planned to convince Reverend Johnson to let him have some private sessions with young Lindy. What happened next would be a matter of her word against his. Who would believe the story of a possessed child-like woman? Reverend Jackson's lips curled up as he smiled at her across the table.

Lindy didn't miss the look Reverend Jackson had given her. She ignored him. She was still basking over the gift Betty had given her the last day at the office. It was five hundred dollars, a going-away present for her trip to Paris.

Later that day people were sitting in the living and dining room waiting to see Reverend Jackson. He was using her grandfather's office for his private consultations. All week the house had smelled like Thanksgiving dinner was being prepared, but today the aroma was particularly strong. Lindy finished what she needed to do for the revival. She decided to take a nap until it was time to get dressed for the night's event.

On the way to her room she found the two Jackson girls sitting on the screened-in back porch. They were so quiet she almost missed them. Lindy decided to go and talk with them for a while. As she opened the door and looked at the two girls, an awful feeling came over her. Both looked into her eyes. Their eyes had a sad dead look about them. She heard the word "wounded" in her head.

Long after she had left the girls, the word "wounded" kept coming to her. The girls were ill; she had figured that much out by studying their auras. While talking to them, she sensed fear and hurt. Someone was hurting these girls, but whom? As she dozed off, Lindy decided to let it go. It was not her problem. She was leaving. Besides, what could she do about it?

The noise from the cars and people arriving woke her up. She hurriedly showered and dressed in the white linen suit that her mother had laid out on the bed for her to wear. The church was filling up fast. Margaret had told her earlier that her grandfather would like them to sit together in the first row.

Several church choirs were singing. They stood out in their white and purple robes. Reverend Jackson had on a purple robe and her grandfather wore a white one. Her mother had coordinated everything. As Lindy took her seat, she could not help but notice the large basket of white lilies on the dais. Instantly, she sensed Mary's presence. Mary was in the church with her tonight. A few seconds later, her mother was sitting down next to her. Lindy looked at her watch. It was seven o'clock.

Across town, Diana also looked at her watch as she lay on the gray wrinkled bed sheets with her legs wide open and her eyes closed. She had arrived precisely at 6:00 p.m. as Nick had told her to do. She had cried all the night before and was still crying when he opened the door to his apartment. Nick pulled her into his arms and gently reassured her that everything was going to be all right. Now here he was sitting partly on the bed next to her holding her hand.

The young med student had arrived a little before 7:00 o'clock. Within minutes he was crouched between her legs. Nick watched the med student as he pulled a long instrument from his bag. The student told Diana that she would feel a pinch and maybe a little pain, but it would be over relatively quickly. He was right. Fifteen minutes later, the student was packing up his bags and leaving. He had demanded that Nick pay him up front before doing the procedure.

Diana just lay there in a fetal position with her back to Nick. Tears started running down her face again. She could not stop them. Nick asked her how she felt. In a muffled voice she said she didn't feel anything. Now they waited. Nick turned on the television and took a seat next to her on the bed. He had a big smile on his face.

Reverend Jackson had brought not only his choir with him but two busloads of his congregants. The energy in the revival tent was high. Several younger ministers and deacons had prayed and read from the Bible earlier. Now the guest choir was singing one of Lindy's favorite hymns, *Sweet Hour of Prayer*. The congregation was clapping and some members were standing up waving their hands. The music went on for over ten minutes or more before the choir sat down and the congregation settled down.

Lindy watched as her grandfather stood at the pulpit looking very distinguished and handsome in his white robe. He gave Reverend Jackson an astounding introduction. Whenever he raised his voice on a particular word, the organist would accompany him. Lindy realized that each year her grandfather would not only be giving an introduction, but his own little sermon.

Reverend Jackson finally took center stage. He started singing in a deep baritone voice that seemed to shake the very foundation of the church. The crowd stood up again, clapping in response to his singing.

They praised God, shouting "Hallelujah!" and "Praise be to God!" Lindy looked at her mother, who was staring at her. Lindy felt an uneasiness come over her. Something was just not right.

Reverend Jackson calmed the crowd as he gave thanks to God, to Reverend Johnson, and to the members of the church for inviting him to the revival. He didn't waste any time before he was demonstrating his healing gift. He called a young man who was in a wheelchair to come forward. Reverend Jackson put his hands on the man's head. There was silence in the large tent as the Reverend asked Jesus to heal this man of his ailments. As he lifted his hands off the man's head, the man jerked in his wheelchair a couple of times and then he slumped over. The people gasped in fear that the young man had passed out or even died.

Slowly, he moved his arms, then his legs. They watched as he stood up, a little unsteady at first. The deacons who stood by his side held him up. He shook them off and took steps toward Reverend Jackson, who held out his arms to him. The young man fell into the arms of the minister, his shoulders shaking with sobs. The crowd went wild with joy and happiness as the choir sang, *"Oh happy days. When Jesus washed my sins away! He taught me how to watch and pray. And live rejoicing every day. Happy day, happy day, When Jesus washed my sins away."*

Reverend Jackson looked into the violet-blue eyes of Lindy. She was sitting directly in front of him. The crowd was still singing and giving thanks for the healing of the young man. For some reason, Reverend Jackson didn't feel elated or energized the way he usually did from these healings. When he locked eyes with Rev's granddaughter, he swore he saw his life pass before him. He could see his future of disgrace and torment.

He stood there at the pulpit, lost for words. He couldn't think. Tears came to his eyes and he began to cry. The melody of "Amazing Grace" played by the organist struck an emotional cord with him. The congregation thought Reverend Jackson was crying out of jubilation as they were. The Holy Spirit had descended upon him and had healed the young man. They figured the Reverend just needed time to get himself together.

"She thinks she is as powerful as God. Nobody is powerful as God!" Reverend Jackson started talking. He looked up as if he was looking up to the heavens listening to someone. He turned and pointed at Lindy. "God is telling me that the demons in you need to be driven out."

The eyes of the congregation went back and forth from Reverend Jackson to Lindy.

Reverend Jackson continued, "Come forth, child, and confess your sins. I was told as I kneeled before the altar that you needed to cleanse your soul now. Hallelujah," he shouted. "God doesn't want us to wait. He wants a healing to take place now!"

Reverend Jackson was back in control. The congregation was clapping and cheering him on. Lindy sat there petrified. Her mother was actually holding her down. Margaret had placed one arm around her shoulder and her other hand was holding Lindy's hand. Lindy began to tremble.

"It's like the song says, child, everything is going to be all right, just trust in the Lord. Let her go, Mother. Let her come forward, ask forgiveness, and get her healing. Let me drive the demons out of her. What did the Lord say, in Isaiah 41:10, 'Don't be afraid, for I am with you. Do not be dismayed, for I am your God. I will strengthen you. I will help you. I will uphold you with my victorious right hand.'"

Reverend Jackson rushed forward and grabbed the Bible from the pulpit. He flipped through the Bible and started reading as he looked directly at Lindy, "'So why are you trying to find out the future by consulting mediums and psychics? Do not listen to their whisperings and mutterings. Can the living find out the future from the dead? Why not ask your God?' That is Isaiah 8:19."

He picked up a white handkerchief from the pulpit and wiped the sweat from his face. "Call out the demon hordes you have worshiped all these years! Ask them to help you strike terror into the hearts of people once again. You have more than enough advisers, astrologers, and stargazers. Let them stand up and save you from what the future holds. But they are useless as dried grass burning in a fire!" he screamed at her.

Lindy looked at her grandfather, who was shaking his head in agreement as he too stared at her. She could hear the shouts and amen's of the congregation. Reverend Jackson continued in his high-pitched voice, "'They cannot even save themselves! You will get no help from them at all. Their hearth is not a place to sit for warmth.' Isaiah 47:12-14."

He reached out his hand to Lindy, and Margaret let go of her tight grip on her.

Lindy felt light-headed. She looked at the lilies and felt the presence of Mary. It gave her the strength to stand up. She didn't go up to the pulpit; instead she stood in front of her seat. The church had quieted down.

Reverend Jackson still had his hand out toward her. He said in a very soft voice, "Confess your sins to each other and pray for each other as that you may be healed. The earnest prayer of a righteous person has great power and wonderful results.' James 5:16." As he uttered those words, his eyes again locked with hers.

In a voice that even Lindy didn't recognize, she said to him: "'And you must confess your sins to each other and pray for each other as that you may be healed.'"

Reverend Jackson was stunned by her response. He looked around at the congregation. First he saw his wife stand up, then his oldest daughter, and lastly his youngest. Their eyes were pleading with him to redeem himself. He started sweating again. Beads of sweat ran down his face. He felt hot inside.

"Jesus!" he called. "Save me! I have sinned, Father. Jesus, save me, I have sinned. I have done some awful things. I have hurt others. Forgive me, Father." He fell on his knees, reciting The Lord's Prayer, and crying like a baby.

The congregation was in shock. They didn't know what to think about Reverend Jackson's behavior. What had he done? Uncanny things were known to happen at church revivals, but this was the strangest yet. They had no idea what caused Reverend Jackson to act that way. However, they presumed that it had something to do with Rev's grand-daughter. She was a strange one. Ever since most of them could remember, she had been different from the other children. They had heard through Cissy and other members of the church that Lindy was on drugs and had had the audacity to challenge their beloved Rev regarding the scripture. She was involved in voodoo or one of those foreign religions. Now she had put a spell on Reverend Jackson right in front of them. They could see it for themselves as Reverend Jackson fell from his knees and laid in a fetal position on the ground.

Rev moved swiftly to help the minister up. *Damn her!* This was no longer his little Lindy. She had too much of her grandmother's blood in her and was too powerful. Now he knew how his father had felt and why he did what he did to Amanda. He had to deal with Lindy just as if he was dealing with any of the devil's disciples. With revulsion in his eyes, Rev looked at his granddaughter and said, "Get thee behind me Satan!"

Lindy looked to Margaret. Her mother turned her head away from her.

Lindy walked down the center aisle of the tent as everyone's eyes were on her. They moved out of her way as if she were a leper. As she walked out into the warm summer night, she could hear her grandfather in the background saying, "I will not let the devil or his disciples live in my house or take over my church."

She could hear the choirs singing as she threw some clothes and other personal belongings into her cream-colored Samsonite suitcases. She would go to Nick tonight and stay with him until it was time to leave. She looked around the room that had been her sanctuary for so many years. Tears formed in the corners of her eyes as she thought of what her grandfather had said to her in front of the whole congregation, "Get thee behind me Satan!" Her mother did what she always did, turn away from her. Lindy was tired of crying. She pushed the tears away as she hurried out of the house she no longer called home.

She decided to stop at Meridian Hill Park one last time. She desperately needed to talk to Mary. The park was full of people. A couple was sitting on Mary's bench. Lindy walked around for a bit and stopped to listen to the drums. The drummers invited her to dance. She graciously declined. She felt free for the first time in her life. The couple finally left and Lindy dashed for the bench. She peacefully waited there for Mary. She waited until it was completely dark, but Mary never appeared, just when she needed her more than ever. Lindy forced herself to leave the bench and headed for Nick's place.

Diana was still curled up on the bed, neither awake nor asleep. Hours had passed and nothing had happened except that she was spotting. Nick was getting anxious. He expected that she would at least be bleeding a little heavier by now. She had not moved much except to go to the bathroom.

Nick felt anxious being cooped up in the apartment. He decided to walk up to 14th Street to get something to eat. He wasn't really hungry. He just wanted to get away from Diana. As he left through the side door of the building, he noticed someone had propped it open with a rock. He left it that way.

Not seconds after Nick left, Diana felt this awful pain rip through her lower body. *Why did he leave me alone?* she wondered. She was scared and wanted to scream. Another pain came, and another one. She had been having cramps for the last hours, but she hadn't told him. Then she felt this gush of blood come out. She had a pad on; nevertheless, she looked down and it seemed that blood was everywhere. She felt dizzy and she wanted to vomit.

Diana pulled herself up. She held on to the bedpost and fell against the wall as she reached the bathroom door. The apartment was so small she only had to go a few feet. Blood was now gushing down her legs. She vomited on the bathroom floor.

She just lay there. She could not get up. Nick would be back soon, she told herself. Maybe she'd better get help. She crawled over to the door and pulled herself up. She opened the door and fell into the arms of Lindy.

The girl was in her arms before Lindy realized what had happened. "Help me!" Diana gasped. "Something's wrong. I'm bleeding badly."

Lindy dragged her back into the apartment. The bed was stained with dark red blood. The girl was going in and out of consciousness. Lindy laid her on the bed and called the emergency number. For the first time, she looked at the girl and recognized that she was Nick's home girl, Diana. The same girl she had seen Nick with his arm around that day near Drew Hall, and the one she had almost hit with her car.

What was she doing in Nick's apartment? Lindy thought to herself as she tried to make Diana comfortable on the bed. She wanted to scream, for around the girl's neck was Nick's panther ring. She heard Mary's voice say, "Help her."

Lindy instinctively put both of her hands on Diana's stomach and imagined the white light going where it needed for a healing. She uttered the words AUM MANI PADME HUM. She kept repeating the words and holding her hands on Diana's stomach until she heard a knock on the door and Nick's voice, "What's going on in there?" The door opened and two paramedics followed Nick into the tiny apartment.

The three men surveyed the room. Diana lay in a pool of blood. Blood was on the floor leading to and from the bathroom. Lindy's new white suit was also covered with blood.

"What happened here?" The paramedic asked Lindy.

"I just got here," she answered in a quiet voice, looking at Nick. "She said," nodding her head toward Diana, "that something happened; she's bleeding."

The paramedics went to work on Diana. Diana opened her eyes and looked at Nick. "Did we lose our baby, Nicky?" Her voice had strength again. For some odd reason, the cramps had stopped.

Lindy looked at Nick and the expression on his face told her everything. As she tried to pass him to leave, he took hold of her arm. "Lindy, it's not what you think."

Lindy shook him off and ran down the flight of steps to the side entrance, the same way she had gotten in earlier. Nick followed, calling for her to wait to give him a chance to explain. He caught her at the bottom landing.

"I know this looks bad. It's not what you think. I did it for us."

"You did what for us? You have been lying to me all the time about her."

"Would you stop for a moment so I can explain?" he asked.

"There is nothing to explain. For once my mother was right. Keep away from me!" she screamed as she slammed the car door. Looking in her rear view mirror, she could see that Nick was still standing there where she left him.

This time she didn't hold back the tears. They poured down her face.

Betty heard the insistent ring of the doorbell. Whoever was ringing the doorbell was leaning on it. She planned to give them a piece of her mind. She wasn't expecting any company. She was soaking in the tub with candles and a glass of wine when the doorbell started ringing and would not stop.

The professor was not home. She had no choice but to answer it. Maybe he'd forgotten his keys or something. Betty fully expected Harvey to be standing on their front steps. Her mouth dropped open when she saw Lindy standing there with blood all over her, her face streaked with tears.

"What happened?" Betty said all at once, taking Lindy's arm. "Come in. Are you all right?"

"Yes. This…isn't mine." Lindy could hardly get the words out as Betty led her upstairs.

"You didn't kill anyone did you?" Betty's law instincts had kicked in. Lindy shook her head, "No."

"You've got to get out of those clothes." Betty escorted Lindy to her guest bathroom and handed her a white terry cloth robe like the one she was wearing. "Clean up, come down, and get some tea. Then you can tell me all about it."

Betty went down and brewed some chamomile tea for both of them. Lindy found Betty sitting in a room off the kitchen that overlooked the swimming pool. The room was decorated with white wicker furniture and beautiful tropical plants. Lindy felt as though she had been transported to an island.

Betty motioned Lindy to sit next to her on the sofa and drink her tea. Lindy poured out her heart in between the tears. She told Betty about Reverend Jackson trying to get her to confess in front of the congregation that she had demons inside of her, about going to Nick's place to find Diana almost bleeding to death, and about discovering the truth about Nick and Diana.

"It hurts! It hurts like hell," Lindy said as she put her head on the older woman's shoulder and cried. Betty remembered how not so long ago she too had felt that pain that pierced the heart. All the human traits of jealousy, betrayal, pain, anger and hurt came with earthly love. Would mankind ever get to that point in evolution where they would learn how to love unconditionally and stop hurting each other?

Right under their noses in a few verses of the Bible was the greatest love story of all, that of Jesus of Nazareth and Mary Magdalene, Betty thought. It shows humanity how to rise up from earthly love to unconditional or divine love. To master divine love, one has to experience many incarnations and lessons of earthly love. *Look how long it took Jesus and Mary to put things right.*

Lindy had had her first lesson in earthly love. Betty remembered reading that everything happens for a reason.

Betty gently stroked the young girl's head as she held her in her arms. She needed to tell Lindy about the lesson of earthly love, but not now. It would not console her. Betty glanced down at Lindy. Her eyes were closed and she was breathing steadily. She had fallen asleep. She had undergone so much in one evening. It had been a long summer. At last she could rest now.

Betty smiled as she thought about what Paul had told Lindy, "that life is never as it seems."

The journey was just beginning.

ABOUT THE AUTHOR

After working for many years as an administrative librarian, **J. J. Michael** decided to pursue her life long dream of writing and traveling. She is the author of two non-fiction titles: *Path to Truth: A Spiritual Guide to Higher Consciousness* and *Sacred Light*. Ms. Michael is the editor of Path2truth.com, an ezine promoting universal healing and peace. She resides in Washington, DC, where she lives with her daughter and two granddaughters. She is currently working on the sequel to *Life is Never as It Seems*. For more information, visit:

www.pathtotruth.com

Excerpt from

PATH OF THORNS

BY

ANNETTA P. LEE

Release Date: August 2005

CHAPTER ONE

On the Shady Side

Thrasher, Thea Carter's three-year-old German shepherd, stayed right at her side in a fast trot. As the two reached the top of the swooping trail at Shasta Park, two men stood to the side with their backs turned. Something about them struck Thea as strange. She shivered as the March breeze drove dated leaves across the path, but slowed only slightly.

She forced herself to keep her eyes focused ahead. The brightness of the sun defied the rain from the night before, but she could smell the damp earth. Ever since she'd moved to Kensington, Colorado from Whispering Pines, Mississippi nine years ago, she hadn't quite gotten used to the seasonal differences.

Keeping his eyes trained on the men ahead, Thrasher lowered his head. Spiking his ears, he crooned a low growl, but remained close to Thea.

"Hush, Thrasher," she whispered, shortening the leash. "Be nice."

Warily concentrating on the path ahead, they began their descent. Suddenly, one of the men backed onto the trail. Her speed as well as the elevation barred her from veering off. Although she called out, it was already too late.

The impact was jolting. Thea bounced against the deceptively slender man as if he were a brick wall. Tumbling with a thud onto the pavement, she cringed at the sound of Thrasher's yelp. Momentarily dazed, she sat up and tugged at the leash she still held. Thrasher immediately limped toward her and happily moistened her cheek with wet slurps. He was OK, she thought with a sigh of relief.

Just as she looked toward the man she'd run into, she saw a stir at the edge of her vision. As she surveyed the area, she realized, with some alarm, that the ground around them was littered with what looked like hundreds of fifty-dollar bills.

Before she could gather her thoughts, a large pair of hands from the second man pulled her to her feet. "Th—thank you," she said, holding onto Thrasher. While the man moved to help his companion, Thea glanced around with a sense of anxious awareness. But no one was on the path. She silently scolded herself for declining Mac's offer to share her run. Why did she get so irritated with him? What harm would it have done?

Thea stared at the men. The one she'd bumped into was short, slender and blue-eyed with straggly, shoulder length, blond hair. In contrast, the second was tall, silent and black. His head was covered with the hood of his sweatshirt. Somehow his presence made her feel a little less afraid.

She turned her gaze back to the first man to apologize. But the rage in his eyes seemed to bore holes through her. Curse words filled the air as he angrily shoved his associate aside. Thea stiffened and pulled herself to her full height, inadvertently signaling Thrasher.

The dog's tail ceased fanning her leg. Once again, she heard his low growl. The lean man froze and glared at Thrasher. His companion moved toward the bench beside the trail. Thea watched in dismay as he anxiously shoved something into an attaché case.

Fighting panic-stricken tears, she glimpsed over the contents and gasped in shock. Although he hurriedly closed the case, she had already made out the small plastic bags inside. She couldn't be certain but had a pretty good idea what was in them. Her earlier sense of kinship and support instantly vanished.

The sound of her pounding heart distracted her from lucid thought, and her breathing became more labored. The cool breeze hastened the warmth from her body. She wasn't sure if the shudder that raced through her was due to it or the fear welling up inside. She glanced down at Thrasher, who was poised to attack.

"I—I'm sorry, sir," she said again, "but you backed onto the trail too late for me—"

"Shut up, you stupid menace," the thin man said through clenched teeth.

Fearful that his tone might set off the dog, Thea slowly began to back away from the two men. She silently appealed to Thrasher by lightly tugging on the leash. Despite the intense agitation, the dog obediently limped to her side. A breeze sent some of the bills floating about the landscaping. The second man hurried after them. In a matter of seconds, the gentle waft turned into a brisk gust that scattered the bills all over the hillside.

The angry man turned away from Thea and shouted, "I told you the park was a bad idea! You've got your goods, now get your hands off my money!"

Grateful for the distraction, Thea turned to run. But before she and Thrasher could make their escape, she felt a hand firmly clasp her wrist.

"Where do you think you're going?"

Thrasher sprang toward the man, knocking him to the ground once again. As he fought the dog, his jacket flung open, revealing a handgun shoved into the waistband of his trousers. Thea's face grew warm with an adrenaline surge.

Aware of him reaching for the weapon, she screamed and rushed to pull Thrasher to safety. Before she knew what was happening, she was knocked backwards against the hand railing. Despite her desperate attempt to regain her footing, the stumble plunged her head first over the embankment.

She splashed into the frigid water ten feet below the trail canopy. Her breath caught in her throat as her face plunged beneath the surface.

Pain shot through her the instant she tried to move. But she had to get back to Thrasher before the man hurt him. Frantically swimming toward the edge, Thea slipped and fell back into the water. Her entire face was covered with an icy sludge. In frustration, she slammed her flattened palms against the surface of the water.

"Thea! Oh, God. What happened?"

As she wiped the remaining murk from her face, she glanced up and saw Mac charging toward her like a knight to her rescue. Relieved, all her emotions surfaced and burst forth. She didn't know which was more intense—the fear, humiliation, or frustration.

Mac pulled her from the pond then removed his jacket and wrapped it around her. She collapsed into his embrace and sobbed.

"Shh!" he said against her head. "Calm down. Are you OK?"

Anxious to get back to Thrasher, she withdrew. Between her shivering and shortness of breath, she didn't know whether she could make him understand the problem. "Mac…Thrasher…he's got a gun."

"Who has a gun?"

Thea pointed toward the rising that she had tumbled down. "Up there…two men."

His eyes were suddenly dark and cold. "Will you be OK for a few minutes?"

"Mac, no. You could be hurt."

"My car is in the usual spot, Thea. Go get inside."

Thea moved toward the small parking lot, pulling the jacket closer around herself. Mac's tall, athletic form sprinted up the hill toward the trail where she'd left Thrasher. Though tense, he moved with relaxed masculine mastery. She hoped the dog hadn't been hurt. She didn't think she had heard a gunshot. Her heart pumped spastically as a wave of acid welled up in her stomach. She couldn't bear to think of Thrasher hurt, but she didn't want

Mac to walk into a hornet's nest either.

Just as she decided to turn back and go after him, both Mac and Thrasher appeared and rushed toward her.

——⟡⟡⟡——

The man sat outside the two-story brick house, glancing around the quiet neighborhood. The motor purred soft enough to dull his senses. His heart thundered as he toyed with the ring hanging on a chain around his neck. He pulled back the hood of his sweatshirt and strained to peer into the big window of the house.

For a moment he thought he felt something crawling up the back of his neck and quickly swept at it with the palm of his hand. Probably just his imagination, he thought.

Anxious to get going, he lightly depressed the accelerator and listened as the motor droned, but he had to know if the woman had called the police. It had been quite some time since he followed them home, and he didn't want to be detected.

Maybe she wouldn't. If the authorities hadn't already arrived, they probably hadn't been called. It was too early to let anyone know he was in town. Maybe he had nothing to worry about. After all, she hadn't been hurt. She didn't get a very good look at him anyway.

His nostrils flared and a scowl formed on his face as his thoughts shifted back to the weasel in the park. Bancroft had disrespected him in front of the young woman. He snorted and grinned. She was a tigress, all right, a real fighter. And she'd had that dog. He chuckled aloud. Bancroft had been scared out of his mind.

Tucking the ring back inside his shirt, he wondered who she was. She was gutsy, that's for sure—and attractive, too. She reminded him a little of someone else—his older sister. He quietly nodded his head in recognition.

The ring had been the last thing she had bought herself, he thought, touching it once again. She had died much too soon. It should have been his worthless parents. Although she had been five years older, she had been his best friend. He let out a bitter snort. He wasn't at all close to his younger sister. His grandparents had taken her away before everything fell apart.

"You're my lucky charm," his older sister had told him when he was fifteen. "I'm gonna save my money and get us out of this dump." Two days later, she'd been found dead in a sleazy motel room.

Convinced that he was in the clear, he put the car in gear and sped down the street.

Cold, wet and befuddled, Thea sat on the sofa in Will and Jessica Morrow's living room wrapped in an afghan. It was closer to the park than her own apartment. Will, her uncle, had taken her aunt to Denver for a few days. She drew Thrasher close and laid her head against his fur. Mac had already looked him over and determined that he hadn't been hurt badly. After insolently refusing his offer to accompany her on the run, she was thankful that Mac hadn't left the park.

While she listened to him move about the kitchen, she sank into a relentless isolation. Loneliness seemed to swallow her whole, as her thoughts became tangled webs. Mac's attentiveness only made the reality more brutal.

Lately, she had even felt the need to distance herself. Circumstances, however, kept placing him back into her path. It was aggravating—as if destiny itself had chosen to torment her by offering unattainable goals.

Walter McAlester Hollings was a dentist and worked at her uncle's clinic. While her uncle's patients were adult, Mac's were all children. He loved children, and she was very much aware that he someday wanted a family.

He was just completing his undergraduate work, under her uncle's direction when she met him. He had been twenty-three at the time, and she was a terrified, grief-stricken sixteen-year-old. She had come to live with her aunt and uncle after the death of her parents. That was nine years and a billion tears ago.

She had developed a gigantic crush on Mac after only a week of him tutoring her in high school. Consequently, he took on a stifling sense of duty and protectiveness toward her—one that still produced a feeling of apprenticeship in her. He had a kind, but firm manner that had somehow joined her in a dark cave of sorrow and escorted her out into the world again.

Mac's presence always gave her a renewed sense of strength. Despite trying to discourage his doting, she always seemed to require his company. She had relied on him for much too long. She was certain that she sent mixed messages, and had to find a way to break free. Thea closed her eyes. She could imagine a posture of herself pushing him away and reaching for him in the same instant. It was ridiculous and impossible. And yet, it was.

Though her crush passed with time, she still thought of him when he wasn't around. She still craved the low hum of his voice in the silence. She still envisioned her in his arms.

Mac's exceptionally good looks had forever ruined her determining preferences. He was six feet, four inches of honey-brown masculinity. His expression, often contemplative, was gentle. When he smiled the world lit up like the sun, and the effects sent soft-tipped darts straight to her heart. He had a long oval face and wore his hair closely cropped. The neatly trimmed beard brought out the rugged set of his jaw. His steely, deep brown eyes were disarming. And yet, one glance could dismantle her thoughts with a tenderness that made her burst with elation.

Thea smiled, recalling the time he persuaded her to attend a picnic with him and a girlfriend. She was still a little awkward and unsociable then, but Mac had insisted the outing would boost her confidence. It wasn't until he had introduced her to Greg and Roz that she loosened up. She instantly connected with Roz, feeling very comfortable around her.

Shortly after realizing she was doing all right with his friends, Mac took off on a walk with his girlfriend. They weren't quite far enough away when she overheard her complain about his obsessive attentiveness to Thea.

"How can you possibly be jealous of a kid?" Mac had asked his friend in dismay.

Thea had been mortified that he actually thought of her as a child. After such a rude awakening, she started rejecting his protective tendencies. It had been her way of releasing the inner shame at even considering him in that way. She eventually buried the hurt and returned to normal around him.

"Hey, beautiful," he said, jolting her out of her reverie. Despite her objections, he had called her that since the day they'd met. Although she frequently snubbed his brand of support, she inwardly enjoyed the reference. "How are you holding up?"

"I'm OK," she said, playfully stroking Thrasher's ears.

Mac handed her the hot tea and sat on the oak coffee table directly in front of her. Still trembling from the park encounter, Thea sat the cup on the lamp table and pulled Thrasher closer. She needed something to busy her hands. Mac's eyes followed her every move. Not unlike herself, he considered the Morrows' residence his home base. They both had keys and knew they had the liberty to come and go as they pleased.

"Thrasher really is OK, you know. He managed to chase those men away, even though his leg was in pain. As soon as you get warmed up, you should go get into some dry things."

Despite Mac's habit of interfering in her life, she trusted him. He was sensitive and supportive. However, since she had broken up with Dorian six months ago, Thea had sensed something unsettling in herself. She suspected it was that old dependence she'd worked so hard to grow out of.

"I want you to promise me you'll make an appointment with Dr. Dyer and have yourself checked out. You took quite a tumble."

"There's no real need, Mac. I'll be fine."

"Promise me, anyway." He held her eyes captive for a few moments.

A wave of heat rumbled through her. She wasn't quite up to challenging him herself. "All right. I'll go."

"I'm sure my secretary wouldn't mind calling."

"Mac!"

He promptly lifted both hands in a gesture of surrender. "All right. All right. I just want to make sure you're seen. You'll probably really feel the need tomorrow morning."

For years now, their relationship had been a string of comradeship and verbal sparring matches. It was important to her that Mac recognized her as an adult, but she wasn't sure why. Maybe it was because he knew so much about her, almost everything, in fact. All except the one thing she couldn't share with anyone.

Only her family was aware that the accident that killed her parents had also taken away her wholeness. Though she once desperately wanted children, she would never be able to have them. One of the most regrettable consequences in that reality was that she couldn't bring herself to tell the one person who could hear her heart—Mac.

She swallowed hard as she thought of her sister, Katie. The fact that she had recently given birth to a son and her best friend was pregnant with her second child stung like a wet slap. She had been doing great around children—especially Jeremy, Roz's little three-year-old. Yet, she had noticed herself becoming more sensitive on the subject.

Thrasher, accustomed to Mac's attention, moved over and placed his head just beneath his hand. "Hello, boy."

He gently rubbed the dog's coat, all the while watching her with concern. Mac had given her the puppy as a sort of peace offering following a petty argument. Unfortunately, her apartment complex did not allow pets, so she had to leave him with her folks.

The doorbell rang. Thea and Thrasher flinched. "I'll get it," Mac said, leaning forward. He lightly touched her arm. "You need to relax."

As his eyes—soft and gentle, yet oddly piercing—searched hers, Thea felt unnerved. How she longed for him to see her as a woman. Under his scrutiny, she sensed the delicate hairs on the nape of her neck rise. For an instant, she worried that he could read her thoughts and shuddered with embarrassment.

The doorbell rang again, rousing annoyance in her. "Who could that be?"

He moved past her. "Might be the police."

"Why would you call them?"

"This needs to be reported, Thea." He rushed to the door. His shoulders slouched slightly as he stepped aside for Regina, his current girlfriend.

Thea immediately sensed a wave of disappointment move through her. Attractive, self-assured, and all dolled up in a violet suit, Regina kissed Mac on the lips. She was awfully chummy for someone who had only known him a couple of weeks, Thea thought. Regina stepped past him into the living room with an air of pre-eminence. Thea straightened and attempted to tidy her appearance.

"How did you know I'd be here?" Mac asked with a lazy smile.

"I drove by to pick you up. When you weren't home, I figured you'd be over here."

Mac slapped his forehead. "Oh, Regina. I'm so sorry. I forgot all about the luncheon."

The woman's face flushed with indignation. "Walter how could you?"

He gestured toward Thea with a slight move of his head. "We've had a situation—"

"Couldn't you have at least phoned?"

Thea got an image in her mind of Regina as a stationary camera, focusing only on one thing. She pondered being more like that, but couldn't see herself in such a self-absorbed mode.

"Hello, Regina," she ventured, hoping to calm the rising tension.

Regina slowly turned and as her eyes took in her form, Thea realized that her feeble attempt hadn't done much to help her mucky appearance. "Thea," she said, her voice softening. "What in the name of heaven happened to you?"

"Thea and Thrasher were attacked in the park," Mac said. As he went on to describe what happened, Thea sat her cup back on the table and nuzzled deeper into the corner of the sofa. Thrasher, restless because of the intruder, began a low growl.

"Settle down, boy," Mac said. "It's OK."

Thea quietly stood and tightened the afghan around her shoulders.

She led the dog through the kitchen, and let him out into the backyard.

When she returned to the living room, Regina had moved to the chair by the window. "I guess this means we won't be attending the luncheon?"

"Regina, I can't leave her like this. I want to be here when the police talks to her."

The woman's eyes widened. "Leave her like what, Walter? Thea is a grown woman."

"I am well aware of Thea's age," Mac said, his brow wrinkled in irritation. "You're perfectly welcome to go on to the luncheon without me."

"I'm sorry. You're right, of course. It's just that I've been looking forward to this." Her voice dropped off when she caught sight of Thea standing in the entryway. "Do you think we can do something later this evening?"

"I need to go by the clinic this afternoon to meet with a patient," Mac said. "Let me call you when I'm done."

"It's Saturday. You should at least let Will handle the after-hour patients. It's not like you're a medical doctor and have to be on call."

"Look," Mac said, impatience hardening his features, "just for the record, Will and Jessica aren't back from Denver yet. And *my* patients are my patients."

Regina lowered her head. Mac stood with his arms folded across his chest. Thea pulled the afghan closer, and moved toward the stairs. "I'm going up," she interrupted, anxious to get out of the wet clothes. "Mac, you should go on with your plans. Regina's right. I can handle talking to the police."

"The decision's made, Thea," he said. "Do you have any clothes over here?"

"Yeah." Thea glanced over at Regina. The woman's artificial angelic smile sent chills through her. "I'm really sorry this intruded on your day, Regina."

Regina shrugged. "I appreciate that, but it isn't your fault. Walter is right. You've had a terrible scare. Besides, if those men had a gun, they're probably dangerous. Have you considered that they could come after you?"

Thea froze and looked to Mac. The thunder in his expression told her that the untimely comment had hit a nerve in him also. She moved up the stairs. The pain in her shoulder and lower back was excruciating, but she kept climbing. Despite her possible intent, Regina was right.

Flashes of the money, drugs and gun resurfaced in her mind. It was obvious the men were doing something illegal, and they had also posed a threat. Adrenaline had been pumping so ardently at the time, Thea hadn't given any thought to whether they'd be concerned that she could identify them.

After hearing Regina's words, reality of the situation hit. The men could very well come after her. The very thought of it took her breath away. For an instant, she wondered if she should even speak to the police. After all, she hadn't been badly hurt, and she hadn't even seen the second man's face. What could she really tell them? If they were brought to trial, could they get off because she couldn't identify the second man? She wasn't even sure she was prepared to face them in court.

Yet, she couldn't shake the image of someone else stumbling upon the two—even a child. They might not have been so lucky. Her conscience wouldn't allow her to take that chance, and she knew it.

Thea showered and dressed, silently praying that the men wouldn't come after her.

Late morning had brightened by the time the police arrived. Mac had opened the drapes wider, making the room appear less depressing. Sgt. Kraft and his partner eyed Thea passively. While squinting against the dance of light and shadow through the window, she gave them a detailed version of the park encounter. Their reflexive by-the-book responses suggested they'd grown a little too accustomed to the daily tedium of crime.

"Miss Carter, would you be able to pick these men out of a lineup if it came to that?"

Thea moistened her lips. "I would recognize the man I bumped into. The white man."

"What about the second man?" Kraft asked. "Do you remember anything at all about him?"

Thea glanced over at Mac and Regina, who were staring back at her in wonderment. The cruel reality of what had happened to her was apparently becoming more evident to Regina. She had actually flinched when she repeated the particulars.

"I didn't get a good look at his face. But he was black, tall—much taller than the guy with the gun." Thea hesitated for a moment, trying to summon up a clearer image of the second man. "He wore a gray sweat suit. The kind with the hood attached. He had it pulled up."

"Anything else?"

"Yeah," she continued. "He had an odd looking scar on his right forearm. I noticed it when he helped me up."

"Anything significant about the scar?" Kraft made several quick notations on his pad.

Thea frowned. She was a little surprised that she remembered such a minor detail. "It looked like the sun—the kind a child would draw. A circle with vertical lines around it for the rays."

The officers glanced at each other then back again. "Miss Carter, can we reach you at this number?"

"No, this is my aunt and uncle's home. My apartment is a couple of miles east, on Wilshire."

The sergeant wrote down Thea's home and work numbers. He closed the pad and handed her a card with his own number on it. "I don't want to alarm you, but we don't know what these guys were up to out there. I suggest you keep your eyes open. If you notice anything out of the ordinary, anyone following you, calling you, be sure and give me a call."

LIFE IS NEVER AS IT SEEMS

2005 Publication Schedule

January

A Heart's Awakening
Veronica Parker
$9.95
1-58571-143-8

Falling
Natalie Dunbar
$9.95
1-58571-121-7

February

Echoes of Yesterday
Beverly Clark
$9.95
1-58571-131-4

A Love of Her Own
Cheris F. Hodges
$9.95
1-58571-136-5

Higher Ground
Leah Latimer
$19.95
1-58571-157-8

March

Misconceptions
Pamela Leigh Starr
$9.95
1-58571-117-9

I'll Paint a Sun
A.J. Garrotto
$9.95
1-58571-165-9

Peace Be Still
Colette Haywood
$12.95
1-58571-129-2

April

Intentional Mistakes
Michele Sudler
$9.95
1-58571-152-7

Conquering Dr. Wexler's Heart
Kimberley White
$9.95
1-58571-126-8

Song in the Park
Martin Brant
$15.95
1-58571-125-X

May

The Color Line
Lizzette Grayson Carter
$9.95
1-58571-163-2

Unconditional
A.C. Arthur
$9.95
1-58571-142-X

Last Train to Memphis
Elsa Cook
$12.95
1-58571-146-2

June

Angel's Paradise
Janice Angelique
$9.95
1-58571-107-1

Suddenly You
Crystal Hubbard
$9.95
1-58571-158-6

Matters of Life and
  Death
Lesego Malepe, Ph.D.
$15.95
1-58571-124-1

2005 Publication Schedule (continued)

July

Class Reunion
Irma Jenkins/John
  Brown
$12.95
1-58571-123-3

Wild Ravens
Altonya Washington
$9.95
1-58571-164-0

August

Path of Thorns
Annetta P. Lee
$9.95
1-58571-145-4

Timeless Devotion
Bella McFarland
$9.95
1-58571-148-9

Life Is Never As It Seems
J. J. Michael
$12.95
1-58571-153-5

September

Beyond the Rapture
Beverly Clark
$9.95
1-58571-131-4

Blood Lust
J. M. Jeffries
$9.95
1-58571-138-1

Rough on Rats and
  Tough on Cats
Chris Parker
$12.95
1-58571-154-3

October

A Will to Love
Angie Daniels
$9.95
1-58571-141-1

Taken by You
Dorothy Elizabeth Love
$9.95
1-58571-162-4

Soul Eyes
Wayne L. Wilson
$12.95
1-58571-147-0

November

A Drummer's Beat to
  Mend
Kay Swanson
$9.95

Sweet Reprecussions
Kimberley White
$9.95
1-58571-159-4

Red Polka Dot in a
  Worldof Plaid
Varian Johnson
$12.95
1-58571-140-3

December

Hand in Glove
Andrea Jackson
$9.95
1-58571-166-7

Blaze
Barbara Keaton
$9.95

Across
Carol Payne
$12.95
1-58571-149-7

Other Genesis Press, Inc. Titles

Erotic Anthology	Assorted	$8.95
Eve's Prescription	Edwina Martin Arnold	$8.95
Everlastin' Love	Gay G. Gunn	$8.95
Fate	Pamela Leigh Starr	$8.95
Forbidden Quest	Dar Tomlinson	$10.95
Fragment in the Sand	Annetta P. Lee	$8.95
From the Ashes	Kathleen Suzanne	$8.95
	Jeanne Sumerix	
Gentle Yearning	Rochelle Alers	$10.95
Glory of Love	Sinclair LeBeau	$10.95
Hart & Soul	Angie Daniels	$8.95
Heartbeat	Stephanie Bedwell-Grime	$8.95
I'll Be Your Shelter	Giselle Carmichael	$8.95
Illusions	Pamela Leigh Starr	$8.95
Indiscretions	Donna Hill	$8.95
Interlude	Donna Hill	$8.95
Intimate Intentions	Angie Daniels	$8.95
Just an Affair	Eugenia O'Neal	$8.95
Kiss or Keep	Debra Phillips	$8.95
Love Always	Mildred E. Riley	$10.95
Love Unveiled	Gloria Greene	$10.95
Love's Deception	Charlene Berry	$10.95
Mae's Promise	Melody Walcott	$8.95
Meant to Be	Jeanne Sumerix	$8.95
Midnight Clear	Leslie Esdaile	$10.95
(Anthology)	Gwynne Forster	
	Carmen Green	
	Monica Jackson	
Midnight Magic	Gwynne Forster	$8.95
Midnight Peril	Vicki Andrews	$10.95
My Buffalo Soldier	Barbara B. K. Reeves	$8.95
Naked Soul	Gwynne Forster	$8.95
No Regrets	Mildred E. Riley	$8.95
Nowhere to Run	Gay G. Gunn	$10.95

Object of His Desire	A. C. Arthur	$8.95
One Day at a Time	Bella McFarland	$8.95
Passion	T.T. Henderson	$10.95
Past Promises	Jahmel West	$8.95
Path of Fire	T.T. Henderson	$8.95
Picture Perfect	Reon Carter	$8.95
Pride & Joi	Gay G. Gunn	$8.95
Quiet Storm	Donna Hill	$8.95
Reckless Surrender	Rochelle Alers	$8.95
Rendezvous with Fate	Jeanne Sumerix	$8.95
Revelations	Cheris F. Hodges	$8.95
Rivers of the Soul	Leslie Esdaile	$8.95
Rooms of the Heart	Donna Hill	$8.95
Shades of Brown	Denise Becker	$8.95
Shades of Desire	Monica White	$8.95
Sin	Crystal Rhodes	$8.95
So Amazing	Sinclair LeBeau	$8.95
Somebody's Someone	Sinclair LeBeau	$8.95
Someone to Love	Alicia Wiggins	$8.95
Soul to Soul	Donna Hill	$8.95
Still Waters Run Deep	Leslie Esdaile	$8.95
Subtle Secrets	Wanda Y. Thomas	$8.95
Sweet Tomorrows	Kimberly White	$8.95
The Color of Trouble	Dyanne Davis	$8.95
The Price of Love	Sinclair LeBeau	$8.95
The Reluctant Captive	Joyce Jackson	$8.95
The Missing Link	Charlyne Dickerson	$8.95
Three Wishes	Seressia Glass	$8.95
Tomorrow's Promise	Leslie Esdaile	$8.95
Truly Inseperable	Wanda Y. Thomas	$8.95
Twist of Fate	Beverly Clark	$8.95
Unbreak My Heart	Dar Tomlinson	$8.95
Unconditional Love	Alicia Wiggins	$8.95
When Dreams A Float	Dorothy Elizabeth Love	$8.95

Whispers in the Night	Dorothy Elizabeth Love	$8.95
Whispers in the Sand	LaFlorya Gauthier	$10.95
Yesterday is Gone	Beverly Clark	$8.95
Yesterday's Dreams, Tomorrow's Promises	Reon Laudat	$8.95
Your Precious Love	Sinclair LeBeau	$8.95

Order Form

Mail to: Genesis Press, Inc.
P.O. Box 101
Columbus, MS 39703

Name _____
Address _____
City/State _____ Zip _____
Telephone _____

Ship to (if different from above)
Name _____
Address _____
City/State _____ Zip _____
Telephone _____

Credit Card Information
Credit Card # _____ ☐ Visa   ☐ Mastercard
Expiration Date (mm/yy) _____ ☐ AmEx   ☐ Discover

Qty.	Author	Title	Price	Total

Use this order

form, or call

1-888-INDIGO-1

Total for books	
Shipping and handling:	
$5 first two books,	
$1 each additional book	
Total S & H	
Total amount enclosed	

Mississippi residents add 7% sales tax